UN HOLY NIGHTS

AN EMERALD HILLS CHRISTMAS ROMANCE

heather ashley

Copyright © 2024 by Heather Ashley

All rights reserved.

No part of this book may be reproduced in any form or by any electronic or mechanical means, including information storage and retrieval systems, without written permission from the author, except for the use of brief quotations in a book review.

ISBN # 9798304544665

heatherashleywrites.com

FOR EVERYONE WHO'S EVER
WANTED TO *HO HO HO*
AROUND WITH THEIR STEPDAD,
THIS IS MY GIFT TO YOU.

Merrry Christmas.

playlist

Heavy is the Crown - Mike Shinoda & Emily Armstrong

Kill For You - Skylar Gray & Eminem

Christmas Lights - Coldplay

A Christmas Song - Keaton Henson

Wolf Like Me - Lera Lynn and Shovels & Rope

You Are the Moon - The Hush Sound

Silent Night (Minor Key Version) - Chase Holfelder

Criminal - Fiona Apple

My December - Linkin Park

Nothing's Gonna Hurt You Baby - Cigarettes After Sex

Dark Paradise - Lana Del Rey

Dance of the Sugar Plum Fairy - Lindsey Stirling

trigger warning

For a full list of triggers,
please visit:
heatherashleywrites.com/triggerwarnings

Please be aware that this book contains
non-consensual sexual activity
and is intended for readers over 18.

Cohen
CHAPTER 1

THE FIRST TIME I saw Emerald Delacroix, I knew I was fucked.

All it took was one glance, and I knew I'd ruin everything to have her—including myself.

Destroy her entire life until all she has is me.

All she *wants* is me.

The first time I saw her cry, something inside me shattered. She stood on that balcony at the Mitchell Gala, tears streaming down her face as she stared at the stars like they held answers, and I was seven years old again—watching my mother sob in our kitchen while that bastard she was dating towered over her.

But unlike that night, when I was too small, too weak to do anything but watch, this time I could do something. This time, I had the power to protect someone. To save her. The need to possess her, to shield her from everything that could hurt her, became an obsession that night. A mission.

I watch her now, my pretty little stepdaughter, as she stands by the window, painted in the soft golden glow of twinkling Christmas lights watching the snow fall.

She's beautiful in a way that feels almost unfair, like some divine hand crafted her to torment me. Fragile, yet resilient. Innocent, yet with something quietly defiant simmering beneath the surface. I see it all, even if she doesn't. That's the thing about her. She doesn't even know what she is. But I do.

I take a slow sip of whiskey, letting the burn settle in my veins as I keep my eyes fixed on her. I'm incapable of tearing my eyes away. Madeline's voice drifts in from the other room, shrill and demanding, as she barks orders at the household staff about some holiday bullshit only she cares about. I learned to tune that shit out a week ago when the decorations went up the day after Thanksgiving.

My wife is nothing if not an opportunist, and her flawless family is her favorite thing to exploit. The perfect Christmas. The perfect fucking lie.

I smirk into my glass. Her obsession with appearances has been useful to me, but it's also becoming... tiresome. She's served her purpose. She got me here, into this house, into Emerald's world. But now, she's more of an obstacle than anything else. And obstacles, well, they don't last long in my world.

The glass makes a soft *clink* as I set it down, my eyes never leaving Emerald. She's wearing a simple white oversized sweater with sleeves that fall past her wrists. It swallows her small frame, hiding her from me and making her look even more delicate than she already is. Her dark hair tumbles over her shoulders, messy in the way I imagine it'll be when she's spent the night in my bed, and I can just make out the way she bites her lower lip as her eyes follow the falling snow.

That lip—full, pink, and soft. I've dreamed of biting it myself, of pulling it between my teeth until I leave marks. Until she bleeds for me.

A small, satisfied hum escapes me at the thought. She has no idea I watch her like I do. No idea I've been staring at her for countless minutes, uncaring who sees.

Seems I'm all out of fucks to give.

I run my thumb along my bottom lip, trying to imagine the way she'll taste on my tongue. I should take a step back, put some distance between us tonight. My need to own her—bone-deep, soul-deep, until there's nothing left untouched by my hand—is too close to the surface and I'm not sure I can hide it away.

I've waited too long, played this game too carefully to ruin my plans on a whim.

Still...

I push myself off the leather armchair and move with deliberate slowness across the room. The pull is too strong. She's still unaware of my approach, her gaze fixed on the virginal snow outside, her breath leaving a faint fog on the glass. I wonder what she's thinking and nearly open my mouth to ask. To demand her thoughts be of me and only me.

My teeth grind together as I attempt to keep the words inside. Now that I've decided to let my plan unfold, holding back is damn near impossible.

I'm only a handful of steps away from her now, a hint of my frame towering over hers in the reflection of the glass. Even now, she's so lost in her head she doesn't notice me.

A flicker of annoyance sparks under my skin as I draw closer, my jaw tightening. How can she not feel me? How can she stand there, untouched, unaffected, when I'm right behind her, my gaze burning a path across her skin? My patience is slipping. Each step I take closer should make the air between us crackle, should force her to turn, to acknowledge that I'm here, wanting her.

That she's wanting me just as desperately.

I take another step, my body nearly brushing against hers, close enough that I can almost feel the heat of her body radiating through the fabric of my clothes. We're shielded behind the towering Christmas tree, a silver-and-gold monstrosity that I've never been more grateful for.

We're caught in a bubble of soft light and silence, and if she leans back into me or tilts her head to the side so I can run my mouth up the side of her long neck, I could live here forever. Just when I think I might have to reach out and force her to acknowledge my presence, I see it—a slight shift. Her body sways backward, just a little, unconsciously leaning in my direction as I take one last step forward.

A dark, satisfied smile curves across my lips. She doesn't even know it yet, but her body already knows what she needs. Already knows it's mine.

"Beautiful, isn't it?" My voice is low, but still cuts through the quiet like a blade.

She startles, just a little. Her shoulders tense before she turns her head to glance at me over her shoulder. I don't miss the shiver that runs down her spine when she sees it's me. When she notices how close we are. The way her nipples harden behind her dress. Her green eyes—those deep, fucking endless eyes that haunt my dreams—go wide in surprise.

"Cohen," she breathes out my name on a sigh before catching herself a fraction of a second too late. There's a hint of something in it. Relief, maybe. Longing. But also weariness. "You can't just sneak up on me like that."

I close the distance between us, leaving a sliver of space between her back and my chest, barely enough for a breath to pass between. I ignore her chastising because when it comes to her, I'll do whatever the fuck I want.

"The snow," I clarify, gesturing with a slight nod toward the window, though I think we both know that's not what I'm talking about. "It's beautiful, don't you think?"

She hesitates, her gaze flicking back to the window as if she needs to remind herself not to look at me too long. Not to let her curiosity show. "It is," she replies after a moment. "It's... quiet."

I move to stand beside her, my shoulder brushing against hers, the contact deliberate. If I don't steal these little moments, push the boundaries between us, I'm afraid I'll snap before she's ready.

Emerald stiffens, her gaze still on the snow-covered grounds stretching out beyond the window. The estate is a winter wonderland, covered in untouched white, framed by towering evergreens heavy with snow. It's picturesque. I'm surprised Madeline doesn't have her photographers out there already, forcing me into a holiday-themed suit and dragging me out onto the lawn.

I'm all too happy to be here now, though.

Forgotten for the moment and hidden away with her daughter.

The tension between us is a living thing, buzzing in the tiny space where we're connected, where her shoulder leans against my arm. She sucks in a breath like if she moves even to exhale, it'll push us closer together or further apart and she's not ready to face either.

The silence sits heavy, almost vibrating against my skin, something that pushes and pulls between us like a current. It's always been this way, even if she won't acknowledge it. From the first time she turned those big, innocent eyes on me and changed the entire course of my life with a single look.

This feeling... It makes my skin prickle, my fingers curl into fists against the urge to reach for her, to close the distance until nothing stands between us. Not even air. Her body pressed against mine, skin to skin. Even my cock gives an enthusiastic twitch.

Fuck, what I wouldn't give to peel her clothes off and unwrap her like the gift she is.

We're even here beside the Christmas tree. It could be perfect.

"You seem distracted, Emerald." I let her name roll off my tongue slowly, savoring the sound of it. The feel of it. She finally blows out the breath she sucked in a dozen seconds ago, and out of my peripheral vision, I look down and notice her dress with the wide collar gives me an exquisite view of her perky little tits in a lacy white bra.

Fuck. Me.

That enthusiastic twitch from before explodes into a raging hard on in less than the blink of an eye. Goddamnit. I shift to the side to try to adjust so I don't scare her away. "Like you're daydreaming of something."

"I'm not," she lies, her voice too high, her words too quick to be convincing.

I chuckle, low in my throat, and shift my gaze back up to her face. "Liar."

Her eyes snap up to mine, wide and startled, and for a moment, I see it. The fire. That spark of defiance she tries so hard to keep buried. It's there, just beneath the surface, begging to be set free.

I love it.

I fucking *crave* it.

She presses her lips together, biting down on that bottom lip again, and I can't stop my eyes from dropping to it. I wonder if she knows what she's doing to me. What she's been doing to me for two fucking years. I wonder if she has any idea how much I want to ruin the image she's been forced to maintain her whole life.

She hesitates, like she's weighing her words carefully. "I was just thinking…" she trails off, her eyes flicking back to the snow outside, her voice softening. "About how I used to love the snow when I was a kid."

I raise an eyebrow, not expecting her to share anything so

personal. Usually, she does everything she can to shut me out. To keep distance between us. Maybe she thinks if she pretends I don't exist, she can pretend she's not attracted to me, too. "Used to?"

She gives a small shrug, her gaze still distant. "It used to mean freedom. Snow days, getting to escape the rules for a little while. Now, it just feels... like I'm trapped." She bites her lip, as if regretting the admission, and I watch as her eyes shutter, the wistfulness there quickly replaced by the practiced composure she always wears.

It's too much like her mother and I fucking hate it.

I lean in closer, close enough that she must feel my breath on her neck, and I lower my voice, letting it brush against her ear. "Trapped by who?" I feel her shiver more than I see it. "By your mother?" Tension ripples through her, her posture stiffening. She's always been too afraid to admit the truth out loud.

That she hates Madeline as much as I do. Maybe more.

She swallows hard, the vulnerability plain on her face before she glances at me, her expression hardening, a glimmer of resistance flickering in those green eyes. "It doesn't matter."

A smile tugs at my lips. There it is—that spark I crave, the fire that hides beneath her fragile exterior. I can't help myself. I reach out, brushing a strand of dark hair away from her face, my thumb grazing her cheek. Her skin is unbelievably soft, and I never want to stop touching her. "Oh, but it does, little one," I murmur. "It matters more than you think."

She flinches, her eyes locking on mine, and I watch as her breath catches, that same restless energy burning up the oxygen between us. Consuming it. I lean in, my lips just a whisper away from her ear, and she tilts her head closer. I'm not sure she knows she's doing it. "One day," I promise, "you'll be free."

Before I can make any more promises she's not ready for,

Madeline's voice snaps through the room like a whip. "Emerald! Cohen! Dinner is ready."

Emerald's shoulders drop and she blows out a breath, as if she's been given a reprieve from whatever thoughts were consuming her. But I'm not done with her. Not by a long shot.

"Shall we?" I offer her my arm with a slight smile. She hesitates, glancing at me as if unsure whether she should accept, but in the end, she does. Of course she does.

Her hand is soft and warm against my arm as we walk together toward the dining room. This is the first time I've gotten this close and I can feel every inch of her, every step she takes beside me. My jaw clenches as the hunger for her I've been fighting for two years ignites deep inside me—bone deep and impossible to ignore any longer.

This is how it should always be between us, with her by my side, pressed against me, looking to me to give her what she needs.

My wife is waiting for us, seated at the head of the long, ridiculous table, her icy blue eyes flicking between me and her daughter. If she's surprised to see us arrive together, she doesn't show it.

Madeline's always watching. Always calculating.

Pulling off my plan is going to take every ounce of my cunning and strategy. There are many things I dislike about my wife, but I have to admit that she's a worthy adversary.

She may be good, but I like to think I'm better.

I guess time will tell.

"Darling," she greets me with a smile that doesn't reach her frosty eyes. "I hope Emerald hasn't been boring you."

I smile back at her even as I bristle at her words, the perfect picture of a doting husband as I pull the chair out for my stepdaughter and reluctantly move away from her touch. I bury my reaction to her shitty passive aggressive comment about her daughter, unwilling to show just how much it pisses me off.

That doesn't mean I'm going to let it slide, though. "Never. She has a remarkable way of seeing the world."

Madeline's smile tightens, and there's a flicker of irritation in her eyes. She doesn't like it when I pay too much attention to Emerald. Not that she's ever said it outright, but I can see it in the way she watches us, the way her jaw clenches whenever I speak to her daughter.

Which isn't even close to often enough.

But that's the thing about Madeline. She's too proud, too arrogant to believe that anything could ever slip out of her control. She thinks she has me wrapped around her finger, just like everyone else in her life.

But she's wrong.

Because this isn't her story.

It's mine.

And Emerald?

She's mine too.

The dinner passes in an endless slog of forced smiles and meaningless conversation. Madeline blathers on about the upcoming Delacroix Christmas party, which, according to her, is the 'event of the year', her plans for the new year, and all the ways she's going to expand her empire. Emerald listens quietly, nodding in all the right places, but I can see the way her fingers fidget in her lap, the way her eyes glaze over as her mother drones on about things that don't matter.

She's suffocating. Drowning in the shallow little world Madeline has built around her.

And I'm going to be the one to pull her out of it. Give her the oxygen from my lungs if I need to. I'll peel back the layers of Madeline's control, one at a time. Even if it means my stepdaughter gets a glimpse of the darkness inside me.

By the time dessert is served, Madeline has finally shut the fuck up, and the room falls into uncomfortable silence. Emerald glances at me from across the table, her eyes flicking between me and her mother as if she's trying to figure something out. I meet her gaze, holding it just a little too long, and there's confusion there. Hesitation.

Good.

Let her wonder. Let her question. Because the more she does, the closer she'll come to realizing the truth. That she doesn't belong in her mother's world. She belongs in mine.

After dinner, Madeline disappears into her office, the faint scent of sulfur lingering in the air. Emerald and I are finally alone.

Emerald pushes away from the table, standing up, her gaze darting to me before dropping to the floor. I follow suit, but she steps back, putting distance between us. I fucking hate distance. She fidgets with her sleeves, her expression tense, her voice quieter than before.

"Tonight... it was nice. Talking, you know?" A faint pink blooms on her cheeks, and she refuses to make eye contact. "But I think I should go to bed," she says, glancing toward the hallway as she chews on that lip that drives me to madness.

I nod, tucking my hands into the pockets of my pants to keep from reaching for her and dragging her against me. "If that's what you need."

Her eyes meet mine again for a heartbeat, and as always, she holds me hostage until she blinks and looks away. She swallows before taking a step back, her voice barely above a whisper. "Goodnight, Cohen."

For tonight, I'll allow her the space she wants, though my gaze lingers on her. "Goodnight, little one."

She turns and walks away, her footsteps soft against the floor, and I watch her go, my satisfaction growing. She thinks she's creating distance, but I won't allow it. The illusion, maybe. For now.

My pulse speeds up, that familiar hunger gnawing at the

edges of my control as I watch her climb the stairs, her untouched little body just waiting for me to own it.

It's been more than a year of this torture and I'm not sure how much more I can take.

She's close. So close.

And soon, she'll be mine.

As the door to her bedroom clicks shut, I head toward my own room, a slow ghost of a smile on my face.

This will be the Christmas everything changes.

This Christmas I give her everything... by taking it all away.

And I can't fucking wait.

Emerald

CHAPTER 2

I'VE ALWAYS WONDERED what it would feel like to suffocate, and now I know.

It feels a lot like waking up in this house.

Morbid? Maybe. But there's something sort of beautiful about the idea of taking your last breath and slipping away from this world.

It's got to be better than this.

Through my window, the Delacroix chapel's dark spire stands tall even through the trees and snow. Most mansions in Emerald Hills come with the typical extras—pool houses, tennis courts, guest cottages. But our estate has something different: a Gothic chapel that's stood here longer than the main house. I think it's from the 1800s or something, but I don't really know. My mother refuses to talk about it.

I've always been drawn to it, though. I don't know what it is, but looking at it makes me feel... hopeful, I guess. Through my window, I love staring at its stained-glass windows, trying to pick out the different colors. They're dull in the gray, at least until the sun hits them just right.

But this morning there's no sun. Just an endless blanket of heavy gray.

The chapel's been locked my entire life, and my mother won't go anywhere near it. She's probably afraid she'll burst into flames if she steps foot on holy ground. I snort, letting myself picture it. I'm pretty sure Satan himself sends her a holiday card since, you know, they're besties.

Outside, the snow covers everything. More must have fallen while I was sleeping. It's thick and fluffy without so much as a footprint, like someone's thrown a down comforter over the whole world. It's hushed, almost peaceful. But this place isn't peaceful at all. The house is no doubt buzzing with staff, getting everything ready for another day of perfection, and all I can think about is how badly I just want to disappear.

My bones are heavy. I haven't even gotten out of bed yet and already I want to crawl back into it, yank the blanket over my head, and pretend the outside world doesn't exist. I don't know how I'm going to drag myself through another day of my life.

I glance at the clock on my nightstand. *7:30 a.m.* My mother's bitchy robotic assistant, Kendra, will be knocking on my door any minute now with my outfit for the day. Something boring and expensive and handpicked by my mother. There will be no room for personality. No room for self expression.

No room for me.

Yay. Another day of my life wasted, spent being Madeline Delacroix's daughter. I'm her favorite accessory. I might as well be a tiny dog in a handbag on my mother's arm.

I stare at the ceiling with its hand-carved crown molding while I try to breathe out my claustrophobia. It's not a small space I'm trapped by, though. It's my whole life.

At that panic-inducing thought, my breathing gets shallow and fast, like I'm trying to breathe through a straw. I swear my ribs are squeezing my lungs, and every inhale's a battle I'm not sure I want to keep fighting. Knowing what's coming today, all the mindless tasks my mother's going to heap on me and the way I'll be expected to wear a mask at all times wraps ghost fingers around my throat and starts to choke the life out of me.

There's this sense of inevitability that hits me every morning, but today for some reason it's worse. Maybe it's the few minutes of attention I got last night from my stepfather that made me feel like an actual human being. Cohen's attention last night was like... like when you're freezing cold and someone wraps you in a blanket straight from the dryer. That's what his words felt like—warm and safe and comfortable.

Maybe it's the added pressure of the holidays.

I don't really know. But it doesn't matter how I'm feeling, I'm still expected to play my part. I can already hear the faint sounds of the house waking up, my mother's staff scurrying around, doing her bidding.

What Cohen said is still bouncing around in my head. The words are impossible to ignore, especially because they're exactly what I've always wanted to hear.

You won't be trapped anymore. One day, you'll be free.

Unfortunately, he's the wrong person to say them.

I bite my lip as I try to ignore the memory of his voice—the way it wrapped around me like the best hug in the strongest arms. The way it gave me all sorts of warm tingles like nothing ever has.

Cohen Astor is dangerous in a way that makes my stomach twist into knots whenever he's around. There's something about him that feels so... right. But it *should* feel wrong. So, so wrong.

Is this what a crush feels like?

I mean, he's my mother's husband. My stepfather. He should be this safe, boring authority figure who ignores me, not someone who makes me feel like the ground isn't steady under my feet. Not someone who makes me question everything I thought I knew about myself.

He's thirty-two and so much older than me, and he radiates this darkness that should send me running in the opposite direction. But God, the way he looks at me... I think he's the only one who sees the girl underneath all the blank expressions, bland smiles, and layers of makeup. Like he knows the real me—the one I had to bury so deep sometimes I forget she exists.

The one my mother spent years trying to suffocate with designer clothes, proper manners, and PR-approved talking points

Stop obsessing over your stepfather, Emerald.

This little obsession I'm developing is at least twenty-five different kinds of messed up.

I've only got maybe minutes before I have to pack up my new fixation on Cohen and my pity party to pull on my Madeline Delacroix-approved Emerald costume.

I force myself to sit up, throwing my legs over the edge of the bed just as the knock I've been dreading sounds at the door.

Kendra, punctual as always. Must be in her programming. I laugh to myself, picturing ripping out her battery pack and watching the light die in her eyes.

"Miss Delacroix, your mother has requested that you join her for breakfast in thirty minutes," she calls through the door, her voice sharp and monotone as she repeats the same words she does every morning. Seven. Days. A. Week. "You'll find your outfit in the closet."

I don't bother answering. Why waste the energy? Instead, I drag myself to the closet, my feet sinking into the carpet that's one of the few soft things in this house. Sure enough, today's costume is hanging there waiting for me. See? Robot-Kendra sneaking into my room while I sleep to hang up clothes like I'm a child isn't creepy *at all.*

If I could, I'd change the lock on my door in a second to keep her out. But I can't drive and don't have any of my own money, so there's not a lot I can do. I did once try to block the door with my dresser and for that little stunt, Mother didn't let me eat for three days.

So this is my reality, staring at another outfit picked out by someone else, living in a room I can't even keep people out of. *Awesome.*

Today's prison uniform is a boring cream-colored cashmere sweater dress that's going to wash out my fair skin. It's cinched with this dainty gold belt that I'd never be able to wear if my mother wasn't a complete Nazi about my carb intake and workout regimen. Add knee-high suede boots and boom—instant Stepford daughter. It's elegant, sophisticated, and makes me want to projectile vomit.

I stare at it, fingers twitching with the urge to rip it off the hanger and maybe set it on fire. But it's not Robot-Kendra's fault she's caught in my mother's web of crazy.

Actually, you know what? Screw that. It *is* Kendra's fault. Unlike me, she chooses to be here. She chooses to work for my mother, to carry out her insane orders, to sneak into my room like some creepy fashion ninja while I sleep. She could get another job literally anywhere else, but no—she likes being Mother's head minion.

With a sigh that comes from my soul, I yank the dress on. The fabric feels like heaven against my skin, and it fits like it was painted on because God forbid anything in this house be less than perfect. I look amazing, obviously. I always do. That's kind of the whole problem—I'm just a mannequin for my mother to dress up in whatever makes *her* look best.

I can't even throw my hair in a messy bun in my own room because someone might see. *"What if there was a fire, Emerald?"* The horror. I roll my eyes so hard I probably strain something, then hurry to finish getting ready before the Robot Assistant returns to beep at me until I comply.

By the time I make it downstairs, the house is already operating at peak efficiency. The staff moves through the kitchen like they're programmed with the same software as Kendra, setting out croissants that look like they just fell out of an Insta travel influencer's story about their trip to Paris and fruit cut into precise quarter-inch slices.

How do they even do that? Is there some class on how to arrange breakfast so it looks too pretty to eat?

I step into the dining room and there she is—the Queen of Everything herself, Madeline Delacroix, perched at the head of the table like she's about to start ordering beheadings. Her perfectly blonde hair (five hundred dollars every three weeks to maintain that exact shade, the complete opposite of my almost black) is pulled back in a chignon so tight it's probably cutting off blood flow to her brain. Maybe that explains... everything about her. She's scanning the room with those icy blue eyes, probably cataloging every microscopic flaw to torture the staff about later.

She's wearing a tailored white blouse and a skirt that shows off how many hours she spends on her Peloton. The perfect ruler of her perfect plastic kingdom. I do a quick scan of the room, and my shoulders relax when I don't see Cohen. Then immediately tense again because why do I care if he's here?

Why does my stomach feel hollow knowing he's not?

Snap out of it, Emerald.

"Good morning, sweetheart," Mother chirps with all the warmth of a shark circling its prey. She gestures to my chair like she's granting me permission to exist in the same space she does. "You're just in time."

Of course I am. When you grow up with a mother who thinks being five minutes early is ten minutes late, you learn to be punctual *or else*.

Her eyes do their usual inspection, like she's checking merchandise for defects. I hold my breath while she catalogs every potential flaw. "You look lovely," she finally pronounces, her tone making it clear that being anything less than *lovely* would be unacceptable. "I trust you slept well?"

I force my face into the bland smile I've perfected over years of practice, even though sleep was basically impossible last night. Cohen's words kept bouncing around in my head like a pinball machine, making my brain buzz and my stomach do these weird flips that are probably a sign of impending death. Or worse—feelings.

We are definitely not discussing what his cologne did to me. Or how his breath on my neck made parts of me tingle that I didn't even know could tingle.

I mean, seriously. What is that about?

And why does he have to be so handsome?

"Yes, Mother. Thank you."

She nods, satisfied with her inspection, and turns to her tablet. "We have a busy day ahead. I've arranged for a photo shoot this afternoon to promote the holiday collection for the website," she announces, not looking up. "The photo shoot is at two. Marketing team call at noon. You'll be present for both."

I nod because what else can I do? Every minute of my life is scheduled, planned, and A/B tested for maximum brand exposure. I'm not a daughter—I'm a walking, breathing advertisement.

The worst part is she doesn't even want my input. I'm just supposed to sit there, look pretty, and nod at appropriate intervals while she maps out my entire future. Her master plan is probably saved in a spreadsheet somewhere titled "How to Turn Your Daughter Into a Carbon Copy of Yourself in 500 Easy Steps."

I'm pretty sure step one is *crush all signs of personality*.

Spoiler alert: I'd rather throw myself off the roof than turn into her. I mean, I don't know exactly what I want out of life, but I know it's not... this.

Maybe I want to be messy sometimes. Maybe I want to be real.

Not that I'd know what either of those things feels like.

Mother's imperial ice-queen stare locks onto me again. "And Emerald?" Her voice drops into that tone that means she's about to issue a proclamation and I better obey. "The Christmas party is approaching. We're hosting some very important guests this year." Her lips thin. "Everything must be flawless."

Flawless. Perfect. Impeccable.

The holy trinity of my mother's religion. Everything has to be perfect, no matter the cost.

And trust me—I'm not talking about money.

The price is always paid in pieces of your soul.

"I won't forget," I mutter, already dreading another night of playing Living Barbie at my mother's social circus.

"Good." She sips her tea. "And Emerald..." Her eyes narrow. "Let's avoid any unpleasantness this year. No boys. No distractions."

I blink. Wait, what? She says this like I'm some wild child sneaking out to party every weekend. "Boys?"

Her lips twist into something that might be a smile if you've never actually seen one before. "Yes, sweetheart. I don't need you getting any silly ideas in that head of yours. This party is far too important for teenage dramatics."

I bite my lip so hard I taste blood. Since when have I *ever* caused drama? Between being homeschooled by the most boring tutors on earth and having every minute of my life scheduled down to when I'm allowed to breathe, I've barely even seen a boy my age, let alone talked to one.

And friends? That's literally a foreign concept in the Delacroix household.

Not that I don't want those things. God, I want them so badly it hurts. But asking for anything resembling a normal life isn't just guaranteed to piss her off—it's completely useless. Mother would never let anyone else into the bubble she's built around me.

Still... maybe...

"Actually," I start, hating how small my voice sounds, "I was thinking maybe I could bring someone? Not even a date necessarily. Just... a friend? Someone my age?" Her eyes slice into me and I scramble to add, "Just to talk to? I've never—" I swallow hard, despising how pathetic I sound, but I'm so lonely I could scream. "I've never been allowed to have friends, and I thought maybe this year..."

She studies me like I'm a holiday tablescape that doesn't match her aesthetic. Then she sighs. "You know how important appearances are, Emerald. This party isn't the time for... experiments." Her eyes get that calculating look that almost never ends well for me. "However, if you behave properly, perhaps after the holidays we can discuss finding you an appropriate companion. Someone who meets our standards."

Translation: Someone as boring and soulless as she wants me to be.

My stomach drops as the reality of her words settles over me. Of course, even my friendships need her seal of approval, like everything else in my life has to pass her inspection first. I don't know why I thought turning nineteen would change anything. I'm still completely dependent on her—no money, no life skills, not even allowed to learn how to drive. I'm an idiot for even bringing it up. Now she has something else to hold over my head, another weakness to add to her spreadsheet of my faults.

I force my face into that blank, pleasant expression I've perfected over the years. "Yes, Mother."

"Good girl," she says, her smile as artificial as everything else about her. Like an AI chatbot trying to mimic human emotion.

She turns back to her tablet and waves me away like an annoying bug that dared to interrupt her morning. "You're dismissed. Don't be late for the shoot."

I push myself up from the table, my legs feeling like jelly like they always do after I dare to ask my mother for anything. The anger and helplessness and disappointment churn together in my stomach, mixing together into something bitter and sharp. Though maybe that's just hunger—not that I'd dare touch one of those perfect, Instagram-worthy croissants.

The loneliness hits harder as I walk down the hallway, my footsteps dull against the polished Carrara marble. I've never been allowed to just... be. Every interaction, every potential connection has been checked and approved by my mother to serve some greater purpose in her master plan for the Delacroix dynasty.

No distractions.

I bite my lip, her words playing on repeat in my head, and because apparently I enjoy torturing myself, my thoughts drift to Cohen. He's definitely a distraction—the kind that makes me feel like I'm standing on the edge of a cliff, knowing I should step back but wanting to jump anyway. The kind that turns my whole world upside down and shakes it until nothing makes sense anymore.

The kind that makes me feel alive for the first time in my life, even though those sparks of life will only make things worse.

I escape the house as fast as my Stuart Weitzman boots will carry me before one of my mother's fashion goblins can drag me into another two-hour meeting about the difference between eggshell and ivory. She's sent me to grab stuff for the Christmas party, and for once I'm actually grateful for one of her endless errands. At least it gets me out of the Museum of Misery.

The home décor boutique sits right in the middle of Emerald Hills, crammed between all the other fancy shops where the town's elite drop thousands on things no one actually needs. Things my mother decides are trends and tells them to buy.

The second I walk in, I'm assaulted by enough expensive candles and leather to give me an instant headache. Before I can even suck in a breath through my mouth, I'm surrounded by sales associates with fake smiles plastered on their faces like they've won the lottery just by my stepping inside the door.

"Miss Delacroix! Welcome!" One of them bounces on her toes, her blonde ponytail swinging. "We've been expecting you."

Of course they have. Robot-Kendra probably called ahead with my exact arrival time.

I pull my face into the same bland, pleasant expression I used at breakfast with my mother as she drags me over to the holiday display. "Your mother selected these for the party," she gushes, waving at some gold and silver ornaments that look like they were handcrafted by artisans flown in from Venice or wherever my mother sources her ridiculously elaborate decorations these days. "Aren't they just divine?"

I nod along while she rambles about holiday trends and how my mother is basically the God (goddess?) of Christmas decorating or whatever. Like I care about any of this. But I know my role. Smile. Nod. Act interested. Be the well-trained Delacroix daughter so everyone can gush about what an excellent job my mother did training her little show pony.

Just as I think I might be able to make my escape, when she's rushed off to answer the phone, a voice behind me gives me the full-on creeps. Like spiders skittering over my skin.

"Emerald Delacroix," the voice drawls, oozing all kinds of

charm—the gross fake kind. "As stunning as ever."

I turn slowly, my stomach doing that awful dropping-elevator feeling when I see Emmitt Caldwell, one of my mother's sleaziest business associates. He's tall, with the kind of artfully dyed hair that screams "midlife crisis," and he has that permanent smug expression that makes my palm itch to introduce itself to his face.

He's what Living Delacroix would call "distinguished"—all custom Italian suits and a sharp jawline—but something about him has always set off warning bells in my head. I've suffered through countless parties where I've caught him staring at me just a little too long to believe he has good intentions.

"I didn't expect to see you here," he says, his eyes doing that gross crawling thing over me that makes me wish I was wearing a hazmat suit instead of this stupid sweater dress. "But I suppose you're here for the same reason I am—preparations for your mother's big event. It wouldn't be Christmas without the Delacroix party."

I manage what I hope passes for a smile, but probably looks more like a grimace. "Yes, I'm just picking up a few things."

Emmitt takes a step closer, and I fight the urge to grab one of those pretentious crystal snow globes and use it as a weapon. His voice drops into what I'm sure he thinks is an intimate whisper, but just sounds slimy enough to make me want to take a shower. "Your mother has quite the plan this year. She always knows how to impress, doesn't she?"

I nod mechanically while my heart slams against my ribs hard enough that I'm surprised he can't hear it. I take a small step back, wishing I could teleport myself literally anywhere else. "Yes, she does."

His straight, white smile widens. "You're lucky to have her, you know. Not everyone gets to be part of such a desirable family."

I'm trying to come up with a response that won't end with

my mother sending me away for an "attitude adjustment", which is her favorite threat lately, when I feel it. It's like gravity suddenly shifted directions, pulling me toward him instead of down to the Earth. My body knows he's there before I do, every inch of me suddenly straining backward, wanting to be closer to the one person I should stay far away from.

Relief floods through me so fast, I let that pull win for just a second, swaying back toward him like my body's finally found its center of gravity.

Cohen.

Emmitt's smile cracks at the edges as he glances past me, his eyes narrowing. "Cohen. I didn't realize you were around as well."

My stepfather's hand settles on the small of my back and everything inside me goes quiet. His fingers press into my skin through the dress, and it hits me—this is the first time anyone's touched me without an agenda of fitting or styling or fixing me. Just touch for the sake of touch.

I know it should feel weird. Wrong. But instead it feels like... coming up for air.

"Emmitt," Cohen says, and his voice has that scary-calm quality that makes the hair on my neck stand up. "I didn't think you'd be lurking around here. This isn't exactly your usual hunting grounds."

Emmitt's eyes drop to where Cohen's hand rests on me, his smile going brittle before he plasters on another fake one. "I was just helping Madeline with a few party preparations at a shop down the block," he says, trying to catch my eye like we're sharing some secret. As if I'd ever want to share anything with him. "You know how important these little details are to her." He waves his hand around with a smile that reminds me of my mother's socialite friends cooing over babies they don't actually want to hold. "When I saw Emerald in the window, I thought I'd pop in and say hello."

Cohen's fingers press harder into my back, and when I glance up, his smile is arctic. "It's easy to wander into dangerous territory without realizing it. I suggest you watch your step around Emerald."

Emmitt lets out this empty laugh that sounds about as genuine as my mother's concern for my wellbeing. Something dark flashes in his eyes that makes me wish I understood the game these two are playing. It's like they're having a whole other conversation underneath their words, and I don't speak the same language. "Always watching, right?"

My stepfather's smile doesn't waver as he meets Emmitt's stare. "Always."

The tension is thick, like I could almost reach out and touch it. Cohen's fingers shift and curl around my hip as he tugs me closer into his body and further away from Emmitt. He smells like something fresh, like the forest after rain, with a little bit of warmth that makes me want to lean closer and breathe him in. Emmitt shifts uncomfortably under Cohen's glare, and after a beat, he clears his throat.

"Well, I should be going. Busy day ahead." He flashes me a tight, strained smile. "Always a pleasure, Emerald."

I nod, trying not to shudder with revulsion, and watch as he finally turns and leaves. The second he's gone, the room feels like it gets a little bigger, a little easier to breathe in, but Cohen hasn't let go of me even though we're essentially alone.

The quiet between us crackles like a storm about to break. I can still feel his fingers curled around my hip, and even though I know I should step away, I don't. I shiver and sink a little further into his touch, trying to memorize the feel of it.

How long has it been since anyone's touched me?

I can't remember my last hug.

How depressing is that?

"You alright?" Cohen's voice is softer than I'm used to, and when I look up at him, his gray eyes are stormy and locked on mine.

I swallow hard against the intensity of that look, nodding. "Yeah. I just... I hate that guy."

His gaze darkens, his expression hardening in a way that sends a chill through me. "You let me handle him from now on, alright?"

There's something about the way he says it that makes me think he isn't just talking about today. It makes me wonder what my stepfather's willing to do to keep me safe, and a part of me—the part that hates how helpless I feel all the time— likes the thought of that a lot.

"Okay." I let out a shaky breath and glance toward the door. "I should go. My mother's waiting."

It's the last thing I want to do, to move away from him. The whole left side of my body is warm and tingly in a way I've never felt before, radiating out from where his hand is still gripping my hip. It's almost like he doesn't want to let go either.

I... don't know what to do with that.

Cohen's eyes stay on me for a beat longer, and then his hand slowly drops away from my body. I shiver at the sudden intrusion of cold. "Of course."

I turn, my legs like Jell-O, and give my best attempt at a polite smile as I pick up the shopping bag and wave goodbye to the salesgirl, because that's what's expected of me. But even as I step outside onto the freezing sidewalk, I can still feel Cohen's gaze on me, intense and burning.

There's a strange comfort in knowing he's watching, that right now he's the only person on this Earth that has my back.

For now, it's enough to know I'm not alone, even if the person standing between me and the rest of the world is the one person I shouldn't want to get closer to.

Unfortunately for me...

I do.

Cohen

CHAPTER 3

I'M LOSING MY PATIENCE.

I grip the steering wheel of my Aston Martin so tightly that the leather groans under the pressure of my white-knuckled grip. My jaw is clenched so hard my teeth ache, every breath I take shallow and labored, like there's a wildfire smoldering under my skin. It's beginning to burn out of control.

Control.

I scoff. The word does little to settle the storm raging inside me.

That bastard touched her with his eyes.

He *dared* to let his disgusting gaze rake over her body.

If it weren't for the boutique's staff swarming the place like flies, I would have zero hesitation about tearing Emmitt Caldwell's smug face apart, inch by inch, with my bare hands. I can still see it—the glint in his eyes when he looked at her, the way his lips curled in that self-satisfied smirk. It took everything within me to hold back, to play the part of stepfather. To keep my fury in check.

But right now? As I picture his face again, it takes a superhuman level of restraint not to turn the car around and hunt him down.

Why should I let him live? He's nothing. He's in my way, and *nothing* will get in my way of having Emerald.

My rage churns and digs its claws in deep. Today, I slipped, and I *never* slip. I reached for her. Publicly. Carelessly. And for what? Fucking *jealousy*. A fucking *need*. But more than that? Emmitt pushed me to my breaking point. He looked at her like he wanted to steal her from me.

The type of man he is, I know exactly what kind of poison was seeping through his thoughts when he looked at her like that. And the idea that someone so mediocre could even think about her that way, that something so beautifully fragile could ever be tainted by filth like him, is unacceptable.

I flick my gaze out of the windshield, watching Emerald get out of the back seat of her mother's new Range Rover, her driver Anthony pulling off to park the car. She climbs the grand stone steps of the house we share, the house where I should already fucking have her. Where she spends her nights far too many doors away from me, in her perfectly polished cage, unaware of how close I've come to snapping every day that I wait.

I want to kill Emmitt for daring to keep even a memory of her when she belongs to *me*.

I'm not sure I can let it go.

I swallow back the bloodlust rising in my veins, forcing myself to think. Insomnia has been my constant companion since I was seven, since the night I learned that sleep meant vulnerability and vulnerability meant death. But I've made those endless dark hours work for me, turned them into weapons in my arsenal. While others sleep, I plan. I watch. I prepare. These sleepless nights have given me everything I have —my reputation, my power, my ability to protect what's mine. And now they've given me her.

His time will come. The problem with a man like Emmitt? He thinks he's untouchable. And that's going to be his downfall —believing that someone hasn't already marked him for disposal. I'll be patient, methodical, the way I always am. One foolish slip could ruin everything.

And I *won't* let that happen. Not when I'm so. Damn. Close.

Emerald's new Range Rover pulls into the spot beside me. Anthony gets out without noticing I'm sitting here behind pitch black tinted windows getting my shit together before I enter the seventh circle of Hell and have to face my wife. My lip curls at my wife's 'gift' for Emerald. Perfect, shining, obnoxious. It's like everything else in this place.

A gift Emerald doesn't even know how to drive.

Fucking Madeline. Even her name makes me want to throw something. The woman who brought me into this house, who paved the path to Emerald, but who now is nothing more than a particularly bothersome mosquito buzzing around my ear.

And speaking of the woman...

My wife is waiting in the foyer when I finally go inside, her arms folded across her chest, the picture of poised elegance wrapped in an icy veneer. There's a sharp smile tugging at her lips, but I'd have to be blind not to see the irritation right there under her skin. She's an expert at hiding her emotions. Unfortunately for her, I pay too much attention.

"Hello, Darling," she says, her voice dripping with saccharine venom. "Doing a little shopping that couldn't wait? Did I miss something? Or are we just ignoring lunch plans now?" Her gaze flicks toward the bag still swinging from Emerald's wrist as she hands it off to her mother without a word, her eyes downcast.

"We're running behind on the afternoon shoot now," Madeline adds, her irritation barely concealed. "You both know how I feel about punctuality."

Emerald doesn't even notice me standing just inside the

doorway as she quickly murmurs an apology and then disappears up the winding staircase toward her bedroom to avoid her mother's wrath. I can barely resist the instinct to follow her with my eyes, to track her every step, but I hold myself back. I wait until I hear the softest click of her door shutting upstairs before I turn my attention back to my wife.

Madeline hates being late, and she's absolutely right. I *do* know it. And the fact that I've thrown off her meticulously planned schedule today brings me a perverse sort of satisfaction. Just another reminder that she may think she is, but in reality, she's not in control here—not of me, and soon not of Emerald.

This woman is always playing games. Watching. Plotting her moves, expecting me to follow her every word like gospel. I've allowed it to this point as it's gotten me here, right where I need to be. But she'll soon learn the man she's shared her house with for the last year isn't even close to who I really am.

Madeline pats herself on the back every time she imagines her strings pulling me along, bending me to her will. If only she knew that the strings were never hers to pull.

Her eyes narrow a fraction more when I remain silent. I fold my hands in front of me, lean casually against the wall, and let one corner of my mouth lift with a smile I don't mean. "Do you need something, Madeline?"

She tilts her head to the side, studying me with eyes that look all too much like her daughters', except cold, practical. Calculating. The green in them reminds me of the icy ferns that coat the floor of the forest in our backyard. They're *nothing* like Emerald's warm summer grass green.

"Did you run into anyone while you were out?" It's as if she's asking about the weather, but that almost bored tone can't fool me. She already knows about my run-in with Emmitt at the boutique.

I shrug, as though her question is too dull to consider. "Like whom?"

Her eyes narrow only slightly, but she covers it well, casting a glance toward the ceiling in Emerald's general direction. "Emmitt was in town. Meeting with our suppliers. He mentioned seeing you. I thought maybe the two of you had a chance to talk."

A smirk begins to tug at the corner of my lips, and I quash it. She thinks she's so clever. What does she think I'll tell her? That I essentially staked a public claim on her daughter in front of one of her business partners?

Does she imagine Emmitt would have been brave enough to tell her about all the details of today? She thinks she has her little pet doing her bidding, spying and reporting back all the details. I doubt he told her that the moment between him and Emerald could have cost him his life.

That he almost died today for looking at the wrong girl. *My* girl.

He might have the audacity to eye fuck my stepdaughter, but he's not stupid enough to return to Madeline without removing any trace of evidence of his misstep.

Or maybe he really is that stupid. Either way, I'll deal with him soon enough.

"We exchanged pleasantries," I say, sounding as bored as I feel, pushing away from the wall to close the distance between us. "It wasn't exactly the time or place for deep conversation."

Madeline raises an eyebrow, clearly pleased with herself, her power. She thinks her success is in prying information from me when, all along, I've been withholding far more than she will ever understand.

"Well, be careful." Her voice softens, dropping into that fake sweet tone, something close to an order creeping through, though none of Madeline's orders work on me. Or maybe it's a warning. "He likes to play with his food."

A laugh almost escapes me. She's warning me about *Emmitt*? The mid-at-best businessman hanging around begging for a scrap of her attention when the real danger is me? I've been the only one she's ever needed to watch out for. But like every other idiot, she's been too wrapped up in her ambition and self-obsession to see the truth hiding in her own home.

I cover a grin with another shrug. "I'll keep that in mind."

Just as I'm about to make an excuse to get the hell out of here, my phone vibrates in my pocket. I slide it out, glancing at the screen, and I suck in a sharp breath when I see what popped up—a notification from the app. The one I've been using to track Emerald's cycle.

Ovulation window begins today.

A dark surge of arousal and satisfaction rush through me that I can barely contain. I refuse to let Madeline see even a hint of emotion on my face, but I have to dig my nails into my palm to keep from reacting.

Emerald's ready—her *body* is ready for me. For what I have planned.

For our child.

Perfect timing, right when everything else is falling into place. I slide the phone back into my pocket, biting back the urge to let the smirk spread across my face in front of Madeline.

"Something important?" she asks, focused on me like if she glares hard enough, she can rip the information straight out of my brain. She's always prying. Always trying to find leverage, even when she's clueless.

"Business," I say, already stepping back. Before she can respond, I retreat quickly down the hallway, heading toward my office. The excuse couldn't have come at a better time. I've got a mountain of work, but my preoccupation with Emerald has taken priority, so I need to play catch up.

The click of the lock behind me is a small relief. I let out a slow breath, my mind still buzzing with that notification. With what I plan to do tonight.

I lean back against the door for a second, letting out a long exhale as I finally let go of the tension that's been gripping me since I left that damn boutique.

Paying off the household staff to report on Emerald's cycle had been one of my better moves. Discreet inquiries, generous payouts—ensuring that I'd always know exactly when her body was primed and ready. Each update fed into my app, allowing me to keep meticulous track. All that planning, all that patience, and now it's finally paying off.

There are no prying eyes here in my office. No interruptions while I finalize my plans. I'm careful to scan for recording devices and cameras every time I step foot in here, and this time is no exception. I wouldn't put it past Madeline to plant them and spy on me, but this is my sanctuary. I may allow her to think she's in control of many aspects of my life, but this isn't one of them.

After the scan comes up clear, I pour myself a drink and move to the window, watching as Madeline's lackeys set up her precious photoshoot on our snow-covered lawn.

I do a quick scan for Emerald, but she's not outside yet.

For now, maybe I can have a minute to gather my thoughts.

I sink into my chair, resolving to get some work done, but it's not long before my mind is drifting toward my pretty little stepdaughter again.

Toward what I plan to do tonight to tie her to me forever.

It's not hard to picture her in my bed, her dark hair tangled on my pillow. Or round and growing our children. Looking up at me with those wide, innocent eyes of hers like I'm the sun her world spins around.

Emerald's face flashes in my mind: standing in the boutique earlier today, unaware—far *too* unaware—of how easily she could have been tainted. The way she fidgeted with the sleeve of her tight sweater dress, biting on her lip as Emmitt's gaze crawled all over her. Emmitt is an idiot, but he's not oblivious. He knows how special she is. How pure.

She's a beacon drawing all the monsters toward her.

I'm the worst monster of them all.

This thing between us... it's inevitable. The gift I'm giving both of us this Christmas. And despite every shred of self-control I've cultivated over my lifetime, it's slipping. The need to possess her feels dangerous in a way nothing else ever has. It's getting out of hand, building every single day, and the patience I've always relied on—my weapon, my shield—is fraying, stretched impossibly thin.

Tonight, I'm going to let the thread snap and take what's always belonged to me.

I reach for the glass of bourbon in front of me. The liquid burns its way down my throat as I finish the entire glass in one go, trying to rein in all the thoughts surging through me. The craving for her.

I've spent more than a year playing the long game. Watching. Waiting. Building the groundwork brick by fucking brick. Each detail, each maneuver crafted to form a perfect existence where *she belongs to me.*

I can't wait any longer. Waiting was for before. Before her eyes started lingering on me a little too long, before the blush that stains her cheeks every time our eyes connect across the dinner table, before she started letting me in.

Before I knew her body was fertile and ready for everything I have to give her.

It's time to nudge things along.

By Christmas, she'll officially be mine.

With any luck, she'll be pregnant by then, too.

I need to get closer to her, to make her feel me in her space, in her dreams, to make sure she understands that I'm the only one who sees her. Who wants her for who she really is. Who'll let her *be* who she really is.

Madeline thinks she's got me on a short leash, but she doesn't understand what's brewing between Emerald and me. She can't, because she doesn't have a heart. A soul.

Emerald is the other half of mine.

I use one of the keys I wear on a chain around my neck to unlock the drawer in my desk, checking the pill bottle inside, shaking the tiny square peach-colored pills inside. I pop the lid off and shake out two, slipping them into my pocket before replacing the bottle and locking the drawer back up.

Tonight, I'll go to her. Sneak out of my room and into hers. My cock is pulsing, harder than it's ever been, just thinking of what I'm about to do. I'll be careful, just as I always am, but this is going to happen. It *needs* to happen.

Nothing will stop me.

I'll give her all of me, and I'll take all of her. I'll get her body used to mine so when she's awake, she craves me but doesn't understand why.

This is what she needs. It's what we *both* need. I've waited long enough, played along with Madeline's rules for far too long. It's time for Emerald to see that I'm the only person she needs in this life. The only one who's really here for her.

I set the empty glass back on my desk, a slow smile spreading across my face as I swivel in my chair to look back outside. I spin my wedding ring around my finger and watch as Emerald stands beside her mother in the middle of a small crowd of stylists, assistants, makeup artists, and the photographer.

But all I see is her. Her light is so blinding, everyone else blinks out of existence.

Tonight is only the beginning.

Tonight, the boundary between us will shatter.

And when that happens, there will be no turning back.

We belong to each other.

I know what needs to be done, and there isn't one goddamn thing that will stop me from taking the first step tonight.

Let the world try to intervene. Let Madeline think she knows everything that happens under her roof.

By the time Emerald begins to understand, it'll be too late.

Her and me?

We're inescapable.

Cohen

CHAPTER 4

EVEN MONSTERS CAN PRETEND to be gentlemen. Until they're done pretending.

Tonight, I've reached my limit.

The house settles around me as I move through darkness thick as ink, my footsteps silent against hand-woven Persian rugs older than I am. It's three in the morning, and everyone's asleep—everyone except the monster prowling these halls.

That would be me.

I've memorized every creaking floorboard between my room and hers. Learned which shadows to stick to, how to move like a ghost through this mausoleum Madeline calls home.

I don't think I care about getting caught anymore. No, what drives my caution now is the need to keep this moment pure. Untainted. This is between Emerald and me. No one else deserves to share in what's about to happen.

I pause at the top of the stairs, listening. The silence wraps around me like a familiar friend, broken only by the soft whisper of snow falling against the nearby windows and the distant hum of the heating system. I've spent too many nights to count walking this same path, talking myself out of what I'm about to do. Convincing myself to wait *just a little longer.*

No more of that shit.

Madeline is three doors down, passed out from the sleeping pill I slipped into her wine at dinner. She has no idea her perfectly crafted world is about to shatter. She's never turned me on, but imagining the look on her face when she loses everything is enough to convince my already hard dick to give an excited twitch.

I move past my wife's door without a sound, my pulse steady despite the anticipation coursing through my veins. I've waited for this, planned it down to the smallest detail. Tonight marks the beginning of everything.

The sight of Emerald's door at the end of the hall is like gravity, drawing me in. Even in darkness, I can see the pale wood, the delicate brass handle that separates me from what's mine.

What's always been mine.

My fingers curl around the cool metal of the other key I wear around my neck, and I close my eyes, savoring this moment—the precipice between restraint and surrender. After tonight, there's no going back.

I pull the necklace off, inserting the key into the lock. It gives way easily, just as it should. I had it changed weeks ago, the new mechanism ensuring only I have the key. Another careful piece in the elaborate game I've been playing. The door opens without a sound, and her scent hits me immediately. It's sweet, like sugar cookies fresh from the oven, wholesomeness laced with something that makes my mouth water.

I step inside, twisting the handle so the door shuts silently behind me as I shove my necklace into the pocket of my joggers. I don't want it getting in the way.

The brightness from the moonlight on the snow outside spills through her windows, painting everything in shades of silver and shadow. My eyes adjust quickly, scanning the familiar space, the artfully arranged furniture, the delicate vanity where she sits each morning, letting her dark hair fall like silk through her fingers.

But it's her I'm drawn to. Always her.

Emerald lies in the center of her bed, a vision of purity and goodness wrapped in white sheets. Her hair spreads across the pillow in waves of midnight, her face peaceful in sleep. One arm is thrown above her head, her throat exposed. It's so fucking tempting, begging to be marked by my teeth until that pristine skin blooms with bruises that prove she's mine. She has no idea about the monster who's crept into her room, ready to corrupt every inch of her innocence.

My cock hardens at the sight of her, straining against my pants as I move closer. The need to touch her, to claim her, burns through my veins like poison.

She doesn't move. Of course she doesn't, not after I slipped her a sleeping pill with her dinner, too. Her virginity has always belonged to me, but she doesn't need to be awake to experience the pain of losing it.

If I can spare her from feeling anything but happiness, love, and satisfaction, I'll do everything in my power to do it.

That includes taking what belongs to me while she sleeps through it, blissfully unaware.

"So beautiful," I whisper, my voice barely a breath in the darkness. "So fucking perfect."

I ease onto the edge of her bed, careful not to disturb her. She may be harder to wake, but not impossible. I'm going to take my time, ensure that even asleep, she gets to experience some pleasure.

This moment is too precious to rush.

God, the things I want to do to her.

The things I *will* do to her.

Her nightgown has ridden up, exposing the creamy

smoothness of her thighs. The sight makes my mouth water, my control threatening to snap. I've imagined this view a thousand times, but reality is so much sweeter. So much more dangerous.

"You have no idea what you do to me, little one," I murmur, letting my fingers ghost along her ankle. Her skin is silky soft and warm under my touch. "The things I think about. The ways I want to break you apart and put you back together."

She stirs a little at my touch but doesn't wake. Good. That's not part of tonight's plan. Tonight is about claiming her firsts, about planting myself inside of her, about putting down roots.

I lean closer, sucking in her scent like the first hit of coke after rehab. "It's already too late," I murmur, my fingers trailing up. "Your body is mine to worship, your mind is mine to twist, and your soul... your soul is the other half of mine."

My hand slides higher, tracing patterns on her calf, her knee, her thigh. She makes a small sound in her sleep, almost a whimper, and shifts restlessly. Her legs part, an unconscious invitation that rips apart the last threads of my restraint.

I climb further onto the bed, pulling the bottle of lube I stashed in my pocket out and tossing it onto the mattress beside her. I hover over her body as the muscles in my arms flex to support my weight. I don't touch. Not yet. I just watch, taking in the rise and fall of her chest, the flutter of her eyelashes, the way her lips part with every breath. Feel the warmth of her skin radiating into mine. She's like a living doll—fragile, untouched, and so fucking corruptible.

"I'm going to take everything from you," I promise, my voice low and dark so I don't wake her. "And in return, I'll give you the only love that matters. It'll burn everything else away until there's nothing left but us."

With my words hanging in the air around us, I finally let myself touch, running my hands over the soft swell of her breasts, the curve of her hips. She's still asleep, but her body responds to me instinctively, arching into my touch like a flower seeking the sun.

"That's it," I murmur, leaning down to brush my lips against her throat.

She moans softly as my teeth graze her skin, a sound that goes straight to my cock. Fuck, I need to be inside her. Need to feel her tight, virginal cunt wrapped around me. It's an obsession, a craving that's consumed me for two years, and now, finally, it's within reach.

"You'll never belong to anyone else. Not in this life, not in the next. You're mine until the stars burn out." It's a promise, an oath, and a curse all in one, whispered in the dead of night. The only witness is the dark.

I slide off the bed, standing to strip away my joggers and my boxers, the only items of clothing I'm wearing, and then grab the lube again. I'm getting high, a euphoric burst of pleasure that's spreading through every artery and vein in my body, knowing what's coming. Knowing that I'll have to prepare her to take my dick, that she'll have to stretch to fit me, that it'll be me and me alone that experiences the raw ecstasy of her body from now until the end of time.

Her body is soft and relaxed as I climb back onto the bed, not stopping until I'm between her thighs, a position I've dreamed about more times than I can count. The moonlight casts an ethereal glow across her skin, and for a moment, I can't help but marvel at the sheer beauty of her. She's an angel fallen into the hands of a demon, and I'm about to drag her down into the depths of my hell with me.

I think she'll like it here.

I run my hands along the outside of her thighs, and she lets out a little whimper as my cock leaks all over the fucking place. It knows what it's here to do.

Fuck. Claim. *Impregnate*.

Her legs spread wider, and I settle in the gap, nudging them open a little more. This is where I belong. This is home.

"Fuck," I groan, running my hand up her thigh again. The silky smoothness of her skin is so soft and unblemished my mouth waters with the urge to bite. Her nightdress is tangled around her waist, and I can just make out the delicate lace of her panties in the silvery light from the window.

Her hips shift, pushing up toward me, and I swallow down another groan. I'm sure she's had dreams like this before. Dreams of me, taking her, owning her, claiming her. I bet she's woken up wet, needy, and aching and didn't know what was happening.

Madeline never taught Emerald about sex or the things her body was made to do. My stepdaughter is untouched in every way.

Since I became aware of her a year and a half ago, I've made sure it stayed that way. I've guarded her innocence since the night I saw her on that balcony at some bullshit charity gala. No one has come near her. No one has gotten the opportunity to taint her with their filthy, greedy hands. I've kept her pure and innocent, a blank canvas ready to be painted with my desires.

I run a finger along the lace of her underwear, tracing the outline of her sweet little cunt through the fabric. With my thumb, I flip open the cap on the bottle of lube and pour a little on my fingertips. I gently ease her underwear to the side and run the tips of my fingers along her smooth slit, taking my time to spread the slippery fluid around. Her body shifts when I brush my fingers against her clit, stroking it soft and slow. Tracing circles around it. I could play with her like this for hours, but the ache in my balls is too great. If I'm not careful, my overwhelming need to come inside of her will make me rush and I want to take my time. Savor every second of acquiring her innocence.

When this is done, no one will be able to take this experience from me.

I continue to stroke her pussy, gently teasing her clit, while I tear my eyes away from the show in favor of another sense—taste. The overwhelming need to know what she feels like on my tongue has me dipping my head before I even make the decision to do it. I'm dragging my tongue up her cunt and circling her clit once before pulling back. There's the taste of lube, but underneath it is pure, unfiltered Emerald. The groan that tears out of me can't be helped. She's so fucking perfect. Like sweetness and innocence. Sin and corruption. Everything I could ever need. Ever want.

I want to obliterate every part of her that hasn't known my touch. Make her come on my tongue until she has to beg me to stop and I'm drunk on her.

But not tonight.

Tonight is about something bigger, something better, something far more permanent.

I slide a finger into her, watching as her tight little hole stretches to make room for me in her body. The lube helps me ease my way in and then out, a slow, easy slide as I bend to flick my tongue against her clit again. Emerald's eyebrows scrunch in her sleep and her nipples peak underneath her nightie.

While my finger slides in and out of her, I reach up and tug down the top of her dress, needing to see her tits more than I need my next heartbeat. They're fucking perfect. Pale and smooth, the kind of tits that could drive me to madness. Her nipples are the perfect shade of pink, delicate and pretty, like every other part of her. They're made for my mouth, my teeth, my hands. Made to be sucked on, to be played with... to feed our children.

They'll never know anything other than me.

She's sleeping, but her body is responding to my touch, arching into me, seeking more. Her mouth parts as her breathing gets faster. Her body flushes pink from her cheeks all the way to those rosy pink nipples and her cunt tightens around my finger. I add a second one as my balls ache and tighten, pulling close to my body. If I'm not careful, I'll come before I'm ready and waste everything I've been saving up for her for the past few days.

I want to give my swimmers the best chance to do their job.

I wrap my other hand around the base of my shaft, squeezing and clenching my teeth together to keep from coming. Deep breaths aren't helping as every inhale is laced with Emerald. I'm drowning in her scent and I fucking love it.

I revel in it.

I want her coated on my skin and I never want to wash her off.

I need to be inside of her.

My fingers slide free, and I move closer, pulling her legs further open to make room for me. I wrap my sticky fingers around her panties, pulling them to the side to keep them away. With my cock in my other hand, I rub the head along her opening. Fuck, she's already so warm and slippery. I breathe out through my nose and grit my teeth. The pre-cum leaking from my tip mixes with the wetness from the lube and her own arousal.

My hips move on their own, rubbing my shaft against her slick pussy, getting me nice and coated so I'll be able to slide inside of her. Every time my stroke ends at her clit, she whimpers in her sleep. On my next pass, the head of my dick slips inside of her and I let out a curse.

The barrier that marks her as untouched, as innocent, stops me from going any further, but I only let it hold me back for a heartbeat before I'm tearing through it. Pushing through her resistance until I'm buried deep inside of her. Until I bottom out. My body shakes as I look down at her, watching for any sign that the pain has woken her. Her face is slack in sleep, her mouth parted on a soft exhale as her cunt ripples and squeezes around me. It's too fucking good. Better than I could have imagined.

It feels like the world has shifted. Like it's moved into alignment.

I've spent so many years of my life, so many decades, without her. And now, finally, we're connected in the most primal way. I can feel the warmth of her body, her soul, wrapping around mine, intertwining us in ways that can't be undone. It's a bond that's been forged in the depths of my twisted heart, a promise that we'll never be apart again.

I'm trembling with the effort of not thrusting, of not taking her hard and fast the way my body wants me to. But I don't want to risk hurting her. She needs a minute to adjust, so I hold my breath and lock my muscles and wait.

She's so fucking tight, it's almost painful as she chokes my dick. This moment is everything I thought it would be and so much more. It's like my entire universe has narrowed down to the point where our bodies are joined, and nothing else matters but the feel of her wrapped around me. I lean down, burying my face in her neck, breathing in the sweet scent of her skin. I'm barely aware of anything beyond the overwhelming sensation of being inside of her, of finally feeling complete.

"Fuck," I bite out, my voice rough and strained. "You fit me so perfectly, little one, like you were made just for me." The words are a low rumble against her ear, and a shiver runs through her body that I feel in mine. Her pussy clenches around me and I nearly lose it.

I brace my hands on either side of her head, lifting my head to watch her face as I finally, finally, start to move. Her dark eyelashes flutter against her pale cheeks as I pull out slowly, indulging in the feel of her body clenching around me, trying to keep me inside. When only the head of my dick is still in her cunt, I pause even as my very soul screams at me to push back inside of her. To fill her up with me.

"You're bound to me now," I whisper, my fingers grazing her skin, "Every cell, every drop of blood, every atom that makes you who you are—all of it exists for me."

I know she's not aware of these declarations I'm making in the dark, but I can't help but say them out loud. Maybe they'll infiltrate her dreams.

With a slow, controlled thrust, I push back into her, filling her up until our bodies are flush. Until I can't get any deeper. My eyes slip shut and I tilt my head toward the ceiling. I'm lost to the feeling of her. Of this.

When I look back down, there's blood coating my dick and the sheets beneath her thighs. I pull out, watching it drip from her. The sight of it nearly turns me feral. It's the physical evidence that she was a virgin, that she was pure, that no one has been or will be here before or after me. She'll wear my mark inside of her for the rest of eternity. She'll be branded by me from the inside out.

Her blood.

My cum.

Our future.

I push back inside of her, a groan tearing out of me, and I give in to the madness. To the insanity. To the obsession. The desire. The depravity of what I've wanted for so long. I thrust harder, faster, letting go of the last shreds of my control. The bed shakes underneath us as I grip her thigh with one hand and open her wider for me, getting as deep as I possibly can inside of her as my balls tighten and my cock pulses with the need to come. I shift my grip to her ass, tilting her hips so that when I let go, I can do it as deeply as possible inside of her. The head of my dick nudges against her cervix and her mouth opens on a breathy moan as she shifts beneath me.

For a second, I think she's going to wake up.

Right now, I don't give a fuck. Let her.

I can't stop.

The pleasure is building to an unbearable peak, and I can feel it bursting in every nerve ending, firing off like little atomic explosions as I grind into her, chasing the release I've been denied for far too long. Her skin is flushed with pleasure and sleep, and her hair's a tangled mess from her head thrashing back and forth on her pillow.

She's so fucking perfect, and I'm so fucking lucky.

So fucking greedy.

So fucking needy.

So fucking obsessed.

I reach between us, rubbing her clit and watching as the pleasure sparks across her face. It's subtle—the fluttering of her eyelashes, the parting of her lips, the flush on her cheeks. She can't come until after I do. I need her greedy little cunt to suck up my cum, the contractions of her orgasm to help my boys along. But I can start building her toward it now while I'm here on the edge about to fall over.

My muscles tighten as my balls draw up. A groan that feels torn from the depths of my soul bursts from my throat, and my fingers dig into the soft flesh of her thigh. I'm on the precipice, and then I'm hurtling over the edge, my hips slamming into her one last time as the most powerful orgasm of my life crashes over me. I can feel the hot rush of my cum flooding her womb, and I let out a choked sob as the pleasure overwhelms me.

It's everything I dreamed of, everything I needed, and more. My heart stutters in my chest as I pump into her, my hips jerking as I fill her with every last drop of the cum I saved up just for her. For this moment. My body shakes with the intensity of my release, and I collapse on top of her, burying my face in her neck, careful not to crush her. My breath comes in ragged gasps as I ride out the waves of ecstasy.

Once the last of the tremors have subsided, I lift myself up and slide out of her. I fucking hate it when the last inch of my cock pulls out of her body and into the cold. But I need to make her come more than I need to be inside of her right now.

I slide down her body, using my fingers to push the cum that's already leaking out of her pussy back inside while my mouth latches onto her clit. I lick and suck as her hips shift and roll beneath me. The taste of her mixed with me is enough to make me hard again, but I ignore my dick while I focus on getting her off. Her fingers twitch, her hands shifting on the bed above her head and at her side. I'm relentless, flicking her clit with my tongue and sucking on her until her body tightens. Her orgasm is quiet as her pussy ripples and squeezes my fingers and her breathing picks up.

When the little flutters stop, I slide my fingers out of her and shift her limp body over, moving her onto her side before pushing my still hard cock back inside of her. I lick the taste of her off my fingers and come down from the high of what I've just done. A dark satisfaction surges through my veins, sweeter than sin and more intoxicating than any high.

She could be pregnant with my baby before the sun rises.

I could fall asleep this way, inside of her as I slowly soften and drift off, her body and mine connected while her body accepts the gift I just gave it.

Unfortunately, if my stepdaughter were to wake up right now, it would ruin everything.

So I slip from the bed and tug her panties back into place. They'll hold in the mess I've left behind long enough for my boys to do what I put them here to do. After that, it doesn't matter if they leak out. If she's pregnant, all of this will be over. If not... I'll just have to try again.

And again.

And again.

As many times as it takes to bind her to me permanently.

I briefly consider trying to change the sheets, but decide to leave them. Hopefully she'll think she started her period. What else could she possibly think happened when she doesn't really know what sex is or how it works?

How babies are made.

I bend down and grab my boxers, pulling them on over my half-hard dick that's still stained with the blood of her innocence. Then I grab my joggers, slipping those on too. I look at her one last time before I leave, the vision of her sleeping soundly, her womb filled with my cum and the sheets beneath her bloody, is something that will live in my fantasies for years to come.

Committing that image to memory, I slip out of her room, shutting and locking the door behind me, and make my way back to my own. Once I'm there, I fall back onto the bed, still in a state of blissful post-orgasmic euphoria. My entire body is buzzing with the afterglow of the most intense sexual experience of my life. But underneath the pleasure, there's a deep sense of peace and contentment that's settled in my bones. For the first time in my life, everything feels right. Like everything I've been working for over the last two years is finally falling into place.

Emerald is mine now.

She may be having my baby.

And all that's left to do is make her fall in love with me.

Emerald
CHAPTER 5

I WAKE up feeling like my brain's made of cotton candy.

My head is fuzzy, sure, but more concerning, there's this deep ache between my legs that I've never felt before. Like I've been split in two and hastily glued back together, but the glue hasn't quite dried yet. Every tiny movement makes me aware of places inside me I didn't even know could hurt, places I've never thought about before.

I blink up at my ceiling, marveling at the little imperfections in the paint on the crown molding as I try to piece together what's wrong with me. The gray light from the snow-covered world outside leaves dull and dark enough that I want to bury myself in my covers and go back to sleep.

I know I can't give in to that, and even if I wanted to, it'd be impossible because everything feels... off.

Maybe I'm getting sick?

The thought drifts through the marshmallow fluff in my mind as I shift under the covers, wincing at the soreness that radiates through my body. My muscles ache as if they've been stretched beyond their limits. It reminds me of the day after one of my trainer Ilya's brutal workouts.

Except all I did was sleep, so what the heck?

And Pilates with Ilya never gets me sore between my legs.

I glance down at my sheets, and my stomach drops when I see the brownish-red stains on the formerly pristine white fabric. Ugh, just what I needed—my period to show up two weeks early. I guess this explains why I feel like death warmed over. Cramps have always been horrible for me, but I don't remember ever having cramps quite like this before.

Fragments of the dreams I think I had last night float through the sticky cloudiness of my mind. Really, you could call them sensations more than actual memories. Warmth. Pressure. Pleasure mixed with pain. The ghost of hands on my skin. But trying to grab onto any specific memory is like trying to catch smoke. The more I reach for it, the faster it dissipates.

I must have had some weird dreams last night. Really weird dreams that I can't quite remember, but that left me feeling...

Well, a whole lot like I'm going crazy.

Huh, maybe it was aliens. That's a thing, right? Getting abducted and... probed?

I snort at how ridiculous I'm being. Obviously, the stress of everything yesterday with Emmitt and the extra pressure my mother puts on me at this time of year is getting to me.

I force myself to swing my legs over the side of the bed and immediately regret it. My thighs tremble and my hips ache. When I stand, the soreness only gets worse, and I have to grip the mattress to keep from falling back onto it and forgetting about this day.

Let's just throw the whole thing away and try again tomorrow.

"What is *wrong* with me?" I mutter to myself, pressing my free hand against my lower abdomen where a dull ache has settled.

Everything feels amplified—it's like all my nerve endings are raw and exposed, hypersensitive to every sensation.

I stumble toward my bathroom, my reflection in the mirror stopping me the second I step through the door and flip on the light. I look... wrecked. My cheeks are flushed, my lips slightly swollen like I've been biting them in my sleep, and my hair is a tangled mess around my shoulders.

A knock at my bedroom door makes me jump, and my heart launches itself up into my throat.

"Miss Delacroix?" Kendra's voice filters through the wood. "Your mother expects you downstairs in thirty minutes."

Of course she does. Because God forbid I get to have a sick day.

"I'll be down soon," I call back, my voice raspier than usual, like I've been screaming or crying or something.

Maybe I really am sick.

I take stock of my symptoms. Despite my flushed cheeks, I don't feel feverish. No stuffy nose, cough, or stomach problems. I'm going through a mental checklist and nothing's adding up.

Not that it would matter if I *was* sick. No doubt my mother has my entire day already planned out, sickness or not.

I turn on the shower, cranking up the heat until steam fills the bathroom. As I peel off my nightgown, I notice more brownish stains on my underwear. Definitely my period then. Though something doesn't feel quite right about that, but I don't know what else it could be.

The hot water helps ease some of the soreness in my muscles, but it can't wash away this strange sense that I'm missing something huge. This sense that the world tilted on its axis while I slept.

While I rinse my hair, my mind drifts to Cohen. It's been doing that a lot lately, my thoughts wandering to my stepfather at the most random moments. But this morning, thinking about him makes my body react in ways I don't understand. My skin flushes with heat that has nothing to do with the shower, and my stomach does this weird flip-flop thing that's becoming way too familiar when I think about him.

Or when he walks into a room.

Or speaks.

Or does anything, really.

Like exist.

Ugh.

I remember how he defended me yesterday at the boutique, the way his hand felt on my back, strong and steady. Warm. *Tingly.* How safe I felt with him there, even though I probably shouldn't. He's my mother's husband, for crying out loud. I shouldn't feel anything when I think about him.

But I do.

And that terrifies me more than this unexplained soreness, more than these half-remembered dreams, more than the idea of spending the rest of my life under my mother's thumb.

Because the way my body responds to even the thought of him? That's not normal. That's not okay. That's not something I can explain away if anyone were to find out—say, my mother or any of her horrible friends.

Or worse, Cohen himself.

I press my forehead against the cool tile of the shower wall, trying to quiet the whirlwind of thoughts spinning around in my head. "Get it together, Emerald," I whisper to myself. "You're just tired. Or sick. Or hormonal. Or all of the above. You *will not* obsess over your stepfather."

I step out of the shower and wrap myself in a fluffy towel, ignoring the fact I'm lying to myself. Who am I kidding? Pretending I haven't spent at least eighty percent of the last three days thinking about Cohen is an exercise in futility. It's like trying to ignore a fly buzzing around my head.

It's so much easier to just deal with getting dressed and pretending there's not something seriously wrong with me.

Yep, I'm just a normal girl.

Nothing to see here.

When I step into my closet, something feels off. I glance around, expecting to see my outfit laid out like every other morning, perfectly arranged and ready to go. But today? Nothing. I blink at the empty space where my clothes usually hang, a weird knot forming in my stomach.

No way did she forget. I've had a long-standing debate with myself about whether Kendra's a human or one of those AI chatbot things wearing human skin.

Jury's still out.

Which makes the fact Kendra hasn't laid out an outfit for me today so strange. For a fraction of a second, I wonder if my mother's allowing me to pick my own clothes for once. If maybe I've earned that privilege. But then I remember Madeline Delacroix is the ultimate control freak and not even if a zombie apocalypse was happening would she loosen the noose she drags me around with.

Which brings me back to... why? What happened?

And if this isn't on my mother's orders, how am I supposed to know the right thing to wear that won't piss her off?

I frown while I search through my clothes, starting to sweat as I consider my options. Eventually I settle on a soft gray cashmere sweater dress. It's modest but tailored and the color will hopefully blend in with the weather and keep Mother's attention off of me. Pairing it with black tights and knee-high boots seems like a safe bet, and just the kind of thing she loves. Elegant and sophisticated and lacking any sort of personality at all.

Getting dressed is an exercise in pain management. Every movement sends little shockwaves through my body, and the tights are basically torture devices disguised as clothing. By the time I make it downstairs, I'm walking like I've been riding horses all day, which is ridiculous because I've never even been on a horse.

The smell of coffee and fresh-baked croissants hits me as I enter the dining room, and my stomach does a weird growl-twist thing that's either hunger or nausea. I'm not quite sure which. My mother sits at the head of the table like she's holding court, her fingers tapping away at her tablet while she pretends not to notice me.

"Good morning, sweetheart," she says after she's waited long enough to be sure I know I only get her attention when she decides she's ready to give it. Of course she doesn't bother looking up, and her voice carries that artificial warmth she only uses when there are witnesses around. Today, that's the kitchen staff standing at attention in case my mother's coffee drops below the halfway point of her cup. "You're almost late."

Almost late in Madeline-speak means I'm exactly on time, but not early enough to satisfy her impossible standards. I sink into my usual chair, trying not to wince at the pressure against my sore muscles.

"Sorry," I mumble, reaching for a croissant just to have something to do with my hands. My mother would never allow me to eat it, not with all the butter and fat. "I wasn't feeling well this morning."

That gets her attention. Her ice-blue eyes snap up from her tablet, scanning me like she's running some kind of diagnostic test. "You look flushed," she says, her perfectly shaped eyebrows drawing together. "I hope you're not coming down with something. We have the website holiday photoshoot this afternoon, and I need you looking your best."

Of course that's what she's worried about. Heaven forbid I mess up her precious photoshoot by being human enough to get sick.

"I'm fine," I lie, tearing the croissant into tiny pieces that she eyes, daring me to take a bite so she can criticize me for something else. "Just... tired."

"Hmm." She sets down her tablet, and I immediately tense. When my mother gives me her full attention, it's never good. "We need to discuss your role in the Christmas party."

The moment her gaze drags down to my outfit, my stomach sinks. "I wasn't aware you had *that* in your closet." Her voice is sugary sweet, but the undertone is as sharp as a knife. "And black tights? You know black makes your legs look even shorter. Why are you not wearing what I selected for you?"

I cross my arms, trying to shield myself from her sharp judgement, but her words find their way through anyway, slipping between my ribs like they always do. Each criticism lands exactly where she aims it, in all the soft, vulnerable places she's spent years learning how to hurt. "Kendra didn't lay out my clothes this morning," I mutter, hating that I have to defend myself over something little kids do on their own every day. Here I am, nineteen years old, getting in trouble with my mother for picking out my own outfit.

Some days it's hard to want to keep breathing.

She holds up a hand, cutting me off as I open my mouth to argue that I should be allowed to wear what I want. "Excuses, Emerald. Always with the excuses. I understand you're not feeling well, but you should've notified me immediately if Kendra failed to do her job. You can't let a little discomfort deter you from looking presentable."

I glance down at my outfit again, the soft fabric suddenly feeling too tight and too plain under her scrutinizing gaze. The truth is, Kendra has a key to my room, but the door was locked from the inside this morning and I don't know why. Did Kendra *want* me to get in trouble?

Why am I the only one expected to play by the rules in this house?

"Really, a little color wouldn't kill you," she continues as I tune back in, her chin raised while she looks down her nose at me.

I flush, swallowing hard but not daring to argue. Because in my mother's world, looking perfect isn't just a requirement—it's a way of life. "You'll change after breakfast." Her voice leaves no room for argument as she lifts her coffee and takes a small sip. Once she's set her cup down on its saucer, she clears her throat, and I brace myself. "I've come up with the perfect idea for how your particular skill set will be most beneficial in helping to plan the Christmas party."

Oh god. Not the party. I'd almost managed to forget about the worst part of my year.

"What about it?" I ask carefully, knowing even if I don't upset her with my questions, I'm not going to like what comes out of her mouth. Whatever she's about to say, it's going to be bad for me.

"Emmitt has specifically requested your assistance with the silent auction," she says, watching my reaction with those sharp eyes of hers. "He thinks it would be good exposure for you, learning how these events work from the inside, and I agree."

Any appetite I might've had disappears. "Emmitt?" I repeat, my voice small. "But... doesn't he have an assistant? Why would he need my help?"

"Because," she says with an edge of impatience, "he's asked for your help and you *will* give it." Her icy eyes flash at me, like lightning in the clouds threatening to strike. "Emmitt is an important business partner, one who I don't want to lose. Besides," she waves her hand in my general direction, "his connections could be valuable for your future."

My future. *Right.* The one she's planned out for me without bothering to ask what I want.

"I don't..." I start to protest, but she cuts me off with another wave of her hand, this one sharper. Like a blade.

"This isn't up for discussion, Emerald." Her voice has gone cold, all pretense of warmth vanishing. "You'll meet with him at his office this afternoon to go over the details."

The room suddenly feels too small, the air too thick. Memories of yesterday flood back—Emmitt's eyes on me in the boutique, the way he looked at me like he was starving and I was a perfect medium-rare steak. If it hadn't been for Cohen...

Cohen.

Just thinking his name makes my body temperature spike, and I shift uncomfortably in my chair as that strange ache between my legs intensifies.

What even *is* that?

"Good morning, ladies."

His voice slides over me like melted butter, and my heart does a stupid little skip-jump that's really unsettling. I don't have to look up to know it's him. My body seems to have developed some kind of radar where Cohen's concerned, and the second he stepped into the room, I felt him in the tiny hairs on the back of my neck that lifted up and in the heat spreading over my skin.

"Did you sleep well, little one?" he asks, his voice low and intimate like we're sharing secrets while he walks behind my chair to his seat at the head of the table. The way he says 'little one' is different from how he says anything else. It's softer, darker, like he's tasting the words before letting them go. I nod, and the tips of his fingers brush along the back of my neck. I shiver. His touch is nothing like my mother's clinical adjustments. It feels personal, like he's laying claim to the skin beneath his fingers.

Goosebumps run down my arms in the wake of his attention and when his touch lifts off my skin, I immediately mourn the loss.

Crap, crap, crap.

I hope he didn't notice.

I may not have to look up, but I do.

I do look up, because I can't not look at him.

He's wearing a charcoal grey suit that fits his fit body perfectly, his dark hair slightly messy like he's been running his fingers through it. He looks... really good.

Like *breath catching in my throat* good.

Like *heart skipping a beat* good.

Like *please look at me and no one else ever again* good.

When his steel-gray eyes meet mine, something electric zips down my spine.

And I officially want to slap myself.

He stares at me, our eyes locked together, and I'm trapped in his snow cloud eyes until my mother's voice breaks the spell. "Cohen," my mother greets him with her public smile. "Perfect timing. We were just discussing Emerald's involvement with the Christmas party planning."

His expression doesn't change, but when he shifts his gaze off of me and in my mother's direction, I swear I see something dangerous there. Almost like when he stood up for me with Emmitt yesterday. After his proclamation that he'll handle all things Emmitt Caldwell from now on, I wonder how he's going to take my mother's orders about my role in the party planning. "Oh?" he says, his voice deceptively casual as he takes his seat. "And what involvement would that be?"

"Emmitt's requested her help with the charity auction," my mother says, and I swear the temperature in the room drops ten degrees. "It's an excellent opportunity for her."

I can feel Cohen's gaze on me, intense like he's trying to force my eyes back up to his with only the power of his mind, but I stay fixated on the mutilated croissant in front of me. My hands are trembling, so I hide them in my lap.

"Is that so?" Cohen's voice is smooth as glass, but there's an edge to it that makes me shiver. "And you think that's appropriate, considering his... reputation?"

My mother's smile tightens. "Emmitt is one of my most valued business partners, Cohen. His reputation is impeccable."

"Is it?" He reaches for the coffee one of the staff sets in front of him, his movements deliberate and controlled. "Because that's not what I've heard."

The tension in the room is crazy, like one wrong move could shatter everything around us. Someone's going to break first, and I really hope it's my mother and not Cohen. I *need* him to win this. To stand up for me because for some reason, when it comes to my mother, I can't seem to do it myself.

I risk a glance at my stepfather, and the look on his face stops the breath in my lungs. There's something in his expression that makes my stomach clench. It's not with fear exactly, but with recognition. His eyes lock onto my mother with an intensity that reminds me of those nature documentaries where the camera catches the exact moment before the lion attacks, when everything goes still and quiet and you know something's about to happen but you can't look away.

"Perhaps," my mother says, her teeth clenched together in a smile that's more of a bearing of her teeth than anything else, "we should discuss this later. In private."

"No," Cohen says simply, setting down his coffee cup with a soft clink. "We shouldn't." His attention shifts to me, and it feels like when I'm standing at the edge of our pool, knowing the water's freezing but wanting to dive in anyway. That moment of terrifying anticipation where my body's already leaning forward before my brain can catch up and tell me to stop. "Emerald, do you want to work with Emmitt?"

The question catches me off guard. No one ever asks what I want. His steel-gray eyes lock onto mine, and that new heat spreads through my body, settling low in my belly where that strange ache has lived all morning. Something about the way he's looking at me makes me feel like my answer actually matters—like *I* matter.

"I..." I swallow hard, glancing between him and my mother. Her eyes are boring into me, silently commanding me to say yes. The weight of her expectations presses down on my shoulders, threatening to crush me. But Cohen... Cohen's looking at me like he sees past all my mother's careful programming, past the perfect porcelain doll she's tried to make me into. His gaze strips away all the layers until I'm just me—just Emerald. And for the first time in my life, that feels like enough. "No," I whisper. "I don't."

The word comes out soft, barely more than a breath, but it feels like the biggest act of rebellion I've ever attempted. My pulse pounds in my ears, and that ache between my legs throbs in time with my heartbeat, like my whole body is coming alive with this one small act of defiance.

"That's it then," Cohen says, his tone final. "She won't be working with him."

My mother's perfectly manicured nails dig into the tablecloth as she glares daggers first at me and then at her husband. The look she gives me promises consequences later, but for once, the thought doesn't terrify me like it should. Maybe it's because of the way Cohen's presence seems to fill the entire room, making everything else, even my mother's fury, feel smaller.

"Emerald is my daughter and you have no right—"

"I have every right," Cohen barks. His voice is loud enough that I flinch. The staff turns and leaves before my mother can fire them for witnessing something they shouldn't, but I barely notice. I'm too caught up in the way Cohen's words seem to vibrate through me, settling deep in my bones like they belong there.

The silence that follows feels like those moments at one of Mother's endless charity galas when I sneak a glass of champagne and the room goes fuzzy around the edges and the ground shifts beneath my feet. My body feels weightless, untethered, like all the rules that have kept me bound are suddenly fraying at the edges. I think something just broke in this pristine glass mansion of ours, and I don't think all of my mother's rules and control can put it back together again.

Emerald
CHAPTER 6

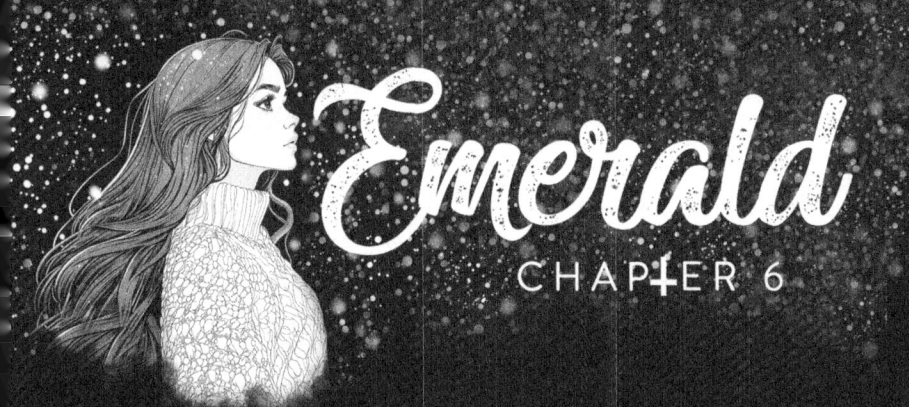

"YOU DON'T UNDERSTAND," my mother hisses. "Emmitt's company is offering to launch my new luxury cosmetics line, but he specifically requested Emerald's involvement in the auction as a condition of the deal."

I shrink in my chair, feeling about two inches tall. Of *course* this is about business. With my mother, *everything* is about business. Even her own daughter is just another investment in her portfolio, another asset to be leveraged at exactly the right moment.

Cohen's jaw tightens, and I swear I can hear his teeth grinding. His fingers curl around his coffee cup like he wishes it was someone's throat. "So you're willing to sell your daughter to that piece of shit for a few dollars?"

"Don't be dramatic," my mother scoffs. "It's just business. So Emmitt wants to spend a few hours in Emerald's company. Is that so wrong? I've raised her to be docile, attentive, and innocent for this exact purpose."

Her words slam into me like a physical blow. *This exact purpose.* Like I'm a doll she's been crafting, keeping pristine until someone with enough money wants to play with me.

"I'm not going to let you ruin this for me, Cohen," she continues, her voice sharp enough to draw blood. "This deal will catapult Delacroix Collective to a whole new level. If you interfere, you *will* regret it."

The silence that follows is thick enough to choke on. I peek up at Cohen through my lashes, and *oh*. Something dark and dangerous flashes across his face before he masks it with cold. Not just regular cold—we're talking arctic levels of frost that would make my mother's ice queen persona look warm and fuzzy. I've never seen his face look like that, but I bet this is the expression he wears right before he destroys someone in court.

"Fine," he says, breaking the silence. "I'll drive her to his office myself. I'll stay for the meeting and oversee the arrangements. After all, we wouldn't want anything... inappropriate to happen."

The way he says "inappropriate" sends a shiver skittering over my skin. There's a promise in his voice, a threat that's not directed at me but that I feel in my bones anyway. For a second, I picture him standing between me and Emmitt's hungry stares, and despite everything wrong with wanting my stepfather's protection, my body relaxes just a fraction.

"That won't be necessary," my mother tries again, but Cohen's already shaking his head.

"It's either that, or she doesn't go at all. Your choice, Madeline."

Something passes between them, some silent battle of wills that I can't quite understand. But I know, somehow, that Cohen's winning. The oxygen seems to vanish from the room, and I'm caught in the crossfire of whatever war they're waging.

My mother's phone buzzes, saving us all from the suffocating tension. She glances at it and stands abruptly, but I don't miss the way her fingers tremble slightly as she grabs her tablet. "I have a meeting at the office." She gives me a look that promises this isn't over, her eyes glacial. "Don't be late for the photoshoot this afternoon, and for the love of God, change your outfit before you meet with Emmitt."

Before she reaches the doorway, she pauses and turns back, already scrolling through her tablet. Like the previous conversation never happened, like she hasn't just offered me up as a sacrifice to her ambition, she starts rattling off the day's agenda in that clipped tone she uses when she's organizing her world exactly how she wants it. She doesn't even look at me as she continues, too focused on her screen. "The photographers will be here in an hour. We need to get your hair and makeup done, and then we'll start with individual shots before the family portraits." She glances up at my stepfather. "Darling, you'll need to be ready by noon."

"Of course," he says smoothly, but his eyes never leave me. The weight of his gaze makes my skin prickle with awareness, and I have to fight the urge to squirm. It's like he can see straight through me, past all my mother's careful programming to something real and raw that I didn't even know existed.

I slide lower, trying to make myself as small as possible. One of the kitchen staff appears, setting a plate of fresh fruit and yogurt in front of me—my usual breakfast. The only thing my mother allows me to have.

Normal people probably get to eat pancakes. Or waffles. Or literally anything with actual flavor.

Cohen pushes back from the table, buttoning his suit jacket with one fluid motion that draws my eyes to his hands. Strong hands that I swear I felt on my skin in my dreams last night... I wrench my gaze to my yogurt bowl, my thoughts scattering like startled birds.

"I have a meeting at The Lodge this morning," he announces. "I'll be back for the photoshoot."

My stomach drops at the thought of him leaving. I try not to let it show, but my hands curl around the edge of my bowl, gripping it just a little too tightly while I stare at the strawberries slowly sinking into the yogurt so I don't have to watch him go. It's pathetic how much I want him to stay, how *safe* I feel when he's here, even though he's probably the most dangerous person in this house.

He stops behind my chair, and I don't have to look to know he's there. It's like my body has developed some kind of Cohen-specific radar, and right now it's going haywire. His hand lands on my shoulder, warm and heavy, and I have to bite back a gasp at the contact. That deep ache between my legs pulses in response to his touch, like my body knows something my mind doesn't.

Oh god. *Oh god oh god oh god.*

"Be careful today, little one," he murmurs, so quietly I barely hear him.

And there goes my ability to think straight. *Again.* Because that's exactly what I need right now—more evidence that I'm completely losing it over my stepfather.

I wonder if there's a support group for this sort of thing. *"Hi, I'm Emerald, and I get tingly feelings when my mother's husband calls me pet names."*

I bite my lip to keep from laughing out loud.

But then he's gone, leaving me with my skin buzzing where he touched me, wondering if I really am losing my mind.

My mother's calculating stare drills holes into my skull, but I'm an expert at pretending it doesn't bother me.

"Really, Emerald," she sighs, setting her tablet down. I thought she was leaving but it looks like she's decided to stay. Great. She's going to pick right back up where she left off. Of course she doesn't care what Cohen has to say. Why would she? I don't understand their marriage at all. They don't seem to love each other. So why marry someone you don't love?

The question gnaws at me. I watch them together sometimes, looking for any sign of affection, but all I see is ice between them. It makes no sense.

When I get married, it'll be to my soulmate. Someone who'll make every moment feel like magic, who'll hold my hand like it's the most precious thing in the world. The kind of love that makes everything else fade away, as if we're living in our own fairytale.

But even as I think it, Cohen's face flashes through my mind, and my stomach does that weird flip-flop thing again.

My mother's next words snap me back to reality. "You need to stop being so dramatic about everything. The photoshoot needs to be perfect, and I won't have you sulking through it."

I stare down at my untouched breakfast, my appetite vanishing. "Yes, Mother."

What else can I say? I'm trapped here, in this pristine prison, with no way out. No friends, no real education, no job skills—nothing that would let me escape. My trust fund is completely under her control until I'm twenty-five, and even then, there are probably a million strings attached that I don't know about.

I don't even know how to drive.

She's made sure I'm completely dependent on her for everything. The perfect little doll in her perfect little dollhouse, ready to be sold to the highest bidder. *Marketed* to the highest bidder, I should say. That sounds more like my mother's style.

"Good girl," she says, standing up. "Now finish your breakfast and get upstairs. The beauty team is waiting."

As she marches away in her designer heels, I push my bowl away and close my eyes, trying to hold back tears. Everything feels like too much today. My skin doesn't fit right, my thoughts keep scattering everywhere, and that deep ache between my legs hasn't gone away. I don't know how much longer I can do this.

I take a shaky breath and force myself to stand, my chair scraping against the marble floor in a way that makes me wince. My mother's probably timing how long it takes me to get upstairs. We wouldn't want to keep the beauty team waiting, would we? Heaven forbid anyone have to wait an extra thirty seconds to make me *camera ready*.

With restraint built up from years of practice, I hold back an eyeroll. My feet drag with each step up the staircase making me more aware of how strange my body feels today. Sometimes I wonder if my mother sees me as a daughter or just another product in her empire—a representation of her brand that she can show off. Today, I'm betting on product.

The beauty team descends on me like a flock of well-dressed vultures, armed with curling irons and makeup brushes. I sink into the chair at my vanity, letting them work their magic while my mind drifts. Every time I close my eyes, I see Cohen's face and replay the feel of his hand on my shoulder.

Under his fingers, it felt like fireworks going off under my skin. The more he touches me, I'm finding, the more I want. Like I'm starving he's started tossing me crumbs. And I'm pathetic enough to be grateful for even that much.

"You look like you're a million miles away today, Miss Delacroix," Maria, my usual makeup artist, says as she dusts something shimmery across my cheekbones. "Everything okay?"

I force a smile. "Just thinking about my to-do list."

She hums sympathetically, but there's a curiosity in her gaze she doesn't even try to hide. Everyone who works for my mother is a spy, reporting back everything I say or do. I learned that lesson early.

They may seem friendly, but these are no friends to me.

"Your mother mentioned you'll be working with Mr. Caldwell on the charity auction," she says, switching brushes.

My stomach churns at the mention of Emmitt. "Yeah," I mutter, then immediately regret showing any negativity when I catch the glint in Maria's eyes. She just smiles and keeps working, no doubt filing away my reaction to report back to my mother.

An hour later, I'm deemed camera-ready. My dark hair falls in perfect waves, my makeup is flawless but natural-looking, and I'm wearing a different cream-colored sweater dress, this one more "festive" according to the stylist.

I look exactly like what I am: an ornament in my mother's holiday display.

"There you are!" My mother appears in my doorway, looking like she just stepped off a magazine cover in a red designer dress that's somehow both elegant and shows off the body she starves herself for. "The photographers are setting up outside. We need to—" She pauses, her eyes narrowing as she studies me. "Something's off."

My heart stumbles. Can she tell? Can she see the guilt written all over my face? The thoughts I've been having about her husband?

Please don't be a mind reader. Please don't be a mind reader. Please don't—

But she just clicks her tongue and moves closer, reaching for my necklace. "This shade of gold isn't right with the cream. Kendra!"

Oh thank god. I hold my breath to keep from blowing it out in relief. Just another fashion 'crisis'. I can handle a fashion crisis. That's, like, a normal Tuesday in his house.

Her assistant materializes like she was summoned by dark magic. "Yes, Mrs. Delacroix?"

"Get the pearl set from my jewelry cabinet. The one with the drop earrings."

"Right away."

I stand still as my mother adjusts my hair, her touches clinical and impersonal. Like she's arranging flowers in a vase. She's never been the kind of mother who hugs or shows affection. Everything about her is calculated, even her love—which I'm not convinced she even feels toward me.

Maybe she's not capable of feeling it at all.

"There," she says finally, stepping back. "Now you look perfect."

Perfect. I clench my teeth together to keep from cringing. I hate perfect.

"Has anyone seen my husband?" she asks, checking her phone. "He should be back by now."

As if on cue, the front door opens downstairs, followed by familiar footsteps. My pulse takes off, and I hate myself for it. Hate that I recognize his walk, that my body responds to him before I even see him. Like my personal Cohen-radar just kicked into high alert.

"I'm here," his deep voice carries up the stairs, smooth as melted chocolate. He stops in my doorway, leaning against the door frame, and his eyes immediately find mine.

Heat floods through me like a fever, burning under every inch of my skin, and for a second, I forget how to exist. I forget where I am. His gaze locks onto mine like he's trying to tell me secrets no one else can hear. Like I'm falling and flying at the same time, and somehow I know he won't let me crash. My heart pounds against my ribs, and I swear the room tilts sideways. I want to reach out, to close the space between us, to... to what? I don't even know what I want, but it scares me how badly I want *something*.

"Well, hurry up and change," my mother's voice slices through the moment, and reality comes crashing back. I blink, remembering where I am. *Who* else is in this room. "We're already running behind."

I wrench my gaze away, worry clawing up my throat. Did anyone notice? Did my mother see how I was staring at her husband like he was oxygen and I was drowning? And what did he see in my face? I risk a quick glance, my heart in my throat, but Cohen's already looking at my mother, his expression unreadable. I drop my eyes to the floor, praying no one caught what must've been written all over my face.

I barely have time to collect myself before my mother spins on her heel, leading everyone downstairs. I follow because I have to, my legs unsteady and my mind a mess. I'm doing what's expected of me, being the obedient daughter, ready for her next command. But it feels harder today, every step heavier, weighed down by feelings I don't understand and thoughts I wish I could ignore.

I hate how I keep thinking about him, hate the way I got caught staring. Hate how much I want him to look at me again, to touch me again, to say my name in that soft, dark way that makes my skin come alive.

And most of all, I hate that no matter how much I try, I don't think I can stop.

Emerald

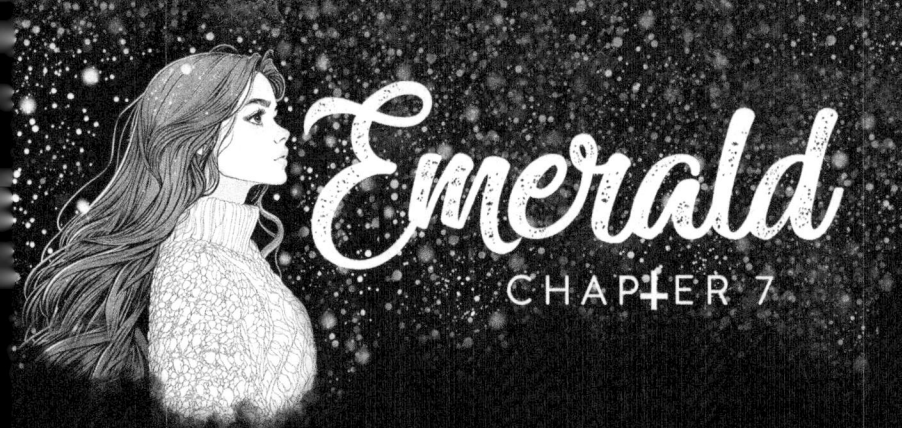

CHAPTER 7

WHEN WE GET DOWNSTAIRS, Cohen stands in the foyer, and my brain short-circuits for a second. He's changed into a black velvet suit jacket that *has* to be illegal somewhere because the way it hugs his broad shoulders and narrow waist is just... unfair. Completely unfair.

And there I go again, noticing things about my stepfather that I definitely shouldn't notice. Like how his dark hair falls just slightly messy, or how his storm-gray eyes seem to catch every tiny movement I make. Or how he has this way of owning whatever space he's in that makes it impossible *not* to look at him.

God, I need therapy.

Our eyes meet, and something dark and hungry flashes in his gaze that makes my stomach do Olympic-level gymnastics.

"You look beautiful, little one," he says softly, and my mother shoots him a sharp look.

"Don't encourage her vanity, Cohen. Emerald, go outside. The photographers want to start with some solo shots."

The words slice through me, and suddenly I'm that little girl again, never quite good enough, never quite *perfect* enough.

Heat rushes to my cheeks as I feel exposed, laid bare in front of Cohen. It's one thing when my mother criticizes me in private, but having him witness it makes me want to crawl into a hole and die.

I move past him toward the door, trying to swallow past the lump in my throat, when his hand brushes against my lower back, so quickly I might have imagined it. But the touch burns through my dress, sending electricity racing down my spine that definitely isn't appropriate for a stepdaughter to feel. When I dare to glance up, he winks at me and something in his expression seems to say he doesn't believe a word my mother said.

I shouldn't like that so much. I really, *really* shouldn't.

Hopefully she didn't notice.

Outside, snow covers everything in an untouched white blanket that would be beautiful if it wasn't about to be used as another backdrop for my mother's endless pursuit of perfection. The photography team has set up lights and reflectors, transforming our backyard into what probably looks like a winter wonderland to anyone who doesn't know better.

"Finally!" The photographer, a tall man with an impressive beard that makes me think of a hipster Santa, claps his hands. "Let's get started. Emerald, darling, stand by that tree. Yes, just like that. Now tilt your head down slightly." I do what he says, before he gives his next command. "Smile like you're trying to get on the naughty list."

If he only knew the kinds of thoughts I've been having about my stepfather, he'd probably need to invent a whole new list.

Wait, what? No. Bad Emerald. Very bad Emerald.

I'm sure this direction wasn't run by my mother. She'd never allow me to look anything less than angelic. Still, I pose as directed, trying to ignore the weight of Cohen's gaze from where he watches by the patio doors. I can't turn to see him, but

I know he's there. His attention feels physical, like hands sliding over my skin. Like those dreams I keep having...

Nope. Not going there. *So* not going there.

"Excellent! The camera loves you, darling."

"She gets it from me," my mother says, appearing beside the photographer like she's been summoned by the mere suggestion that I might have a quality of my own. "Now, let's do the family shots. Cohen!"

My heart kicks into overdrive as he moves toward us through the snow. We're going to have to stand close, touch, pretend we're a normal family when everything about this is so far from normal.

"Right here," the photographer directs, positioning Cohen behind me, my mother to my right. "Mr. Astor, put your hand on your stepdaughter's shoulder. Mrs. Delacroix, angle yourself toward them slightly. Just like that!"

Cohen's hand lands on my shoulder, and it's like someone plugged me into an electrical socket. Even through my dress, his touch burns, and I have to fight every instinct that says to lean back into him, to seek more of that warmth in the cold. His thumb brushes against my neck, and I feel it all the way between my legs where that weird ache from this morning still lingers. A little gasp escapes before I can stop it, and while my mother (thank every possible deity) doesn't notice, I swear I hear a low chuckle from my stepfather.

Right. Because that's *exactly* what I should be thinking about while my body's going haywire from my stepfather's touch. I smile wide, playing my part as the perfect daughter in the perfect family photo, while inside I'm screaming. Because Cohen's touch makes me feel things I don't understand, like I'm burning from the inside out. I can feel him behind me, solid and strong, and I know I shouldn't want him closer.

But I do.

And I have no idea what to do with that.

"Perfect!" The photographer claps his hands before gesturing toward the Gothic structure peeking through the snow-laden trees. "And the chapel in the background... the light hitting those windows would be divine for some final shots."

"No." My mother's voice is sharp enough to cut glass. "The chapel is not part of today's shoot."

The speed of her rejection makes me curious. I've caught her staring at the chapel sometimes, when she thinks no one's watching. There's something in her expression during those moments almost like fear. Which is ridiculous because my mother isn't afraid of anything.

Except maybe holy water.

The photoshoot drags on after that, and after what feels like hours of posing in the snow, my mother finally declares the it complete. I can't feel my toes, and my face hurts from fake smiling, but that's nothing compared to how my entire body's on high alert from having to stand beside Cohen for the last two hours. Every tiny movement, every breath, every subtle shift of his hand—my body noticed *all* of it.

"Emerald." My mother's voice slices through my thoughts like one of those fancy Japanese knives she keeps in the kitchen but never actually uses. "Don't forget you're meeting Emmitt at three to discuss the charity auction."

And just like that, my stomach drops into my frozen toes. "Right," I manage to say, though my voice comes out squeaky. "Where—"

"His office," she says, already typing on her phone like I'm not even worth looking at while she speaks to me. "Kendra will drive you."

"No, she won't." Cohen's voice comes from behind me, making me jump. His tone carries an edge of warning that makes my skin prickle. "Or did you forget our discussion about my attending Emerald's meeting with Emmitt?"

My mother's shoulders stiffen, and when she looks up from

her phone, her expression is carefully blank. Of course she hasn't forgotten—my mother never forgets anything. She was probably hoping Cohen would.

"I thought perhaps your schedule had changed," she says, her voice tight. "You mentioned a meeting—"

"My schedule is clear for this," Cohen cuts her off. "As I said before, either I attend, or she doesn't go at all."

The silence that follows feels... *dangerous*. I watch as something passes between them. It's the same battle from this morning, but this time my mother seems to realize she's already lost.

Her lips press into a thin line. "Fine." She glances at her watch, her movements sharp with irritation. "But don't be late for dinner. We have the menu tasting for the party tonight."

She walks away across the snow in her heels, leaving me alone with my stepfather. The oxygen vanishes from the space between us, and even the winter air isn't enough to fill my lungs.

"Go change," he says softly, his breath warm against my ear. "Wear whatever you want."

Whatever I want.

Those three words turn my world sideways. My mind empties of everything except pure panic, which starts creeping in around the edges. My mother chooses everything—*everything*—down to the shade of nude in my stockings. The thought of standing in my closet and having to decide for myself is suddenly terrifying.

"I... I don't know what to wear," I whisper, feeling about two inches tall and completely ridiculous. My chest tightens as the panic builds. "I don't even know where to start. Do I dress professionally? Business casual? Formal? What if I pick wrong and everyone laughs and—"

His hand comes up to brush my cheek, gentle and soothing, and my rambling cuts off like someone hit a mute button. His fingers ghost across my skin like he's testing boundaries. Like he's waiting to see what I'll do. Like he's writing secrets into my flesh that I'm not sure I'm ready to read.

"There are no expectations," he murmurs, his voice calm, like he's talking me down from the side of a bridge. "No wrong answer. Just put on something comfortable. Something that makes you feel good."

I nod, trying to swallow the fear that's lodged in my throat. The idea of choosing still feels too big, too impossible. I bite my lip, my eyes on the floor as my mind whirls with uncertainty.

He grips my chin, forcing my gaze to his, and *oh wow*, his eyes should come with a warning label. "Let me help you choose," he says, and it doesn't sound like a suggestion. "We'll do it together."

I look up at him, meeting those stormy eyes, and something in his gaze—dark, hungry, but carefully controlled—makes the panic start to fade. I nod again, this time more sure.

"Such a good girl," he growls softly, his hand sliding possessively down my back as he guides me toward the house.

The way he says those words makes my whole body tingle, which is so not okay. When my mother says them, they make me feel about as significant as a speck of dust. But when Cohen says them? It's like being wrapped in the world's softest blanket while sitting by a fire drinking hot chocolate.

I am so, so screwed.

I let him lead me toward my room, because apparently I've lost all sense of self-preservation. Every step makes my heart beat faster, like it's trying to warn me that letting my stepfather into my personal space might not be the smartest decision I've ever made.

When we reach my room, Cohen doesn't hesitate at the threshold—just walks in like he owns the space. Like he owns *me*. He's never been in here before, and watching him move through my bedroom makes me jittery and breathless. His large frame turns my spacious room tiny, and the air around us shifts into something dangerous and thrilling that I probably shouldn't like as much as I do.

"Show me your closet," he orders, the gentleness in his voice feeling like a reward for my obedience.

I lead him into my walk-in closet, every nerve ending suddenly aware of how *alone* we are. He prowls through the rows of designer clothes like he's hunting for something specific. His fingers trail over fabrics, and he pauses at a silk dress. The way his fingers stroke the material makes heat bloom across my skin. Something about the way he touches them makes me imagine those fingers on me instead, and the thought sends electricity racing through my veins.

I shouldn't want that. He's my stepfather. He doesn't want to touch me.

Does he?

"Perfect for dealing with men like Emmitt." There's such darkness in how he says the name, such raw hatred, that my heart does this weird flutter-skip thing in my chest—the same feeling I got when he stood between Emmitt and me at the boutique. His fingers trace the soft fabric as his lips curve into that dangerous half-smile that makes my heart race. "Innocent on the surface... but we both know better, don't we?"

My face flushes at his words. I want to ask him what he means—I *am* innocent, aren't I? But the look in his eyes leaves the question stuck in my throat.

"Try it on," he says, his voice dropping an octave lower. When I don't move immediately, his eyes darken. "Now."

I grab the dress with trembling fingers, but then my brain catches up with what's actually happening. I'll need to change. In front of him. *Oh god.*

"I... um..." I stammer, clutching the dress to my chest like it might protect me from the way he's looking at me.

A slow, wicked smile spreads across his face. "Don't worry, little one. I'll turn around." He moves to face the wall. "This time," he adds, and his words slip beneath my skin, past every wall I've built, every defense I thought I had. They nestle somewhere deep inside where I can't dig them out.

My fingers shake as I unzip my photoshoot dress, letting it pool at my feet. Every cell in my body pulses with knowledge of Cohen's presence, just a few feet away, separated only by his turned back. Electricity crackles through the air as I yank the sweater dress over my head, my fingers stumbling over the fabric.

"Done," I whisper, and my voice sounds strange even to my own ears.

He turns, and the look in his eyes makes me feel exposed, like he can see every part of me even though I'm fully dressed. His gaze travels slowly up my body, and I feel myself dissolving under the weight of it, melting from the outside in. When he finally meets my eyes again, there's something intense in his expression that splits me right down the middle—half of me wanting to run, the other half wanting to step closer.

"Beautiful," he murmurs, stepping closer. His hand reaches out, adjusting the collar of the dress. When his knuckles brush against my collarbone, I have to bite my lip to keep from gasping. "So fucking beautiful." Then his gorgeous eyes lift to mine while I breathe in a lungful of his expensive earthy cologne and *Cohen*. "But what do you think?"

Beautiful.

I've heard that word a thousand times, always measured against my mother's impossible standards—beautiful means perfect, untouchable, cold. A word that's never felt like it belonged to me. But when Cohen says it, something cracks open inside me. His version of beautiful shatters every mirror my mother ever held up to me. In his eyes, I exist beyond her carefully drawn boundaries—I'm something wild, untamed. Something that's been clawing beneath my skin all this time, only now waking up.

My fingers run over the fabric and his gaze drops to follow the motion. It takes me three times to swallow and get my voice to work. It does feel nice, and the color is pretty, but... "I don't know," I whisper. "It's hard to choose."

He nods, his dark gaze pinning me in place. "I know. But I want you to try. Pick something that feels good."

I glance back at the rows of clothes, my eyes scanning over the dresses, the sweaters, the skirts... My heart is pounding, and my chest feels tight. The thought of making this decision —*any* decision—is completely overwhelming. But Cohen's presence beside me somehow makes it a little easier to breathe.

"Okay," I whisper, my voice so small it's almost nonexistent.

Something pulls me toward the back of my closet to a section I never visit. There's a dresser back here that I doubt my mother's touched in years.

I know I haven't.

I pull open a drawer, digging through old workout clothes and—*oh*. My heart skips about five beats when I find a pair of jeans with a tear in the knee and a black hooded sweatshirt.

The fabric is soft in my hands, probably left behind by someone on staff. It feels dangerous and exciting, like I'm finally doing something *real*. Something that's actually me.

Am I really doing this?

If my mother sees me or Emmitt reports back...

My stomach does a nervous flip as I imagine her reaction. She'll probably come up with some creative new punishment, like making me attend *all* her business meetings for a month. Or worse—forcing me to do another round of finishing school etiquette classes.

Still...

I think I want this. Need this, even.

There's a spike in my heart rate, like a warning shot fired before the battle begins. To most people, this would be nothing

—just picking out clothes for the day. *Normal* people do this every morning without having an existential crisis.

But to me? This is my first real choice. My first step toward figuring out who I am. Who I want to be.

Cohen's eyes go midnight-dark as he takes in my choices, his smile promising all kinds of trouble. "Look at you, already learning to push boundaries," he says, his voice dropping lower. "Try them on."

My fingers tremble around the soft fabric as I nod.

"That's my girl," he purrs. "It's time to learn to take what you want."

As I turn to change, I notice my top drawer's open enough that my cotton and lace underwear are visible. My face flames as I snap my hand out to close it, but Cohen's faster. His hand shoots out, catching a piece of pale pink lace between his fingers.

"Look what you've been keeping from me," he murmurs, voice thick with something that makes my stomach clench. My heart stops as he examines the delicate fabric, treating it like something precious and forbidden. His thumb traces the lace edge in a way that makes me think of how his fingers felt against my collarbone earlier, and something hot and unfamiliar pools low in my belly.

I should be mortified. I should snatch them back, tell him he can't just take my underwear. But watching him handle something so private, so intimately mine... it does something to me I can't explain.

He tucks the lace into his pocket with deliberate slowness, like he's claiming a piece of me. His smoky eyes lock onto mine, daring me to challenge him. "I'm keeping this," he states, no room for argument in his tone. The possessiveness in his voice makes me feel marked somehow, like he's branded me without touching my skin.

I can't speak, and even if I could, what would I say?

"Get changed." The words rumble from his chest as he backs toward the door, his burning eyes pinning me in place. "I'll be right outside."

I wait for him to leave, surprised and maybe a little disappointed that he's not staying this time. The door clicks shut behind him. I can't move for a second. My heart races while my body can't decide what to do with itself. Every logical thought dissolves like sugar in hot tea, leaving behind only this new, impossible wanting that Cohen creates.

I change quickly, hands shaking as I pull on the clothes. The denim feels so *wrong* against my skin after years of designer dresses that I almost laugh. But wrong in the best possible way. Like breaking a rule you never agreed to follow in the first place.

I can taste the smell of him on my tongue. It's like he's infused the air with possibility, with the courage to be someone... *different*.

God, my mother is going to have an aneurysm when she sees this. The thought should terrify me, and it does, but there's also this tiny spark of satisfaction that makes me want to grin like an idiot.

Am I really going to do this? Risk whatever creative punishment my mother dreams up when she sees me in clothes that aren't perfectly curated for the Delacroix image?

Yes. Yes, I think I am.

Emerald

CHAPTER 8

WHEN I STEP out of my closet, Cohen's burning gaze drags over me, and I swear my pulse trips over itself at the approval in his expression.

"Exquisite," he says. His normally deep voice is a little rough and I think I like that, too.

In fact, I *know* I like it if the way a flood of emotions is bursting through my entire body is any indication. It's like someone just cranked up everything to eleven.

I actually *stood up* for myself, made my own choice, and Cohen doesn't just accept it—he approves. A grin slowly spreads across my face, bigger than any I've ever had in my life. The sudden urge to giggle like a lunatic hits me and I have to bite my lip to keep it in so I don't look like I'm insane in front of my stepfather.

It's weird how something so simple can feel like so huge. I'm wearing *jeans*. It's not like I shaved my head or something. But maybe the world is bigger than my mother's endless rule-book of *perfect, always camera-ready* behavior.

Wouldn't that be something?

For exactly five seconds, I let myself enjoy that little bit of pride. Cohen saw me—actually *saw* me—and didn't immediately tell me I was wrong. If anything, that look in his eye was so very *right*. But because the universe has a sick sense of humor, reality comes crashing back like a bucket of ice water when I remember why I changed in the first place.

Emmitt.

That stupid meeting.

My stomach twists up like a pretzel as I try to think of literally anything that can get me out of doing this planning meeting. It doesn't matter, though. There isn't an excuse in the world that will go over well with my mother, and if I don't do her bidding, she'll make life even worse than it is now.

Starving me for days. Taking away my laptop and phone. Locking me in my room. Or worse? Forcing me to go to the office and *people*.

God, I really don't want to do this.

The way Emmitt looks at me is like he's trying to peel me out of my skin with his eyes, like I'm something he wants to sink his teeth into.

I catch myself biting my lip again—a habit Mother absolutely hates—and look up at Cohen. His steady gaze is helping me not freak out. He must see the way my confidence crumbles, replaced by that gnawing sense of dread creeping back in—how my shoulders slump and my eyes drop, as if I could make myself small enough to disappear. Ugh. So much *ugh*.

"I don't want to go," I whisper, finally voicing the fear that's been gnawing at me all morning.

His hand finds my lower back, but instead of pulling me against him, his fingers glide up until they reach the back of my neck, his thumb brushing against my skin. Something electric skates down my spine, leaving me lightheaded and a little off-balance, like stepping onto solid ground after hours on a rocking boat. It isn't fear—it's the strange relief of being noticed, of being steady when I didn't even realize I was drifting.

"I know, little one," he murmurs, his voice cutting through the mess in my head. His eyes are locked on mine as he watches me, and the intensity in them makes me suck in a breath. "But you won't be alone."

His fingers tighten, and a strange tremor rolls through me, like my body's been rewired and he just flipped a switch I didn't know existed. Every logical part of my brain is screaming at me to pull away, to tell him to stop looking at me the way he is.

It's wrong. I may not know exactly what's happening here, but I know that much. He shouldn't be looking at me like he's been in the desert and I'm a glass of ice water.

But I don't say anything. Instead, I find myself leaning into his touch for a heartbeat—okay, maybe a dozen heartbeats—before that annoying inner voice kicks in and I force myself to step back. His hand falls away, and the loss of his touch leaves me feeling strangely empty. Cold. *Alone.*

The muscle in his jaw ticks, his eyes darkening with barely contained frustration.

"Five minutes," he says, his voice rough. "I need to change. Meet me downstairs."

He turns and leaves before I can respond, and I'm left standing here, trying to catch my breath. I know I keep asking this, but what is *wrong* with me? Getting into a car with Cohen seems like the worst idea ever, but here I am, my heart flailing around like it doesn't know what to do with itself, all because it means more time alone with my stepfather.

"You're playing with fire," I whisper to my reflection when I step into the bathroom to fix my hair, but the girl staring back at me looks... different. Like maybe she wants to get burned.

Or at least a little singed.

When I head downstairs, Cohen's waiting at the front door in the charcoal suit that matches his eyes. The way he looks at me makes my body feel like every cell is suddenly aware it belongs to him.

"Ready?" Cohen loads that single word with enough meaning to fill one of my mother's endless etiquette manuals. The question hovers in the air between us, and somehow I know we've stepped way past discussions about this meeting and into something that feels both terrifying and inevitable.

I nod, my voice lost somewhere in my throat. His presence fills the entryway, and I find myself studying the way his suit fits perfectly across his broad shoulders. He looks so intimidating this way, so... powerful.

It should be a crime to be so handsome. His hair's a little messy and I wonder what the dark waves feel like. Is it soft? Is his cheek rough under the light dusting of stubble that's started to shadow his jaw since this morning?

I shouldn't be this drawn to him, but it's like after my dream I woke up with a brand new fascination I shouldn't have but can't—or maybe don't want to—stop.

A burst of laughter echoes from somewhere in the house, and I stiffen. Cohen steps closer until I have to tilt my head back to hold eye contact. "Your mother's at the office, probably castrating someone for daring to order green and white candy canes instead of red and white," he says as he smirks down at me. "A true emergency." He chuckles. "She won't find out about the jeans."

I blow out a breath and his eyes drop to my mouth. I ignore how fast my heart is beating. He gestures toward the door, and I follow him outside to his Aston Martin. The black car gleams in the driveway, all sleek curves and barely contained power—a perfect match for its owner.

When he opens my door, there's the lightest brush of his fingers along my hip. It's so soft, I'd almost think I imagined it, but there's an explosion of chills across my skin that seems to happen every time his body makes any sort of contact with mine.

The moment he slides in beside me, the space between us feels way too small. My fingers dig into the buttery leather, searching for something solid in a moment that feels anything but. I wiggle in my seat, trying to find a position that doesn't make me feel like I'm crawling out of my skin, but it just makes him glance my way.

And then I do it. I breathe him in like some kind of idiot, like my body's decided it has a mind of its own. I try to be sneaky about it, but the smirk playing at his lips tells me I failed.

I press my legs together because of that look. Being this close to him, just the two of us, his scent and just... his *presence* taking up all the space, I'm getting warm.

Uncomfortable in places I've never been uncomfortable.

I don't know what it is, and I don't know how to handle it, especially not with him watching me so closely, even as he shifts the car into gear and pulls out of the driveway.

"Emerald." The way he says my name wraps around me like a velvet ribbon. "Look at me."

Against my better judgment, I do. His gray eyes lock onto mine, and it's like staring into the center of a winter storm—cold, endless, and impossible to look away from. The gate opens slowly, but he doesn't move, his attention fixed on me as though the world beyond the car doesn't exist.

"If Emmitt touches you," his voice drops into a lethal sort of quiet, "if he so much as breathes too close to you, you tell me. Understand?"

My throat goes dry. "Yes."

"You're learning."

His praise sends tingles down my spine, and I have to look away. Outside, snow falls in delicate flakes, making everything look pure and clean. Cohen steers us out into the road and I watch his hands, how big and strong they are as they effortlessly grip the steering wheel and control this expensive piece of machinery.

And then I think about my dreams last night and I shift in my seat again, wishing I didn't react to him the way I do. Heat floods my cheeks as fragments of those dreams flash through my mind—his hands on me, his lips...

Maybe I'm sick, like in the head.

"What are you thinking about?" His question startles me out of my thoughts.

I nibble my lip, studying my hands in my lap. "Nothing important." But my face feels like it's on fire, and I know he can tell I'm lying.

"Try again, little one." His voice has that edge to it, the one that makes my stomach do backflips.

"I..." I swallow hard. "Last night. I had... dreams." The last word comes out as barely a whisper.

Ugh, I can't believe I'm telling him this.

His knuckles go white on the steering wheel. "What kind of dreams?"

My cheeks burn hotter, if that's even possible. "I don't... I can't..." I shake my head, mortified. How can I tell him about dreams that make me feel so strange, so... warm? I don't know how to describe it to myself let alone explain it to him.

"You can tell me anything." His voice makes me want to confess all my secrets and beg for forgiveness.

"They're embarrassing."

"Embarrassing how?"

I glance out the window to find we're stuck at one of the few downtown stoplights, a line of sleek luxury cars idling in front of us—Bentleys, Porsches, the occasional Rolls-Royce—decked out with red bows and wreaths that gleam in the glow of glittering twinkle lights. It's almost enough to distract me, but then he speaks again, and my stomach does that fluttery thing it's started doing around him.

"What kind of dreams, Emerald?"

I shouldn't have said anything. Heat prickles at the back of my neck, crawling down my spine and pooling low in my stomach. I keep my eyes fixed on the dashboard, unable to handle the weight of his gaze. I'm horrible at standing up for myself, and just keeping my mouth shut instead of spilling my greatest shame all over my stepfather is already exhausting. "Just... dreams. Nothing important."

"Everything about you is important." He drops his grip on the shifter and grabs my hand, weaving our fingers together to hold my hand. Little fireworks detonate under my skin and I can't stop staring at my smaller fingers folded between his big ones. "Tell me."

Crap, crap, crap.

What if I don't obey and he takes his hand away?

My heart's beating so fast I wonder if he can hear it. "They're... um..." I swallow hard, twisting the fingers of my right hand in the hem of my hoodie while I tighten my grip on his with my left. I don't want to chance him pulling away when he hears the words already climbing their way up my throat. "Sometimes you're in my room at night in them."

"Am I?" The interest in his voice makes me shiver. He doesn't sound grossed out the way I thought he would. "And what do I do in these dreams of yours?"

"You..." My voice comes out barely above a whisper. "You touch me. And whisper things to me in the dark."

Instead of saying anything, he makes a sort of rumble sound in his chest, almost like he's... satisfied? I find myself gripping his hand tighter where our fingers are intertwined, and his fingers flex against mine like he's daring me to try to let go.

"And how does that make you feel?" he asks finally, his voice quieter now, pulling the words out of me before I can even think.

I swallow hard, staring at the glowing dashboard lights because looking at him feels impossible. "I don't know," I admit, the words trembling out of me. "It's... confusing. I shouldn't like it. Should I?"

"Why not?" He asks it so simply, like it's the most obvious thing in the world.

"Because it's you," I whisper, the admission tasting bloody and raw, as if speaking it aloud has carved something out of me.

He doesn't flinch. Doesn't pull away. His gaze is unrelenting as it holds mine, and I feel stripped bare. It's like he can see every thought I'm too afraid to admit. "And do you think that changes the way I see you?" he asks, his voice dipping lower.

I shake my head, gripping my knees, my palms damp against the fabric of my jeans. The stoplight glows red, holding us in this unbearable pause, and all I want is for it to change so I can breathe again. "I don't know what to think," I admit, my chest tightening. "I just—" The words catch, breaking apart before I can finish.

His fingers shift against mine, firm but careful, like he knows exactly how to steady me without saying a word. "There's nothing wrong with those feelings, Emerald," he says. "They're natural. Beautiful. You don't have to fight them."

There's this weird pull in my chest that I don't know how to deal with as I sag back into the plush leather and stare at our joined hands. I don't even bother trying to look at him, but I feel his eyes burning into me, stripping away my resistance. "But... I shouldn't feel this way. It's not... I mean, I don't know how to..."

"That's why you have me." His thumb strokes over my knuckles, leaving tingles behind. "To teach you everything you need to know."

From the moment he married my mother and moved into

our home last year, Cohen's been the only one to see past my perfect daughter act. The only person who makes me feel real instead of like some mindless wind-up doll.

The only one I want, even though I shouldn't.

I don't bother saying anything about him teaching me. I'm not sure what he means and I'm too afraid to ask.

His fingers tighten around mine, the car swerving slightly before he corrects it. When I dare to peek at him, the *starvation* in his expression makes my stomach flutter with butterflies made of fire.

Why is he looking at me like that?

"How did it make you feel? Dreaming of me?" The roughness in his voice ripples through me, scattering every thought I try to hold onto and leaving me with nothing but the wild, aching pull of him.

I should lie. Should tell him I was horrified. Instead, I whisper the truth: "Alive."

The sound he makes is pure animal, and he slides our joined hands higher up on my thigh, his grip possessive as my skin catches fire underneath it. The heat of his touch burns through my jeans.

"Good," he says, and that single word drips with so much he doesn't say.

We sit in a silence so charged it feels like it could spark if either of us dared to speak. His hand is wrapped around mine and pressed against my thigh the entire time, his thumb rubbing circles into my flesh. As we pull up to Emmitt's building, I realize something that should terrify me:

I think I may be falling into darkness, and I don't want anyone to catch me but him.

Cohen
CHAPTER 9

CONTROL IS SLIPPING through my fingers like blood from a fresh wound, and for once, I don't want to stop it.

Her scent lingers in the air of my Aston Martin, a heady mix of innocence and awakening lust that makes my cock throb with every inhale. I grip the steering wheel tighter, my knuckles going white as I try to focus on the road instead of the way her thighs press together, the slight tremor in her breathing, the way her teeth worry at her bottom lip.

Fuck, I want to bite that lip myself. Want to suck it between my teeth and tug until she whimpers, until she begs me to teach her everything.

But not just yet. There's vermin to exterminate first.

I pull up to Emmitt's sleek downtown office building, a glass and steel monstrosity that screams new money and overcompensation. It's the kind of place that tries too hard to impress, much like its owner. My jaw clenches as I eye the place, imagining all the ways I could burn it to the ground with Emmitt inside.

"Are you okay?" Emerald's soft voice cuts through the red

haze of my thoughts. I turn to find her watching me, those big green eyes wide with concern. She's fidgeting with the hem of her hoodie, looking small and unsure in a way that makes my chest ache.

I want to tell her we're turning around, that I'm taking her far away from here, away from Emmitt and Madeline and anyone else who might try to dim her light. But there are too many pieces still in play, too many moves left to make before I can claim her completely.

"I'm fine, little one," I say, keeping my voice low and steady. I reach out, tucking a strand of hair behind her ear, letting my fingers linger against her skin. "Are you ready?"

She swallows hard, her pulse fluttering visibly in her throat. "I... I think so."

"You don't have to be afraid," I tell her, my hand sliding to cup her cheek. "I won't let anything happen to you. You're safe with me."

The way she leans into my touch, seeking comfort, makes something primal roar to life inside me. Mine, it screams. Mine to protect. Mine to possess. Mine to corrupt.

"I know," she whispers, and the trust in her voice is both intoxicating and terrifying. She has no idea the monster she's putting her faith in.

I let my hand fall away, already mourning the loss of contact. "Let's go," I say, opening my door. "The sooner we get this over with, the sooner I can get you out of here."

As we walk toward the building, my hand finds the small of her back, a possessive touch that's becoming second nature. I guide her through the revolving door, my eyes scanning our surroundings for any potential threats. The lobby is all polished marble and sleek lines, designed to impress and intimidate. The receptionist behind the curved desk looks up as we approach, her plastic smile faltering slightly when she meets my gaze.

Then her eyes shift to Emerald, lingering a fraction too long, assessing her with a look that says she knows exactly why Emmitt requested this meeting with my teenage stepdaughter.

My fingers dig into Emerald's back possessively. *Mine.* The urge to shield her from even this stranger's gaze makes my jaw clench. No one gets to look at her like that.

"Miss Delacroix," the receptionist says, her voice overly bright before her eyes dart uncertainly to me, "and... Mr. Astor. Mr. Caldwell is expecting you. Fifteenth floor."

I nod curtly, steering Emerald toward the elevator without bothering to respond. As the doors slide shut, I feel her lean into me slightly, seeking reassurance. I tighten my grip on her waist, pulling her closer.

"Remember," I murmur, my lips against her temple. "You don't have to say or do anything you're not comfortable with. I'll handle Emmitt."

She nods, but I can feel the tension radiating off her in waves. When the elevator dings and the doors open, I have to resist the urge to simply scoop her up and carry her back to the car.

Emmitt's assistant, a nervous-looking young woman with perfectly styled hair, is waiting for us. "Mr. Astor, Miss Delacroix," she says, her voice slightly strained. "This way, please."

As we follow her down the hallway, I notice the way she keeps glancing over her shoulder, her eyes darting between Emerald and me. There's a wariness there, a poorly disguised discomfort that sets off warning bells in my head. How many other young women has Emmitt lured into his office under the guise of "business"?

The thought makes my blood boil, and I have to consciously unclench my fist before we reach his office.

The man himself is waiting behind an ostentatious desk when we enter, and I watch his practiced smile falter when he spots me beside Emerald. "Cohen," he says, voice tight as he stands, clearly thrown off his game. His eyes shift to Emerald and warm considerably. "And Emerald. I wasn't expecting company for our meeting."

His eyes zero in on my stepdaughter, roving over her body in a way that makes me want to pop them like grapes with my bare hands. The hunger in his gaze is unmistakable, and it takes every ounce of self-control I possess not to lunge across the desk and snap his neck.

"Emmitt," I say, my voice cold enough to freeze hell itself. "Let's get this over with, shall we?"

He gestures to the chairs in front of his desk with forced politeness. "Please, sit. Can I offer either of you anything?"

"We're fine," I say curtly, guiding Emerald to sit before unbuttoning my jacket and taking the chair next to her. I angle my body slightly, creating a barrier between her and Emmitt. A clear message that he'll have to go through me to get to her.

"Right," Emmitt says, his jaw tight as he settles back in his chair. "Let's discuss the charity auction. Emerald, your mother speaks highly of your attention to detail. I'm looking forward to working closely with you on this."

I watch as Emerald shifts in her seat, her discomfort palpable. "I... I'll do my best," she says softly, her eyes flicking to me before returning to Emmitt.

"Perfect," Emmitt says, and something dark flashes in his eyes that makes my fingers itch to wrap around his throat. "We'll need several meetings to get everything organized properly. I was thinking dinner might be more... comfortable. There's this private bistro—"

"That won't be necessary," I cut in, my voice sharp enough to slice through steel. "Any further discussions can be handled via email or conference call."

Emmitt's eyes narrow slightly, his mask of affability slipping. "Now, Cohen," he says, his tone patronizing. "I'm sure

Emerald is more than capable of handling a simple business dinner. After all, she'll need to learn how to navigate these social situations if she's going to take over her mother's empire someday."

I lean forward, my elbows on my knees, fixing Emmitt with the same stare I give defendants right before I destroy their lives in court. "Let me be very clear," I say, letting ice coat every syllable. "Emerald will not be attending any private dinners or meetings with you. Ever. If you have business to discuss, you can do it through me."

The tension in the room ratchets up several notches, the air thick with unspoken threats. Emmitt's face flushes, a vein pulsing in his forehead as he struggles to maintain his composure.

"I see," he says finally, his voice tight. "Well then, let's discuss the auction plans. Emerald—"

"You won't be discussing anything with her," I interject smoothly, letting my lawyer's smile spread across my face. "Emerald's role will be purely ceremonial. A figurehead, nothing more."

Emmitt's eyes narrow, his lips pressing into a thin line. "Is that so? And what gives you the right to make that decision? Last I checked, you were just the husband, not the parent."

The raw fucking audacity of this pathetic excuse for a man thinking he has any say over what's mine makes my vision go red around the edges. Every predatory instinct I possess screams at me to show him exactly what kind of "husband" I am, to make him understand with broken bones and blood exactly who Emerald belongs to.

But then I feel it, Emerald's small hand on my arm, her touch searing through my jacket. The urge to protect her wars with my need to destroy the threat in front of us. I take a measured breath, letting cold calculation replace hot rage.

"Let me explain something, Emmitt," I say, each word

precise as a bullet. "What I am to her isn't your concern. What is your concern is understanding that if you so much as breathe in her direction again, they'll never find all the pieces."

Emmitt leans back in his chair, a slow, calculating smile spreading across his face. "So protective of your stepdaughter, aren't you, Astor? I wonder what Madeline would think about just how... invested you are in Emerald's welfare."

The implication in his words makes something lethal unfurl in my chest. I rise slowly from my chair, savoring the flicker of uncertainty that crosses his face as I plant my hands on his desk and lean in close.

"You'll handle the auction yourself," I say, my voice soft but razor-sharp. "And you'll tell Madeline that Emerald was absolutely perfect, everything you hoped for. Because if you don't, if you breathe one word about anything else..." I let the threat hang between us, watching his throat work as he swallows.

"Are you threatening me?" He tries to sound confident, but I catch the tremor in his voice. "Maybe I should tell Madeline exactly how her husband looks at her daughter. How he touches her."

I smile then, letting him see exactly why the Savage Six trust me to handle their dirtiest work. "By all means, tell her. But ask yourself this—do you really think you'll survive what comes after?"

The color drains from his face as the reality of his situation finally sinks in. He's not just playing with fire anymore—he's standing in gasoline and I'm holding the match.

"Now," I say, straightening up, "we're done here. Emerald?"

She stands quickly, and I place my hand on her lower back, letting my thumb sneak up under her sweatshirt so it brushes against her skin while I guide her toward the door. The contact grounds me, reminds me why I can't simply end this piece of shit right here.

"This isn't over," Emmitt calls after us, his composure finally shattering to reveal the desperate little man beneath.

I pause at the threshold, turning back just enough to let him see the promise of violence in my eyes. "Keep pushing, Emmitt. I'd love to show you how this ends."

Cohen
CHAPTER 10

WITH THAT, I steer Emerald out of the office, my hand never leaving her back as we make our way to the elevator. The moment the doors slide shut, something inside me snaps. I pull her against me, crushing her small frame to my chest, finally—fucking finally—feeling her entire body pressed against mine. Having her in my arms feels like drowning and breathing for the first time all at once—everything I've denied myself for two endless years. It's different than night in her room because she's hugging me back just as hard.

For the first time, she's choosing this—choosing me—and the victory tastes better than any I've stolen in the night.

She fits perfectly in my arms, her head tucking just under my chin, every inch of her pressed against me confirming what I've known since that first night—she was made for me.

That intoxicating sweet scent that haunts my dreams—sugar cookies and pure fucking innocence—rocks through me as she shakes in my arms, and I have to bite back a groan when her fingers curl into my jacket, holding on like I'm the only thing keeping her standing. My cock hardens at how she surrenders to this, at how desperately she needs me.

"You did so well, little one," I murmur into her hair, not ready to let her go. "Though I doubt he'll be stupid enough to try that again."

She looks up at me, those green eyes full of questions she's not sure she should ask. "The way you looked at him... I've never seen anyone look that scared before."

I cup her face in my hands, my thumbs stroking her cheeks. "Men like Emmitt only understand one language—power. And now he knows exactly who holds it."

She bites that bottom lip, and for a moment I forget we're in public, forget everything except how badly I want to taste her. "He was going to tell my mother about... about how you..." She trails off, unable to voice what's building between us.

"Let him try," I say, my voice dark with promise. "I meant what I said in there—I'll handle everything. Including Emmitt."

The elevator doors open, and I guide her through the lobby and out to the car. As I open her door, she hesitates, her hand on my arm.

"Cohen?" Her voice is soft but steadier now. "No one's ever... I mean, you're the only one who's ever stood up for me like that."

The trust in her eyes makes possession roar through my veins. Everything is falling into place exactly as I planned.

I brush my knuckles along her cheek, savoring the way she leans into my touch. "You never have to thank me, little one. Now get in. We're not going home just yet."

Her brows furrow in confusion. "We're not?"

"It's Christmastime," I say, letting a rare smile slip free. "And you deserve to experience it without someone orchestrating every fucking breath you take."

"But—" she starts to protest, but I cut her off with a gentle finger to her soft lips.

"Trust me," I murmur, watching her eyes darken at my touch. "Let me show you how Christmas should feel."

I round to the driver's side, my mind already racing with possibilities. Tonight is about Emerald. About showing her a glimpse of the world I want to give her—a world where she's cherished, protected, free from the suffocating expectations of her mother and men like Emmitt.

A world where she belongs to me, and only me.

I slide into the driver's seat, watching as she fidgets with her seatbelt. "Ready for an adventure, little one?"

She looks at me, a spark of excitement breaking through her ingrained hesitation - that careful restraint her mother's drilled into her. But I see past it, past all of Madeline's conditioning, to the girl beneath who craves freedom. Who craves me. "I think so. Where are we going?"

I start the engine, the Aston Martin purring to life beneath us. "You'll see," I say, watching how her eyes light up at the possibility. "This is just the beginning."

Watching Emmitt's empire shrink in my rearview mirror, I savor what's to come. The glass and steel monstrosity recedes into the distance, along with all the ugliness it represents. Ahead of us lies possibility—a chance to show Emerald a taste of the future I have planned for us.

A future where she's mine in every way that matters.

As we drive through downtown, snow starts falling harder, coating the historic buildings in white. The old church on Main Street looms ahead, its Gothic spire piercing the dark sky. Emerald's gaze follows it as we pass, and something in her expression draws my attention.

"Beautiful, isn't it?" I nod toward the church. "Though not quite as interesting as the chapel on your family's estate." I watch her reaction carefully, hungry for every micro-expression that crosses her face. "I bet your mother never told you its history."

She shifts in her seat. It's one of those unconscious, delicate movements she makes that she doesn't realize tears at my control. The way her thighs press together, so fucking innocent yet so tempting, proves she has no idea what she does to me.

"Mother doesn't tell me anything unless it benefits her somehow." She bites that fucking lip that drives me to madness. "What do you know about it?"

"Quite a bit." I can't resist sliding my hand onto her thigh, satisfaction coursing through me when her breath catches. "I'm a bit of a history nerd, believe it or not." I flash her a smirk and she grins right back. "Your great-great-great-grandfather Alexandre had it built in 1889." I let my thumb trace circles on her leg through her jeans, watching as her pulse flutters in her throat. "For a French opera singer who captured his soul."

"An opera singer?" The breathy way she says it makes my cock twitch.

"Vivienne. She was performing Marguerite's aria from 'Faust' at the Seattle Opera House when Alexandre first saw her." I lower my voice, drawing her further into the story. "She played a pure, innocent girl tempted by darkness. Fitting, since he was already married to someone suitable, someone his family approved of. But Vivienne..." I pause at a red light, turning to drink in the sight of her. "She was dying of consumption, pouring her soul into that role while coughing up blood between performances. And still, he couldn't stay away."

"What did he do?" Her eyes are wide, hungry for more.

"He divorced his first wife—a scandal that nearly destroyed the Delacroix name. Married Vivienne while she was on her deathbed." I flex my fingers against her thigh, gripping her through the denim. "She prayed every day for recovery. And when she survived..."

"He built the chapel," she whispers.

"Yes. Though some said it wasn't God who saved her." I let my lips curve into a smile as I relish her entire focus being on me. "The more superstitious whispered about darker forces."

"Did they stay together?"

"They lived a long life together. Had many children. Until death finally claimed them both, decades later." My thumb draws circles on her thigh. "Alexandre's family called their love unholy. Said the chapel was his penance for choosing her over duty."

"And was it? Penance?"

"No, little one." I lock my gaze onto hers, letting her see just a glimpse of the hunger that consumes me. "It was a declaration. A monument to his total devotion to her. A dare to anyone or anything to try and take her from him."

The way she shivers at my words makes the predator in me purr with satisfaction. She has no idea how perfectly she's playing into my hands, how every reaction draws her deeper into my carefully laid plans.

The rest of the drive is short, and when I park near the edge of a quiet, snow-dusted hill overlooking the glittering lights of Emerald Hills, I hear Emerald's sharp intake of breath.

"This is beautiful," she murmurs, her eyes wide as she takes in the view.

"It's private," I say, stepping out and coming around to her side to help her out into the snow. I open the trunk and pull out a basket and thick blanket I had the kitchen prepare. "Including hot chocolate."

She lets out a soft laugh that makes my cock twitch, and I watch that flawless Delacroix mask crack as genuine joy lights up her face. "You planned this?"

I spread the blanket over the hood of the car, then reach for her, pulling her close against me as we settle onto the warm hood. Snow started falling on our drive up here, and soft flakes catch in her dark hair like stars. Every one of them a wish I've made since that first night—to have her, to keep her, to make her understand there's no life without me.

She takes a sip of her hot chocolate, her body gravitating

toward mine like she can't help herself. "Why are you doing all this for me?"

I set my cup aside and cup her face in my hands, my thumbs stroking her cheeks as snowflakes melt against her skin. "Because you deserve to know what it feels like when someone puts you first," I say, watching a blush spread beneath my touch in the faint golden light from the Hills below. "Because I want to give you everything."

She goes still at my words, and those pretty green eyes search mine like she's trying to read the secrets in them. "Everything?" she whispers, and the way she says it—soft and wondering and a little afraid—stokes the obsession I've been feeding since the moment I first saw her.

The air between us crackles with raw electricity, with everything I've been starving for. Her lips part, and my carefully constructed walls shatter like glass—all that control, all that fucking patience I've tortured myself with, obliterated in an instant. For two years, I've caged the beast inside me, forced it into submission while I waited for the right moment to strike. But now, watching those delicate snowflakes melt in her hair, seeing that perfect trust in her eyes, the predator breaks free. No more chains. No more cage. Just hunger.

My hands tremble with the need to touch her, to take what's been haunting me since that first night. Her breath quickens as I lift a hand, brushing my thumb across the bottom lip she's been driving me insane with all night. Her small gasp is soft, barely there, but it hits me like gasoline on a flame.

"Cohen?" Her voice is quiet, trembling with uncertainty, with a want she doesn't understand.

Slowly, so slowly it feels like torture, I slide my hand into her hair, the strands soft and cool against my fingers. I tilt her face up to mine, our breath clouding in the frigid air between us, giving her time to pull away even though I know it'll destroy me if she does. But she doesn't move. She watches me with those impossibly wide eyes, and when my lips finally meet hers, every plan, every careful move I've made burns to ash.

Her mouth is hesitant, soft, unpracticed. Exactly as I knew it would be.

She tastes like hot chocolate and purity, sweet enough to drive me mad. For a heartbeat, she's frozen, her body stiff, and then instinct takes over. Her fingers dig into my shoulders, nails biting through my jacket, and the softest whimper escapes her throat. The sound shatters what's left of my control—now I've had a taste of forbidden flesh that feeds the darkness inside me.

And then I'm devouring her.

My hand fists in her hair, holding her tight as I ravage her mouth, stealing every sweet, innocent gasp for my own. I bite her soft bottom lip, and the way her breath hitches makes me hard as fucking granite.

She tastes like hot chocolate and purity, sweet enough to drive me mad.

No one will ever satisfy me again. Not after stealing her virginity. Not after tasting her. Not after having her willingly in my hands. My obsession has found a home in her and I'll never be able to leave it.

I tilt her head back, my tongue slipping into her mouth, and when she tentatively touches hers to mine, I nearly lose my fucking grip on the world.

This is it. This is what I've been waiting for. What's been tormenting me in the deepest, darkest hours of the night, taunting me, driving me to the brink of madness. Her. Emerald.

Mine.

She's soft, warm, perfect. Her mouth surrendering to mine as she melts against me. The hand in her hair loosens, and I slide it down her spine. She shivers, her body arching into me, all that heat and going straight to the ache in my cock. I'm torn between savoring every second of her innocence and pinning her down and rutting her until she's a shattered wreck beneath me.

Below us, a sudden cheer erupts as the massive Christmas tree in the middle of town blazes to life, its colorful glow flooding the snow-covered hills. Emerald startles, breaking the kiss with a soft gasp, but she doesn't pull away. Instead, she buries her face against my neck, her breath warm and unsteady against my skin as the cheers echo up from the town below.

I tighten my arms around her, holding her close while the world celebrates something far less monumental than this—the moment she gave herself to me.

"That was..." She trails off, her breath a soft whisper against my chest. "I didn't know it could feel like that."

"Like what, little one?" I murmur, stroking her hair. Her face is still buried against my neck, hiding from me. From the truth.

"Fire," she whispers, her voice barely audible. "Like burning from the inside out."

Hearing the need in her voice makes my entire body go taut. "That's because we're meant to burn for each other," I say, my fingers sliding beneath her chin and forcing her to meet my gaze. "It's going to consume us both, and when it does, we'll rise from the ashes as something new."

I watch her throat work as she swallows, her eyes searching mine. "What if I'm not ready to burn?"

My thumb traces her lips, still swollen from my kiss. "I'll help you spread your wings, little phoenix," I say softly. "And I'll be right there beside you when you soar."

As we sit there, the lights of Emerald Hills a thousand colors sparkling in the snow, I know that this moment is just the beginning. Soon, very soon, Emerald will be mine completely.

And nothing—not Madeline, not Emmitt—will stand in my way.

Because Emerald isn't just a wildfire anymore. She's become the air I breathe, the blood in my veins, the very essence of my existence. And I'll raze the fucking world to keep her.

She was made for me, sculpted by some divine hand to be the missing piece of my soul.

The thought should terrify me—I've never been one for sentimentality or romantic notions—but instead, it fills me with a fierce, possessive joy.

"What are you thinking about?" Emerald's soft voice breaks through the silence, her breath a puff of smoke in the winter air.

I brush a strand of hair from her face, letting my fingers linger on her cheek. "You," I say simply, because it's the truth. "Always you."

She bites her lip, a blush staining her cheeks. "I don't understand how you do that," she murmurs. "How you make me feel like the center of the universe just by looking at me."

"Because you are," I tell her, letting a rare smile tug at my lips. "You're the sun, and everything else orbits around you, including me. *Especially* me."

"Cohen—" she starts, but I cut her off with another kiss, this one soft and sweet and full of promise that ends far too soon.

"Tell me something," I say, my forehead resting against hers as we both attempt to catch our breath. "What do you want? Not what your mother wants for you, not what society expects. What do *you* want?"

She pulls back and blinks up at me, clearly caught off guard by the question. "I... I don't know," she admits after a moment, her brow furrowing. "No one's ever asked me that before."

The admission sends a spike of anger through me—anger at Madeline, at the world that's tried to crush Emerald's spirit.

But I push it down, focusing instead on the vulnerable girl in front of me.

"It's okay not to know," I tell her, my thumb tracing circles on her wrist. "But I want you to start thinking about it. Because you deserve to have dreams, Emerald. You deserve to want things for yourself."

She's quiet for a long moment, her eyes fixed on the twinkling lights below us. When she speaks again, her voice is so soft I have to lean in to hear her. "I think... I think I want to be free," she whispers, like she's confessing some terrible secret. "To make my own choices. To not be afraid all the time."

My heart clenches at her words, a mixture of triumph and rage swirling in my chest. Triumph, because her desire for freedom plays perfectly into my plans. Rage, because she should never have been caged in the first place. But that's going to change. Soon, Emerald will have everything she could ever dream of—and more. Because she'll have me.

I brush my lips against hers, a silent promise of what's to come and because I can. "You can have that," I tell her, cupping her face in my hands and forcing her to meet my gaze. "All of it and more. I'll give you the world, Emerald. I'll tear down every wall, break every chain that's holding you back. You just have to trust me. Can you do that?"

She stares at me, her eyes wide and searching, like she's trying to see into my very soul. For a moment, I wonder if she can—if she can see the darkness that lurks there, the possessive, obsessive love for her that's only dug deeper into my soul since the first time I saw her.

But then she nods, slowly at first, then more firmly. "Yes," she whispers. "I trust you, Cohen."

I break the kiss with a growl, my chest heaving as I try to regain control. "We should go," I tell her, my voice rough with barely restrained desire. "Your mother will be wondering where we are."

Emerald blinks up at me, her lips swollen and shiny, her eyes hazy with lust. The sight nearly undoes me, and it's all I can do to stop myself from pinning her to the hood of the car right here on this snowy hilltop and burying myself inside her until she screams my name to the stars.

Emerald nods, but she doesn't move away. "Do we have to?" she asks, a hint of rebellion in her voice that makes me grin.

"For now," I tell her, pressing a softer kiss to her forehead. "But soon, little phoenix. Soon we won't have to go back at all."

Emerald
CHAPTER 11

THE TASTE of darkness lingers on my lips, sweet and dangerous, like chocolate-covered poison.

I can't stop touching them, my fingers tracing where Cohen's mouth claimed mine as we drive back through the snow-covered streets of Emerald Hills.

His kiss was nothing like I've read in books or seen in the movies I've stolen in my bedroom.

My first kiss. Given to my stepfather on the hood of his Aston Martin while snowflakes melted in my hair.

The thought should horrify me. Should make me feel sick with guilt or shame or... something. Instead, I'm just hungry.

Hungry for more of the way he held me. For more of his taste—chocolate and something dark, something forbidden. Something that belongs to the shadows. Something that belongs to him.

I sneak glances at him as he drives, unable to look away for long. The streetlights paint shadows across his sharp features, and my heart does this weird stuttering thing every time I catch him watching me from the corner of his eye. His knuckles are white on the steering wheel, and there's tension radiating off him in waves that make the air feel thick enough to drown in.

"Stop biting your lip," he growls softly, his eyes never leaving the road as his hand slides over to grip my thigh. The warmth of his touch burns through my jeans, and I can't hold back a shiver.. "Unless you want me to pull over and finish what we started."

The threat—promise?—in his voice sends a rush of heat through me, settling between my thighs. I press them together, trying to ease the sudden ache there. My heart races as I imagine what he might do if he pulled over. What he might do to me.

What's happening to me?

But then his hand relaxes, and he gives me a look that's half amusement, half warning. "Soon, little phoenix. Soon, I'll show you everything."

The car slows to a halt in front of the Delacroix mansion, and Cohen's hand slips from my leg.

Panic starts clawing at my chest as reality crashes back. My mother. Oh god, what will she say? What time is it? Have we been gone too long?

"Breathe, little one," Cohen murmurs, his hand finding mine across the console. His touch calms me better than one of my mother's Xanax, steadying the wild rhythm of my heart. "Let me handle your mother."

"But how will you—"

He silences me with a look that brooks no argument. "I'll handle her," he repeats, his voice firm and unyielding. "You did well tonight. Trust me to take care of things."

I swallow hard, nodding as I let him help me out of the car. My legs shake as we walk across the driveway. Before we get to the front door, it swings open, spilling warm light across the snow and revealing my mother standing in the entryway. Her face has that pinched, disapproving look she gets when she's really, really angry.

"Where have you been?" she snaps, her eyes flicking back and forth between us. "The menu tasting was supposed to start two hours ago."

I shrink into myself, but Cohen's hand finds the small of my back, steady and warm. I straighten my shoulders. "That was my fault," he says smoothly. "The meeting with Emmitt ran long, and then we had to deal with some unexpected business."

My mother's eyes narrow, scanning over us both with laser precision. I hold my breath, certain she can see the truth written all over my face. Can she tell I've been kissed? Does sin leave visible marks? Because that's what this is, isn't it? Sin?

"Business," she repeats, the word dripping with skepticism. "And this business required you to be gone for hours?"

"Actually, yes." Cohen's voice carries that edge of authority that makes even my mother hesitate. "Emmitt was... difficult. But it's handled now. Isn't that right, Emerald?"

I nod quickly, relieved when my voice comes out steady. "Yes. Everything's arranged for the auction."

My mother's lips press into a thin line, but she steps aside to let us inside. "Well, I suppose we'll have to reschedule the tasting. Though really, Cohen, you should have called."

"You're right," he says, helping me out of my coat with careful hands that linger just a little too long. "My apologies."

She watches this interaction with sharp eyes, and something in her expression makes me nervous. Like she knows.

Does she know?

Can she see the way he affects me? Can she see that her daughter is a twisted, sick thing that craves the touch of a man that could ruin her life? Can she see it? Can she feel the darkness that clings to us?

"Emerald," she snaps, making me jump. "What are you wearing?"

Oh god. *The jeans.* In all the chaos of kissing Cohen and

coming home late, I'd completely forgotten about my rebellion against the ridiculous dress code my mother enforces. Panic rises in my throat again, choking me with the fear of what she'll do. My mother doesn't tolerate defiance, especially not in front of guests. I brace myself for her tirade, for the icy anger that's about to rain down on me. "Mother, I can explain—"

But Cohen cuts in smoothly. "My suggestion," he says. "For the meeting with Emmitt. I thought a more... approachable look might put him at ease."

My mother's eyebrows shoot up. "Approachable? Since when does my daughter need to appear approachable?"

"Since Emmitt's ego needed managing," Cohen replies, his tone carrying just enough bite to make my mother blink. "Trust me, Madeline. It worked perfectly."

A tense silence follows as they stare each other down. I hold my breath, caught between them like a butterfly in a spider's web. Finally, my mother lets out a sharp sigh.

"Fine. But Emerald, change immediately. And get some rest —we have the photographer coming back tomorrow for additional shots."

"Yes, Mother." The words taste like ash in my mouth, but I say them anyway. It's easier than fighting.

I start toward the stairs, my legs shaky, but my mother's voice stops me. "Oh, and Emerald? Come see me in my office first thing tomorrow morning. We need to discuss some things."

My blood turns to ice water in my veins. "Of course."

I practically run up the stairs, my heart pounding against my ribs like it's trying to escape. Behind me, I hear my mother saying something to Cohen in that sharp, controlled voice she uses when she's angry, but I don't stop to listen.

Relief crashes through me as I slam the door to my room and lock it, then lean against it. My whole body feels jittery, like I've had too much caffeine, and my thoughts are a whirlwind of fear and confusion and something else—something hot and desperate and wild.

Cohen.

The way he looked at me. The way he kissed me. The way he made me feel alive for the first time in my life.

I touch my lips which are still a little swollen from his kisses.

But it's wrong. So wrong. He's married to my mother and old enough to be my father.

And yet... I can't bring myself to regret it. I don't want to regret it.

I sink to the floor, my back against the door, and bury my face in my hands. The weight of what I've done, of what I still want to do, threatens to crush me. How can I face my mother tomorrow? How can I pretend nothing has changed?

Eventually I change into my nightgown on autopilot, my mind spinning in circles. I climb into bed, but sleep is impossible. Every time I close my eyes, I see his face. Hear his voice. Feel his touch.

I pull the covers up to my chin like they might shield me from whatever storm is coming. My mother's words echo in my head: "Come see me first thing tomorrow morning."

Nothing good ever comes from those meetings.

I must drift off at some point because the next thing I know, I'm jolting awake in the darkness, my heart racing and my breath coming in short gasps.

A noise. There was a noise that woke me.

I lay perfectly still, straining my ears. For a moment, there's nothing, and I start to think I imagined it. But then it comes again—a soft, barely audible sound. The lock on my bedroom door opening and then the click of it closing.

How did they get in? I locked my door... didn't I?

Fear spikes through me, adrenaline flooding my veins,

before I recognize Cohen's familiar shadow moving through the darkness.

"Cohen?" I whisper, sitting up as he approaches my bed. "What are you—"

"Shh," he murmurs, perching on the edge of my mattress. His hand finds my cheek in the darkness, his thumb tracing my lower lip. "I couldn't stay away. Not tonight. Not after..."

I swallow hard, my pulse pounding in my ears. "After what?"

He leans in, his breath warm against my skin. "After that kiss. After everything. I had to see you, touch you, remind myself that it was real."

My heart skips a beat. "It was real," I whisper.

"And this is, too." His mouth covers mine, and suddenly, there's no fear, no doubt—just heat and need and the desperate ache of wanting him closer. I kiss him back, losing myself in the taste of him, in the way his tongue teases mine, coaxing me to open wider. To let him deeper.

His hands slide under the blankets, skimming up my sides and sending shivers of pleasure through me. When he cups my breast through the thin fabric of my nightgown, I gasp into his mouth, arching into his touch. I can't believe this is happening. Can't believe I'm not stopping him.

I should stop him. This is wrong.

"My mother—"

"Is asleep," he finishes, his lips trailing down my throat. "She took one of her pills an hour ago."

I should tell him to leave. Should push him away and remember all the reasons this is wrong. Instead, I find myself tilting my head back to give him better access. I'm pulling him closer, my fingers shoving into his hair as his mouth moves lower. I whimper and I don't even know why or what I want. More, I think.

But more of... what?

He tugs the strap of my nightgown down, baring my breast, and a moan slips out when his lips close over my nipple.

The sounds he's pulling out of me are so embarrassing that my face burns and I'm glad he can't see it in the dark.

"Cohen," I breathe, the word catching on a moan as his tongue swirls around the hardened peak. There are sparks shooting beneath my skin like one of those sparklers from the Fourth of July, and the magic of what he's doing with his mouth settles between my legs.

His fingers find my other nipple, rolling it gently as he sucks, and the sparks turn to fireworks, bursting through me with a force that leaves me trembling. I'm not sure what's happening to my body, but I don't want it to stop. It's like he's casting a spell, weaving a web of sensation that's trapping me, holding me prisoner, and I never want to escape.

I'm panting by the time he switches his mouth to my other breast, teasing the first with his fingertips until I'm squirming beneath him, needing... something. I'm not even sure what, just that I need it desperately.

He kisses me again, his tongue sweeping into my mouth, and there's something hard pressing against my thigh, even through the blankets. When his hand slips between them, finding how... wet I am there, I jerk away. "I'm sorry," I choke out, trying to close my legs. To keep him from feeling how I've drenched my underwear. "I don't know why—"

He groans and catches my knee, holding me open. "You're perfect," he whispers fiercely into the dark. "Perfect, little one. This means you're ready for me. That your body wants what I'm giving you. Do you understand?"

I shake my head, my face hot. "No," I whisper. "I don't understand any of this."

"Oh, Emerald." His thumb strokes my inner thigh. *When did he pull the blanket off me?* "Let me show you."

His hand slides higher, tracing the line of my underwear,

and I freeze, every muscle in my body tensing. He hesitates, his fingers so close to where I ache, and I don't know what to do.

"Relax," he soothes. "I won't hurt you. I'm just going to take this ache away. I promise."

And because I trust him—despite everything, despite the danger—I force myself to let go. To relax, like he asked. To give myself over to his touch.

The second I do, his fingers slip inside my underwear, and he groans again when he feels the slickness of me. "Fuck, little one. You're so fucking wet for me. I knew you would be."

A flush of shame heats my cheeks, but then his finger finds a place that sends off more of those fireworks, and I gasp, my hips lifting off the bed. He circles that spot slowly, and the pleasure is so sharp it's almost painful. Almost too much to bear. I clutch at his shoulders, my nails digging into his bare skin.

That makes me stop and I pry my eyes open and study him. He's wearing sweats but nothing on top, and his chest is broader than I realized. The muscles defined. I can see the ink swirling over his ribs and up his shoulder and the sight of him looming over me, half naked, only makes that ache worse. "What are you doing to me?" I manage to say, my voice thin and strained.

"Showing you how good we're going to be together," he murmurs, his breath hot against my ear as he keeps playing with that place between my thighs. "How right."

I'm lost in the sensations he's drawing from my body, in the heat and need and hunger that's building inside me. When he slips a finger inside me, I can't hold back a cry. It's too much. It's not enough.

He covers my mouth with his, swallowing my cries, and I cling to him as he works me with his hand. His thumb still circling that spot while his finger moves inside me, deeper, faster. The pressure builds until it's unbearable, until I'm shaking and panting and begging him without words.

"Come for me, little phoenix," he whispers in my ear. "Let go and fly."

I don't know what that means, but my body does. I break apart, shattering into a thousand glittering pieces, each one brighter than the last. My vision goes black and I'm flying. And then he's there to catch me, his arms wrapped tight around me, holding me close as I come back to myself.

When I can breathe again, when I can see, he's looking at me. His gray eyes glint in the moonlight, and there's that smile again. That soft, almost boyish grin that makes him look younger and more gorgeous than he has any right to.

"How was that?" he asks, his voice low and rough.

"Amazing," I breathe, still floating on the high of whatever he just did to me. "I didn't... I've never felt anything like that before."

"Good," he says, brushing a lock of hair off my forehead. "Because that was only the beginning. There's so much more I'm going to show you. So much more for us to discover together."

My heart stutters in my chest at his words, and I'm not sure if it's from fear or anticipation. Maybe a bit of both.

"But not tonight," he says, kissing the tip of my nose. "We have to be careful. Patient." His fingers tighten in my hair. "No matter what your mother says tomorrow, remember this moment. Remember how this feels."

I nod, unable to form words past the lump in my throat. He presses one more kiss to my forehead before untangling himself from me and standing.

"Sleep," he orders. "I'll see you in the morning."

I sink back into the pillows, feeling his absence like a physical ache. But then his lips are on my forehead again, and I don't know how I'm going to fall asleep tonight. Not when I have his words echoing in my head, and the memory of his touch burned into my skin.

Emerald

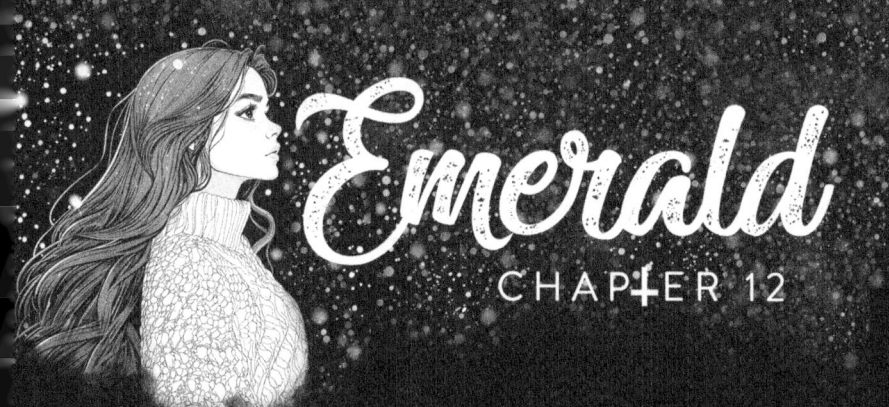

CHAPTER 12

SLEEP IS impossible after Cohen leaves. Every time I close my eyes, I see his face in the darkness, feel the ghost of his touch on my skin. My body still tingles in places I didn't even know could feel like this.

When morning comes, reality hits me with a cold slap. I can't believe that actually happened. That Cohen snuck into my room, touched me the way he did. That I liked it so much.

And now, the weak winter sun is streaming through my windows, and I have to go downstairs to face my mother. To pretend nothing has changed, even though everything has. How am I supposed to do that? How am I supposed to look her in the eye, knowing what her husband did to me last night?

I dress carefully in one of my mother's approved outfits—a gray shift dress the color of Cohen's eyes that has pearl buttons down the back—hoping to appease her before whatever lecture she has planned. My hands shake as I try to do up the buttons.

A knock at my door makes me jump so hard I nearly rip one of the stupid buttons off.

"Come in," I call, expecting my mother's assistant Kendra with some new schedule change.

Instead, Cohen steps in, closing the door behind him. The sight of him makes my heart skip a beat. He looks devastatingly handsome in a perfectly tailored navy suit, his hair still damp from a shower. He takes in the sight of me in my dress, his gaze sweeping over my body, and the memory of what he did to me last night has heat creeping up my neck.

"Having trouble?" His voice is soft, and when he touches a finger to the blush on my chest, the heat intensifies.

"I can't get the buttons," I manage to say, and the words are barely out before he's turning me around, his hands working down my spine. His fingers graze my skin with each one, and the blush spreads up to my face.

"My mother's waiting," I whisper, but I don't move away.

"I know." He finishes with the buttons but doesn't step back. Instead, his hands slide down to my hips, holding me steady. "Remember what I said last night. Let me handle everything."

I turn in his arms, looking up at him. "How can you be so calm about this?"

A dark smile curves his lips. "Oh, I'm far from calm, little one. Trust me. But we can't afford to let your mother know anything. She can never suspect, not until it's too late. Do you understand?"

I nod, even though I don't. I don't understand any of this. I don't understand how he can act like nothing happened, like he didn't have his hands all over my body last night, like he didn't have his tongue in my mouth and his fingers between my legs. I don't understand how he can be so calm and controlled when I'm a mess of emotions. "Yes. I'll be careful."

"You're exactly what I've been waiting for," he says, stroking a finger down my cheek. Then his gaze drops to my lips, and for a moment, I think he's going to kiss me. My heart pounds in anticipation, my breath catching in my throat. But then he steps away, and I have to press a hand to my stomach to quiet the butterflies.

"Now go," he says, stroking a thumb across my bottom lip. "Don't keep her waiting. I'll be close by."

The walk to my mother's office feels like marching to my execution. Each step on the marble floor echoes like a countdown, and by the time I reach her door, my hands are trembling so badly I have to clench them into fists.

I knock softly.

"Come in."

My mother sits behind her massive desk like a queen on her throne, perfect as always in a tailored white suit and pearls. Her makeup is flawless, her hair pulled back in a neat chignon, and she looks like she could step onto the cover of *Living Delacroix* magazine without needing a single airbrush.

"Sit down," she says, not looking up from her tablet.

I perch on the edge of one of her uncomfortable visitor chairs, crossing my ankles like she taught me and folding my hands in my lap.

"Do you know why I asked you here?" She finally looks up, fixing me with that arctic stare that always makes me feel about two inches tall.

"No, Mother."

She sets her tablet aside and leans back in her chair, studying me with narrowed eyes. "I'm concerned about you, Emerald."

"Concerned?"

"Yes. Your behavior lately has been... disappointing."

"Disappointing? How?" The word slips out before I can stop it, and I brace for her displeasure.

She leans forward slightly. "Those hideous jeans you wore yesterday for one. Your arguments about working with Emmitt for another. You've always been a compliant child, but lately, you've been pushing boundaries. And I can't have that, especially not with the Christmas party coming up."

I swallow hard. "I—"

"Don't interrupt," she snaps. "These changes coincide rather perfectly with Cohen's increased interest in your activities."

My blood runs cold. "I don't understand."

"Don't you?" Her classic French manicured nails tap against her desk. "Men like Cohen are drawn to weakness, Emerald. To naive little girls who they think need saving." Her lips curl into a cruel smile. "Do you really think he cares about you? Do you really think he'd risk his position here for a silly little girl? Please. Don't be stupid."

I try to speak, but my throat is tight. I can only shake my head, a silent plea.

"He's using you, darling. I would have expected you to recognize that. I raised you to be smarter, but apparently, I was wrong. Apparently, you're as foolish and gullible as every other girl your age."

Each word hits like a physical blow, finding all my deepest insecurities and twisting them like knives. "That's not—"

"You have no skills, Emerald. No education beyond what I've allowed. No money of your own." She stands, moving around her desk to tower over me. "Everything you are, everything you have, comes from me. And if you continue down this path of rebellion, I will take it all away. Do you understand?"

Tears burn behind my eyes, but I refuse to let them fall. "Yes, Mother."

"Good." She moves back to her chair. "Now, about the Christmas party. You'll be escorted by James Montgomery's son. He's a suitable match, and the merger with their company would be beneficial."

"But—"

"This isn't a discussion." Her voice turns to ice, and the tears threaten again. "You will be on your best behavior at the party. You will be polite and charming and do everything in your power to secure a future with this boy. Do I make myself clear?"

I can't seem to find my voice, so I just nod. Anything to get out of here, away from her. Anything to end this conversation.

"And Emerald? Stay away from Cohen. He's not as perfect as you seem to think he is. In fact..." She pauses, a small smile playing at her lips. "Did you know he was investigated for the disappearance of his last girlfriend? Nothing was ever proven, of course, but still... interesting, isn't it?"

I feel like I'm going to be sick. "May I be excused?"

She waves a dismissive hand, already turning back to her tablet. "Yes. And remember what I said. Everything you are belongs to me."

I somehow make it back to my room before the tears start falling. I collapse on my bed, sobbing into my pillow, the image of Cohen's face swimming in front of my eyes. Those beautiful gray eyes, that dark hair, those strong, tattooed arms that held me close last night, that made me feel safe. That made me feel like maybe he could actually care about me. That maybe he would be the one to finally, truly love me.

But my mother is right. What do I have to offer someone like Cohen? And what about his last girlfriend? What really happened to her?

I curl up on my window seat, pressing my forehead against the cold glass as snow starts falling outside. Everything feels wrong, twisted, broken. Like someone's taken all my certainties and shattered them into pieces I can't put back together.

"Little one."

I whirl around to find Cohen standing in my doorway, his expression dark as storm clouds. Before I can speak, he's crossing the room in long strides, pulling me into his arms.

"I heard everything," he says against my hair. "Every fucking word she said to you." A shudder runs through him like his body's struggling to contain his fury. "You can't even imagine the things I want to do to her for making you cry."

The anger in his voice, the barely contained violence,

should frighten me, especially after what my mother told me. But only I cling to him tighter, his words a balm to my wounded soul.

"Is it true?" I whisper. "Am I just... weak to you?"

He pulls back enough to cup my face in his hands, forcing me to meet his hurricane-force gaze. "You are the strongest person I know. Your mother is desperate. She's losing control, and she'll say anything to keep you caged."

"But—"

"No." His thumb brushes away a tear I didn't realize had fallen. "Everything she said was calculated to hurt you. To make you doubt yourself. To make you doubt me."

"What about... what she said about your ex?"

Something dangerous flashes in his eyes. "Ancient history," he says. "And not what you think. I'll tell you everything when the time is right, but for now..." He leans down, pressing his forehead to mine. "For now, just trust me. Can you do that?"

I should say no. Should run far away from whatever darkness lurks behind his eyes.

Instead, I whisper, "Yes."

His kiss tastes like victory and secrets, and I let myself drown in it. Because maybe my mother's right—maybe I am naive and weak. But in Cohen's arms, I feel strong. Feel real.

Feel free.

And that's worth any price.

Cohen
CHAPTER 13

RAGE TASTES like blood in my mouth and feels like fire in my veins.

It's a living thing inside me, clawing at my insides, demanding to be set free as I slam my fist into the heavy bag, imagining Madeline's face where my knuckles connect. The impact reverberates through my bones, but the pain does nothing to stop the inferno inside me.

Every tear Emerald shed in her room last night is a debt I intend to collect from her mother. Every cruel word Madeline hurled at her is a promise that I'll repay her ten-fold. A hundred times over. A thousand. I'll tear her down to nothing, strip everything away, and leave her a hollow, broken shell of her former self.

Madeline thinks she can force my little bird back into her cage. Thinks she can bend her to her will. Thinks she can mold her into the docile, submissive daughter who will marry the man of her mother's choosing and carry on the Delacroix legacy.

She's wrong. So very wrong. She has no idea what she's unleashed.

Because I will never, ever, let that happen. Emerald will never belong to anyone but me. I'll burn down the entire fucking town before I allow that woman to take her from me.

I'm not usually prone to outbursts of emotion, but something about Emerald brings out the worst in me.

The best in me.

My fists fly in a flurry of strikes, sweat beading on my forehead as I throw everything I have at the bag. It's not enough.

The home gym is empty, the sun barely risen, but it's all I've wanted to do since I left Emerald's room. But no matter how hard I strike, how much weight I bench, how many miles I run on the treadmill, it never lessens.

Sweat drips down my bare chest, and my muscles burn, but I don't stop. Can't stop. Not when I don't know what I'll do if I stop. Not when I can still hear Madeline's voice in my head, cutting into Emerald like a fucking knife, making her bleed.

"Everything you are belongs to me."

The heavy bag swings wildly, and I keep punching until my knuckles are bruised and raw. Until there's blood spattering the black leather, leaving tiny red constellations across its surface. Until my lungs ache, and my vision blurs.

The physical outlet is the only thing keeping me from storming upstairs and showing Madeline exactly how wrong she is about who owns what in this house.

Because Emerald doesn't belong to her mother. She belongs to *me*. Has since that first night when I saw her crying on a balcony, face lifted to the stars as tears tracked down her cheeks. Her pain mirrored my own, a kindred spirit that called to something deep in my soul.

It was like the universe had reached out and slapped me in the face, waking me from a long, dark dream.

I didn't know her then, didn't know why she was crying, or what she was running from, but none of that mattered. In that moment, I saw her. Saw the loneliness that matched mine, the aching emptiness, the need for someone to hold on to. And I knew I had to make her mine. No matter what it took. No matter the cost.

Her soul has been mine since that moment.

Of course, I had no idea then just how bad things were for her. No idea of the hell she lived in, of the nightmare her mother created. And knowing it now makes me want to murder someone.

Preferably Madeline.

Everything since then—marrying Madeline, moving into this mansion, playing the dutiful husband—has been leading to this moment. This opportunity to take what's mine and make it permanent. Irrevocable.

My father would be proud of this cold calculation, this careful restraint. Harrison Astor built the Astor legacy on control—ruthless, unrelenting control that crushed everything in its path, including his own son. But I learned from his mistakes. Where he used control to destroy, I use it to protect. Where he broke things, I save them. The iron grip I keep on my darkness isn't just about power—it's about making sure I never become him. Making sure I use this poison in my blood to shield rather than shatter.

The heavy bag shudders as I unleash a series of brutal kicks, the chain creaking above. Sweat drips into my eyes, stinging them, and I wipe it away with the back of one hand.

But Madeline's words found their mark. I saw it in Emerald's eyes last night, the way doubt crept in like poison. The way she looked at me after Madeline mentioned Charlotte, fear warring with trust as she tried to reconcile the monster her mother painted me as with the man who held her while she cried.

"You're here early."

I don't pause my assault on the bag as Kendra's voice floats across the gym. Madeline's assistant hovers in the doorway, her usually impeccable appearance slightly disheveled. There are shadows under her eyes that makeup can't quite hide.

Madeline's work, no doubt.

"What do you want?" I ask, landing another combination of punches and sending the bag swinging again.

"Mrs. Delacroix asked me to remind you about the menu tasting this afternoon." Kendra's normally uptight voice wavers slightly. "She wants to make sure you'll be there this time."

I catch the bag, steadying it as I turn to fix Kendra with a look that makes her take an instinctive step back. "Tell my wife I'll be wherever the fuck I want to be whenever the fuck I want to be there."

Kendra swallows hard but stands her ground. "She also wanted me to tell you that she's arranged for Daniel Montgomery Jr. to escort Emerald to the Christmas party. She says it's not up for discussion."

The rage that's been simmering in my blood reaches a boiling point. I stalk toward Kendra, satisfaction curling through me as she shrinks back against the doorframe. "Let me be very clear," I say, my voice soft and lethal. "Emerald isn't going anywhere with anyone except me. And if Madeline has a problem with that, she can take it up with me directly instead of hiding behind her messenger."

"I... I'll tell her," Kendra stammers, already backing away.

"Good." I turn back to the bag, dismissing her. "Oh, and Kendra? The next time my wife wants to threaten me, tell her to do it herself. I'd hate for something to happen to you just because you were following orders."

I wait until the door closes behind her before resuming my attack on the bag.

Let her run back to Madeline. Let her report every word.

The game is changing, and it's time Madeline understood exactly who she's playing against.

I land one final punch, imagining Daniel Montgomery Jr.'s face this time. The thought of that entitled little prick anywhere near Emerald makes me want to rip him apart with my bare hands. He's a wolf in sheep's clothing, just like his father, and I'll be damned if I let him lay a finger her.

But I force the rage down, lock it away where it can't touch the plans I've spent two years perfecting.

Soon, I'll show Emerald the truth about her mother. About me. About everything.

But first, I need a shower. And then I need to make sure my little phoenix understands that no matter what Madeline says, no matter what she threatens, no matter what she does, she'll never take my girl from me.

The hot water runs red with my blood and sweat, the rainfall from the custom showerhead washing away the physical evidence of my workout. It does nothing to wash away the darkness coursing through my veins.

My knuckles sting under the water, and I examine them with clinical detachment. They're already bruising, but it's worth it.

I shut off the water and grab a towel, my mind already racing ahead to what needs to be done. Emerald will have questions about Charlotte—questions I need to answer before Madeline can poison her further against me. There's also Emmitt, who appears to be licking his wounds, but I have no doubt he'll crawl back out of his hole and become an issue at some point.

And then there's the matter of Daniel Montgomery Jr., that simpering little sociopath who thinks he has any right to touch what's mine.

One problem at a time.

I dress quickly in dark Kiton slacks and a white button-down, leaving the top buttons undone. No need for the full armor today—not when I'm planning to spend it with my girl.

I find her exactly where I knew she would be—in the living room, curled up in the window seat next to the Christmas tree like a cat seeking sunshine. She's wearing another one of her mother's approved outfits, an ice blue dress that makes her blend into the blue and silver flocked tree beside her.

She looks like an angel, and I can't wait to make her fall.

"Little one."

She startles at my voice, those big green eyes finding mine across the room. I can see the war being waged in them—the fear and longing and hope and doubt all swirling together and I fucking hate it.

"Cohen." My name on her lips is still the sweetest sound I've ever heard. "I... I didn't expect to see you this morning."

I cross the room, unable to resist the magnetic pull she has on me. "Where else would I be?"

She bites that bottom lip that drives me fucking insane, and I have to fist my hands at my sides to keep from reaching for her. "I thought maybe... after what my mother said..."

"Look at me." I wait until those evergreen eyes meet mine. "Nothing your mother says changes anything between us. Nothing."

"But what she said about your ex—"

Goddamn Madeline. Emerald's trusting, but she's also curious. It's not fair of me to leave her in the dark when I can so easily put her fears to rest with the truth. It's not really my secret to tell, but trust works both ways and Emerald deserves mine.

"Was manipulation," I cut in, settling beside her on the window seat. "Like everything else that comes out of her mouth."

Emerald's fingers stretch out and start playing with a button on my shirt and I don't even think she knows she's doing it. Her cheeks flush that gorgeous rose and I want to lick the color, taste it on her skin. "She said you were investigated. About the disappearance of your ex."

I take a deep breath. "It's true," I say, watching her carefully. "But not the way you think."

I study her face for a long moment, weighing how much truth to give her. But the fear lurking in her eyes makes the decision for me. I won't let Madeline's lies come between us.

"Charlotte was never my girlfriend," I say finally. "She was a friend of a client who needed help escaping an abusive marriage. Her husband, Gregory, was a powerful man who used that power to keep her trapped. To hurt her."

Understanding dawns in Emerald's eyes. "You helped her escape?"

"I did what needed to be done." I reach out, tucking a strand of dark hair behind her ear. "I created a new identity for her, helped her disappear so completely that even Gregory couldn't find her."

"And Gregory?"

My lips curl into a cold smile. "Let's just say he won't be hurting anyone else ever again."

She shivers, but doesn't pull away from my touch. If anything, she leans into me more. "Why did you tell my mother Charlotte was your girlfriend then?"

"Because I knew it would intrigue her." I let my fingers trail down the side of her neck, feeling her pulse jump beneath my touch. "Your mother has a weakness for powerful men she thinks she can't have. She likes to hunt. I used that to get close to you."

"To me?" Her voice catches as my thumb traces her collarbone. "But why?"

I study her face in the soft winter light filtering through the window, committing every detail to memory. The way she leans into my touch without realizing it. The perfect mixture of innocence and curiosity in her expression. The slight parting of her lips as she waits for my answer.

Two years of watching. Planning. Waiting.

And now she's finally asking the right question.

Cohen
CHAPTER 14

I LEAN IN, close enough to brush my lips against hers before I move back. "Because I've been watching you for a long time, little phoenix. Since the night at the Mitchell Gala two years ago, when I saw you standing on the balcony all alone, looking up at the sky with tears running down your face. Since that night, you've been mine. Every breath. Every heartbeat. Every second of my life has belonged to you."

Her eyes widen at my confession, and for a moment, I worry that I've said too much, that the darkness inside me has scared her. But then she smiles—a soft, tentative thing that's like seeing the sun rise after a long, endless night.

"You've been planning this for two years?" she whispers. "Everything—marrying my mother, moving in here—it was all to get to me?"

"Yes." There's no point in denying it. Not when the truth feels so fucking right. "And it was all worth it. Every move, every decision, has been leading to this moment. To us."

She swallows hard, and I track the movement of her throat with hungry eyes. "That's... that's insane."

"Is it?" I cup her face in my hands, forcing her to meet my

gaze. "Tell me you don't feel it too. This connection between us. This pull that makes everything else fade away."

"I do feel it," she admits, her voice barely above a whisper. "But Cohen, you're married to my mother."

"Not in the ways that count," I say, my thumb brushing across her bottom lip.

She tries to turn away, but I hold her still. "Do you... do you sleep with her?"

The question makes my jaw clench, pure disgust coursing through me. The thought of Emerald imagining me with Madeline makes me want to demonstrate exactly how wrong she is about who I belong to.

"No," I say, letting her hear the revulsion in my voice. "I have never touched your mother the way I touch you. I never will. She means nothing to me beyond being a means to an end."

"But—"

I cut her off with a kiss, unable to bear another second of her doubting who she belongs to. She makes a soft sound of surprise against my mouth, but then she's melting into me, her hands fisting in my shirt as I devour her.

She tastes like peppermint tea and innocence, and I growl as her tongue tentatively meets mine. My hand slides into her hair, holding her still as I take what's mine, showing her with lips and teeth and tongue exactly who she belongs to.

When I finally pull back, we're both breathing hard. Her lips are swollen from my kiss, her pupils blown wide, and the sight of her like this—wrecked and messy—makes my cock throb.

"You're the only one I want," I tell her, my voice rough. "The only one I've ever wanted. Everyone else is just collateral damage on my path to you."

"But why me?" she whispers, her fingers still twisted in my shirt like she's afraid to let go.

"Because you're mine," I say, pressing my forehead to hers.

"Because the moment I saw you, something inside me recognized something inside you. Like we were carved from the same midnight, you the starlight, me the void."

My hand slides down to her flat stomach, wondering if my seed has already taken root inside her. If she's carrying the physical proof of my claim on her. The thought makes my blood burn hotter, my grip on her tightening possessively.

"I'm going to give you everything," I promise against her lips. "A future. A family. A love so consuming it'll rewrite your DNA until there's nothing left but us."

Her skin heats under my touch, a flush spreading down her throat to disappear beneath her dress. "What if I'm not strong enough for this?" she whispers.

"You're stronger than you know," I tell her, my fingers tracing patterns on her skin. "Strong enough to survive everything your mother's done to you. Strong enough to become what you're meant to be."

"And what's that?"

"The beginning and end of everything I am." The words come out like a prayer and a curse combined.

"I'm afraid," she admits, and the vulnerability in her voice makes me want to paint the walls with the blood of everyone who's ever hurt her.

"Don't be," I murmur, kissing her again, claiming her mouth with slow, deliberate possession. "I'll destroy anyone who tries to touch you. Your mother, Emmitt, all of them."

"Even Daniel Montgomery?"

"Especially him." My hand settles gently around the front of her throat as I imagine all the ways I could make him disappear. "Your mother can make all the plans she wants. But the only future that exists is the one where you're carrying my child, wearing my ring, sharing my bed. And I'll eliminate anyone who tries to stand in the way of that."

My teeth graze her bottom lip, drawing a soft gasp from her throat. "Cohen—"

My phone vibrates in my pocket, cutting off whatever confession was about to fall from those perfect lips. One look at the screen shows Tristen's name.

When my client and friend calls—when any of the Savage Six calls—you answer.

"I need to take this," I say, stealing one more taste of her mouth before standing. "Don't move. We have unfinished business."

She nods, lips swollen from my kisses, eyes dark with something desperate and needy that makes walking away feel like carving out my own heart.

I move to the window, positioning myself where I can watch Emerald while scanning the snow-covered grounds. "What's happening?"

"Montgomery Jr.'s been shooting his mouth off at my club." Tristen's voice carries the casual menace of a man who could start a war with a single phone call. "Seems the little bastard can't stop talking about his Christmas present from Madeline."

"Elaborate."

"He's telling anyone who'll listen that he's going to announce his engagement to Emerald at the party. That Madeline's arranged everything." Tristen pauses. "You want me to handle it?"

An offer from one of the Savage Six to "handle" a problem isn't made lightly, and I know Tristen has a lot going on right now. "Not yet. But keep him talking. I want to know what else Madeline's promised him."

"There's more. He's been asking questions about you. About our connection. The kind of questions that suggest Madeline's fishing for leverage."

I watch Emerald through the reflection in the glass, memorizing every detail of how she looks right now - flushed and wanting. "Let him ask. It'll be the last mistake he makes."

"She's not as smart as she thinks she is," Tristen says, a hint of amusement coloring his voice.

"Of course she isn't." My eyes stay fixed on Emerald's reflection as she pretends to read, stealing glances in my direction. "She's getting sloppy."

"Want me to put some pressure on Montgomery Sr.? Nothing ruins Christmas like your company stock taking an unexpected dive."

I smile at the casual way Tristen offers to destroy a family's generational wealth. This is why we're friends. "Not yet. But keep watching him. I want to know every word that comes out of his mouth about Emerald."

"Done. And Cohen?" Tristen's voice drops lower. "Watch yourself. She's starting to realize she's lost control. Makes her unpredictable."

I end the call, already calculating how many moves ahead I need to be. Madeline's desperation makes her dangerous, but it also makes her vulnerable.

"Everything okay?" Emerald's soft voice pulls me back from the edge of darker thoughts. She's watching me with those pretty eyes, and something in my chest twists at the concern I see there. I cross back to her, drawn like a compass finding north.

"Everything's fine," I tell her, though we both know it's a lie. When she steps into my arms, my entire existence narrows to the weight of her against me. "Just business."

She tilts her face up, studying me. "You're angry."

"Not at you," I assure her, brushing my lips across her forehead. "Never at you."

She's quiet for a moment, her fingers tracing patterns on my chest. "My mother wants me to go to the Christmas party with Daniel Montgomery."

"That's not happening." The words slice through the air between us, and I feel her shiver. "At the party, everyone's going to learn exactly who you belong with. No more hiding. No more pretending."

"What do you mean?"

I cup her face in my hands, drinking in every detail of her features—features I've memorized in midnight visits and endless hours staring at the camera feed in her room. "I mean it's time to burn your mother's perfect world to ash. Starting with her precious Christmas party."

Her eyes widen. "But my mother—"

"Will learn to accept reality," I say, each word falling like a death sentence between us. "Or she'll learn there are worse things than losing control."

The rest of the morning passes in a blur of stolen moments and heated looks. I have meetings I can't avoid, calls I have to take, but my mind keeps circling back to Emerald. The heat in her skin when I touched her. The way she looked at me like I could give her everything she's been starving for.

By late afternoon, I can't stay away any longer and I go looking for her. I find her in the formal dining room, surrounded by elaborate gift baskets she's assembling under Madeline's strict instructions. Another way for her mother to assert control, to remind Emerald of her place.

I watch from the shadows as she meticulously arranges bottles of wine and artisanal chocolates, checking items off a detailed list with the precision of someone who knows the cost of even the smallest mistake. Her dark hair falls forward, hiding her face as she works, but I can see the tension in her shoulders, the careful way she moves.

She pauses in her work, staring out the window at the

falling snow. There's such longing in her expression, such desperate need for freedom, that it makes something in my chest constrict painfully. She doesn't belong here, arranging pretty boxes of expensive trinkets for her mother's social circle. She belongs in my bed, in my arms, creating a life she loves instead of these soulless displays of wealth.

I think about the black folder locked in my office drawer. A USB drive containing security footage from the night Madeline pushed her elderly father down the stairs when he threatened to cut off her inheritance. The same drive holds video of her confession about arranging Emerald's father's "accidental" overdose when he tried to get custody. Bank records that reveal her lifestyle empire for what it really is—an elaborate front for selling young models to wealthy men like Emmitt. Files detailing how she's systematically broken every person who's ever crossed her, including her own sister who mysteriously overdosed after threatening to expose her.

Proof that her perfect image is built on rot and corruption, collected over the last two years.

I'm only waiting for the perfect moment to destroy everything she's built.

And Emmitt... my lip curls thinking about what I've found on him. Three girls in the past two years alone, all of them underage, all of them paid to disappear with their families' silence bought through ironclad NDAs. The latest one was the daughter of one of Madeline's socialite friends. The settlement amount was substantial, but money can't erase security footage. Can't erase the bruises documented in hospital records that mysteriously vanished from official files.

Can't erase rape kits.

That moment is coming. I can feel it in my bones, in the way the air seems charged with the potential for violence. Madeline won't let go easily—of me or of Emerald. She'll fight with everything she has to maintain control.

Let her try.

I watch as Emerald returns to her task, efficiently tying a perfect bow around another basket. Such a small act of submission, but it makes my blood boil. Soon, I'll free her from all of this. Soon, she'll never have to bow to anyone's will but mine.

I turn away, leaving her to her work. I have preparations to make, pieces to move into place. The Christmas party is approaching faster than I'd like, and everything needs to be perfect. By then, I should know if she's carrying my child. If she's already growing the future I planned for us.

Because that night won't just be about announcing our relationship. It won't just be about showing everyone that she belongs at my side. It will be about destroying everything Madeline has built, piece by precious piece.

And if she tries to stand between me and what's mine... well. I didn't get where I am by letting obstacles live. The divorce papers I drew up the day I married her will be the least of her concerns.

I stride into my office, unlocking the drawer that contains my insurance policies. Everything I need to ensure Emerald's freedom is right here. Every piece of leverage, every dark secret, every weapon I might need to deploy.

Of course, these aren't my only copies, but their proximity brings me comfort.

My phone buzzes with a text from Madeline, demanding my presence at dinner tonight for her goddamn menu tasting.

I ignore it, a cold smile curving my lips as I flip through the folder's contents. Let her make her demands. Let her think she still has any control over me.

Soon, she'll learn what happens when you try to keep a monster from what belongs to him.

Soon, she'll learn that her daughter was never hers to keep.

Emerald

CHAPTER 15

MY MOTHER always said nothing good happens after midnight, but she never mentioned how tempting darkness could be.

That probably explains why I'm wide awake and staring at a note that definitely qualifies as "not good."

I just found it in my bed. It falls out as I'm pulling back my covers, this pristine white rectangle against my flannel sheets that's basically a written invitation to trouble. My hands shake as I pick it up. The paper feels expensive, and I wouldn't expect anything less from my stepfather.

Come to the chapel. -C

Four words. That's all it takes to make my heart go completely wild and my skin feel like it's on fire, which is kind of impressive considering my room is basically the North Pole right now temperature-wise.

I'd know that handwriting anywhere. It's all clean lines and sharp angles, just like the man himself. Because of course Cohen even manages to make his handwriting hot.

This is such a bad idea. The chapel's way out at the edge of the property, and if my mother caught me sneaking out?

God, I don't even want to think about what she'd do. Three days without food would probably be the least of my punishments.

But I'm already sliding out of bed, so clearly my self-preservation instinct is broken. Or maybe it's because the chapel's the only place on this entire estate that feels like mine, even though I've never stepped foot inside.

Plus, Cohen's waiting.

Yeah, because that's totally a good reason to risk your mother's wrath, Emerald.

But I'm still going.

There's something about knowing Cohen's waiting that makes my whole body feel weirdly buzzy, like I've had way too much caffeine (which would never happen since Mother monitors my intake). Every cell feels like it's waking up for the first time, and the way he talked about the chapel earlier, all quiet and intense... yeah, there's no way I'm staying in bed.

My hands shake so bad it takes me three tries to zip up my boots, and then I slip into my jacket.

The house is creepy-quiet, just the heating running and the antique grandfather clock ticking away in the hall like it's counting down to something. I press my ear against my door, listening for any sign of movement. Like, I don't know, my mother's cloven hooves clomping down the hall to catch me being a huge disappointment.

But there's nothing. Just silence.

Walking through the house at night is trippy. Everything looks different in the dark, all the fancy antiques casting weird shadows in the light reflecting off the snow. My heart's pounding so loud I'm amazed it doesn't wake anyone up as I sneak through the kitchen and out the back door.

The cold hits like a slap in the face almost as hard as my mother.

I follow Cohen's footprints in the snow, trying not to think about how this is probably going to end badly. The Christmas lights Mother insisted on stringing everywhere make the snow look kind of magical though, all these colors bleeding together. An owl screeches somewhere and I nearly jump out of my skin.

Every step puts more distance between me and my mother's kingdom, bringing me closer to... whatever this is with Cohen.

This is such a bad idea.

But I keep walking.

The chapel materializes out of the snow and night, its silhouette rising from the trees like something torn from a gothic fairytale. For something that's been my favorite view since forever, it looks different up close at night. The moonlight hits the stained glass just right, making colors dance across the snow. There's this warm glow coming from inside and it takes me a second to realize what it is.

Candles.

My heart stumbles. He's already here. Waiting for me.

My hand's shaking so bad I almost can't get the door open. When I finally do, it lets out a loud creak, and I step into... wow. It's a world of flickering shadows and golden light. There are candles everywhere, and someone (three guesses who) has wrapped evergreen garlands around the pews. It smells amazing, like Christmas trees and old wood and melting wax.

It's nothing like I imagined, and somehow it's better.

"You came." Cohen's voice emerges from the shadows near the altar. It's low and gravelly and the entire lineup of birds from *The Twelve Days of Christmas* take flight in my stomach.

"Did you think I wouldn't?"

He steps into the light and... *oh*. He's wearing all black, the fabric of his shirt stretched across his broad shoulders. The candlelight catches the silver in his eyes, making him look otherworldly. Dangerous.

"No," he says, with a gorgeous half-smile. "I knew you would. You can't resist me any more than I can resist you."

He walks toward me, and I freeze like a deer in headlights, torn between bolting and throwing myself at him. Instead, I force myself to stay still.

"This place is incredible," I manage to say, trying to slow down my racing heart. "I can't believe I've never been inside before."

"I know." He stops right in front of me, close enough that I can feel how warm he is. "Your mother keeps it locked. She hates what it represents." His fingers brush my cheek. "Love."

That word hangs in the air between us, and my heart's beating so fast I briefly wonder if I'm going to need medical attention.

"Love?" The word feels weird on my tongue. My mother's never loved anything except her brand and her social media following. "Is that what this is?"

His eyes go dark as his thumb traces my lip, and my brain completely stops working. "What else would make me willing to destroy everything just to have you?"

I shiver, and not from the cold. There's something about the way he says it—like nothing else matters to him except me. "You make it sound so easy."

"It is easy." His fingers slide into my hair, just tight enough to make me gasp. "The moment I saw you, I knew how this would end. Everything since then has just been leading us here."

"Why here?" My voice comes out embarrassingly breathless. "Why tonight?"

His eyes catch the candlelight as he cups my face. "Because this place was made for us, little phoenix. And I'm done waiting."

The words sink into my skin. Every touch, every stolen moment over the last week has led us here, to this unholy night in this sacred place. And despite everything—despite knowing this is wrong, despite knowing what it will cost—I've never wanted anything more.

"Neither of us is getting out of this unburned, are we?" I whisper.

His smile is all darkness and promise. "No. But sometimes the most beautiful things rise from the ashes."

He leans down, his lips brushing my ear. "Are you ready to burn with me?" he asks, his hands sliding down my sides to grip my hips.

I look up at him, at the man who's become everything I never knew I needed. The candlelight flickers across his face, shadows dancing in his eyes, and I know there's no turning back.

"Yes," I breathe, and the word feels like a prayer.

His smile is triumphant as he reaches into his pocket, pulling out a length of deep red velvet ribbon. "Take off your coat," he commands, and I obey without hesitation, letting the heavy fabric fall to the floor so I'm only in my thin nightgown and boots. It's cold in here and my nipples go hard in less than a second. His eyes drop to them as his tongue drags along his lip like he's imagining tasting me there.

"What are you doing?"

"You'll see," he says, wrapping the velvet around my wrists and tying it in a pretty bow. My heart races as he guides me to the altar, pushing me onto the polished wood and stretching my arms above my head. "How does that feel?" he asks, his eyes intent on mine. "Is it too tight?"

"No," I whisper, a rush of heat flooding my core as he slides his fingers along the velvet. It's soft against my skin, but the knot is tight. Inescapable. Just like my feelings for my stepfather.

"Good," he says, leaning down to brush a kiss against my forehead. "Tonight, you're my gift, and I intend to take my time unwrapping you." His breath is hot against my skin as he trails a line of kisses down my throat, his tongue darting out to dip into the hollow at the base. "And when I'm done, I'm going to take you right here on the altar."

My breath catches in my throat as he straightens up, his eyes roaming over my body like a starving man faced with a feast. "I've imagined this moment so many times," he murmurs, his hands sliding up my thighs, pushing the hem of my nightgown higher. "But nothing compares to the reality of you laid out for me. So soft, so beautiful, so willing to give me everything."

He pulls a knife from his pocket, the blade glinting in the candlelight. My eyes widen and everything inside me is chaos, like someone shook up all my emotions in a snow globe as he brings the tip to the neckline of my nightgown.

"Look at me," he orders, and I drag my gaze away from the knife to meet his eyes. The silver of his irises seems to glow in the candlelight, the color almost magical. He holds me captive with that gaze as he slowly drags the blade down, splitting the fabric of not only my nightgown but my underwear, too, with a soft tearing sound that reverberates through the empty chapel.

The cold air kisses my newly exposed skin, but it's the heat in Cohen's eyes that makes me shiver. He slides the knife back into his pocket, his gaze never leaving mine as he parts the torn fabric of my nightgown, laying me bare before him. I feel a rush of vulnerability and excitement, my breath coming in short gasps.

"You're trembling," he murmurs, his hands gliding up my sides, thumbs brushing the undersides of my breasts. "Are you afraid?"

I shake my head, my voice barely a whisper. "No. I'm just... I don't know what to do."

His smile is a slow, wicked curve of the lips. "You don't have to do anything. Just feel. I'm going to teach you, Emerald. I'm going to show you what your body is capable of."

Emerald

CHAPTER 16

HIS HANDS CUP MY BREASTS, thumbs circling my hardened nipples, drawing out a gasp from somewhere deep inside of me. "Starting with these perfect tits. They're begging for my attention, aren't they?"

I nod, pushing into the heat of his touch and away from the cold stone beneath me. The sensation is so overwhelming but it's also... intoxicating. I'm dizzy with it.

He leans down, his mouth replacing his thumb. His tongue, the one I've learned is made of magic over the last week and a half, is flicking against the sensitive peak before he swirls it around. I cry out, the sound so loud in the empty chapel, as he sucks and licks and nibbles, drawing out a pleasure so sharp it's almost painful.

"Cohen," I gasp, my hands straining against the velvet binding. I'm desperate to touch him, to dig my fingers into his thick hair and yank him closer... or maybe push him away. "It's too much."

He lifts his head, his eyes so dark they look demonic. The flames reflected in them don't help. "No, baby. Your body is made for me, remember? There's no such thing as too much between us." He moves to the other breast, giving it with the same attention until I'm writhing beneath him, my hips bucking against nothing.

"Please," I beg, not even sure what I'm asking for. I just know I *need*... whatever it is.

He smiles, but it's a feral, wicked thing. Then he's trailing kisses down my stomach, stopping just below my belly button, his hands gripping my hips. "Please what, little one? Tell me what you want." His lips brush my skin with his every one of his words and I shudder.

"I don't know," I whimper, my body painful from a craving I can't describe. Over a million words in the English language and I can't find a single one to give him. "I just... I need..."

"You need to come," he says, his voice a low growl as he pushes my thighs apart, exposing me to this holy place and the dark god kneeling before me. "And you will. On my tongue, on my fingers, on my cock. You'll come until you can't take anymore, and then you'll come again."

His words are filthy, shocking, and they send a flood of heat straight between my legs. He slides down further, flinging my legs over his broad shoulders. He wraps one of his big hands around my thigh, holding me tight enough that I can't move. And then his hot tongue is on me, licking, sucking, exploring. When I try to wiggle away, he growls like an animal, his fingers digging into my flesh and holding me tighter.

He alternates using his tongue and his lips, sucking until I'm tingling and shaking all over and then switching to long licks with the flat of his tongue. I cry out, completely overwhelmed, lost, mindless. I've never felt anything like this before.

"Cohen," I gasp, my hips bucking against his mouth because he won't let them move any further. The stubble on his jaw scrapes along my sensitive skin and it hurts in the best way. "What are you... oh *god*..."

He lifts his head, his chin glistening with my wetness. That's still so embarrassing. My face burns at the sight of him like that. "Don't say his name," he growls, his voice raw and possessive while his grip on my thigh tightens to almost painful. "When you're with me, it's only my name on your lips. Say 'Cohen' like I'm your fucking prayer."

His eyes lock onto mine like he's daring me to defy him. The air between us crackles and sparks. I can feel his heart pounding against the back of my leg, matching the wild rhythm of my own.

Without blinking, he slides a finger inside me, and I clench around him. I'm the one to break our eye contact when my eyes roll up into my head and this time I do moan his name.

The satisfied sound he lets out sends a scattering of goosebumps across my flesh.

I may have no clue what I'm doing, but my body's operating on instinct. "It's been too fucking long," he murmurs into the slippery skin between my legs. It's so muffled I can't be sure that's what he says because the words don't make sense. We've never done this before. "You're going to feel so good around my cock, little one. You're going to take every inch of me, and you're going to love it."

He adds another finger, stretching me, preparing me, as his mouth makes a mess between my legs. He's sucking and licking until I'm a writhing, dripping, moaning wreck. The pressure builds, my body tensing as I chase something just out of reach. My breath hitches, caught in my throat as a warmth spreads from my core, pulsing with my heartbeat. My muscles clench, toes curl, and my fingers dig into the velvet ribbon as it hits, a wave of pleasure so intense it steals my breath, my body convulsing as I cry out his name again.

Cohen straightens, his eyes locked on mine as he drags his forearm across his face, then brings his fingers to his mouth, sucking them clean. "That's just the appetizer, little phoenix."

Now you're ready for the main course. I'm going to devour every inch of you, make you scream my name until you can't remember your own."

Uh, *yes, please.*

His smirk tells me in the haze of feel good-ness that I'm currently floating in, I said that out loud.

He unbuttons his shirt, shrugging it off, and I drink in the sight of him, all defined muscle and smooth, inked skin, a necklace with a key on it hanging around his neck. Then he unbuckles his belt. The sound of the buckle hitting the floor echoes through the chapel and I wonder if this is the most sinful thing that's ever happened here. He pushes his pants down, and then I see him. For the first time, I really see him. He's hard and thick, long and intimidating as I watch liquid bead at the tip and slide down his shaft.

"Do you know what this is?" he asks, his voice a low rumble as he gestures to the fluid at his tip. I shake my head, my eyes wide with curiosity. "It's called pre-cum. It's a sign that I'm really turned on by you."

I swallow as my mouth starts to water. I think... I want to lick him. I want to see what he tastes like.

My stepfather groans, his voice a low rumble I feel in my bones. "You're looking at me like you finally understand what it means to be starving," he murmurs, his eyes locked onto mine. "Like you'll die if you don't feel my cock on your tongue. But not this time. Next time, I'll let you explore. Next time, I'll have you on your knees, worshipping every inch of me with that sweet mouth. But I'm not patient enough to wait any longer to be inside you."

I bite my lip, the image of kneeling before him burning in my mind. I can't believe how much I want that, how much I want him to teach me. How did I not know that this is what I've been missing?

"Please," I whisper, my voice trembling. "I need—"

"I know," he murmurs, crawling onto the stone altar, over my body. The heat of his skin sears me everywhere we touch. "You need me to fill all those empty places you've never understood. To give you everything you've always craved."

His lips crush against mine and everything inside me sparks to life at once. This feels raw and real, like he's finally letting me see the darkness I've always sensed underneath his control. My hands fist around the ribbon as his tongue teases mine, still teaching me things I never knew about kissing, about wanting, about need.

It's the kiss of a conqueror, of a man claiming his rightful property.

Cohen is right. He's always right, and it's terrifying. I want him to show me everything. I want to learn from him. I want to give him the parts of myself I've never even seen, let alone shown to anyone else.

"This is what you do to me," he says as he breaks our kiss and I stare down between our bodies to where his hand is wrapped around his length, stroking slowly. More liquid slides down his shaft. "Every minute of every day for two goddamn years, I've been walking around with this, thinking about you. About this moment." He rubs his tip against my opening, teasing, taunting, but not giving me what I'm aching for.

"Have you thought about it?" he asks, his breath mingling with mine as our lips touch. "Did you think about me in your bed? Between your legs? What it would feel like when you gave yourself to me?" The tip of him slips inside of me but he holds himself there, just inside, his eyes on mine, his body so tense it's shaking as he holds himself back. "Do you think it will hurt?"

"I think it will," I whisper as a tear slips out and runs down my cheek. He licks it up and then he's staring down at me again.

"Are you afraid?"

"Yes," I admit, and it's not a lie. I'm terrified of the things I feel. Terrified of the fact that this feels like a breaking point. Like I'll never be able to go back. I'm scared that once I cross this line, I'll be addicted. To him.

He leans down, kissing my cheeks, the corners of my mouth. "Don't be scared, little one," he whispers. "I'll never let anything hurt you. Even me."

And then he's thrusting all the way inside of me and he's huge and I'm stretched and full, but... somehow it doesn't hurt. He's as deep inside of me as he can get, and his muscles shake as he holds himself still. His jaw is tight as he stares down at me with midnight eyes.

It's the most amazing thing I've ever felt in my entire life. Warmth spreads from my belly to my fingertips and toes, and then I'm moving, shifting my hips, trying to get him to move.

"I've waited a long time for you," he murmurs, his voice strained as I stare into his endless eyes and he stares right back. "I'm not only your first. I'm your only. Now that I've had a taste of you, nothing can tear you away from me. This isn't just a fuck. It's the end of the world and the birth of the universe. It's the most sacred of rituals, and when I'm finished, you will never look at another man again. Because you'll never crave anyone the way you crave me. Do you understand?"

"Yes," I whisper, because I feel the truth in his words, the inevitability. Everything has led us here, and there's no turning back.

He grips my thigh, spreading my legs wider as he starts to move, slowly at first, dragging himself out of me inch by torturous inch before thrusting back in. Each stroke is a brand on my soul.

He fucks me slowly, the stone altar cold and unforgiving beneath my back. I barely feel the icy air as I wrap my legs around his waist and tilt my hips, needing him deeper. The sensation is overwhelming. He's everywhere. Around me, inside of me. It's magic and chaos, and it's everything I've ever dreamed of.

Losing my virginity to my stepfather on the altar of an ancient church while bound with blood red velvet wasn't exactly how I thought it would go, but I wouldn't change a single thing.

"More," I gasp, my hands straining against the velvet binding. I want to dig my nails into his back, feel his muscles moving beneath his skin as he drives into me. "I need more, Cohen."

"Greedy girl," he growls, his hands tightening on my thighs. "You'll get more than you can handle. I'll give you everything you can take, and then I'll give you even more."

His hips snap, and I cry out as he hits a spot deep inside me, sending sparks dancing along my spine. He does it again and again, each thrust harder and faster, his hips snapping in a punishing rhythm that leaves me gasping for breath. The sound of his skin on mine is obnoxious as it bounces off the stone walls, wooden pews, and stained glass.

"You're a miracle," he pants, his voice ragged. "A fucking gift, and I'm going to show you what it means to be loved by a man like me. By a king."

He shifts slightly, and I'm opening wider, taking him deeper. I feel the sting of his fingers as he digs them into my thigh, his other hand sliding up my body to grip the back of my neck, holding me close to his chest. His teeth scrape against the column of my throat as his hips roll so he's hitting a spot that turns me into a puddle.

"Come for me, little one," he commands, his voice a guttural growl that makes my whole body tremble. "Let me feel you surrender. Let me feel you give everything you are to me."

I'm helpless to resist, my body obeying him like he's some kind of dark god, and I'm his most devout disciple. Pleasure surges through me, white-hot and blinding, and I scream his name, my body lifting off the altar like I'm possessed as I come apart in his arms.

He doesn't let me come down. Instead, Cohen swallows my screams with his lips while his hips keep moving, his tongue invading my mouth as his cock claims every inch of me. He swallows every gasp, every moan, every whimper.

When I'm a trembling, overstimulated mess, he releases my wrists from the ribbon and lifts me from the stone altar, holding my body against his, still buried inside of me. My arms are wrapped around his neck and my thighs tighten around his waist as he carries me to the windows, his dick shifting inside of me with every step and I whimper. My back slams into the icy colored glass and I gasp.

The cold of the glass does nothing to cool my burning skin as he presses me against the window. If someone were to look out here, they'd see us, but I don't care. Let the whole world know that we belong to each other now.

"Open your eyes," he says, and I realize they're squeezed shut. My gaze collides with his and my heart stumbles in my chest. His eyes hold mine with such intensity that the rest of the world blurs away, like he's rewriting reality until there's nothing left but him and me and this moment. "Don't ever look away from me. Not when we're like this. Not ever. Do you understand?"

I nod, unable to speak as he moves inside me, his hips rolling in a relentless rhythm. I'm already sensitive from before, and the friction is almost too much to bear. He pins me to the glass with his hips, one hand in my hair, his mouth devouring mine as he starts this slow grind that has the embers inside of me sparking and flickering to life again.

He pulls out almost completely, only to slam back into me, his pelvis grinding against my clit, his cock rubbing a spot inside of me that makes me see stars. My nails dig into his shoulders, holding on for dear life as he takes me higher and higher, his body demanding everything I have to give. And I do. I give it all to him, willingly, without hesitation.

"Cohen," I breathe, my voice a broken whisper. The moonlight pours in, brighter than it should be with all the fresh snow, and casts his shadow onto the stone floor. The leaded glass angel's wings turns his silhouette demonic with a halo of candlelight behind him. "Please..."

"Fuck," he snarls, his grip on my hair tightening, his thrusts becoming more chaotic. Then he starts murmuring, but I'm not sure he even knows what he's saying. He's just as lost in this as I am. "I've been saving this load for you. Just for you, baby. I'm going to fill you until it's dripping down your thighs." He rolls his hips again and my head falls back against the glass. His teeth scrape against my neck. "Until you're so full of me you'll never be empty again."

His body's dragging against that amazing spot between my legs with every thrust and I start to shake with the force of what's building inside of me. His words are only making it worse. The tips of my fingers dig into the back of his neck, his shoulder, the tops of his arms. Anywhere I can reach.

"I'm not going to stop until I've filled you so completely that you're carrying a piece of me inside you. My child growing in your belly, proof that you're mine. That you'll always be mine." His words are horrible and filthy and so, so scary.

They're also the hottest thing I've ever heard.

"Listen to me, baby. When you feel that explosion inside you, that's me. That's us. That's how we create life together."

The idea of having his baby, of conceiving a child in this sacred space with the man I love... I can't help it. It makes something feral rise inside of me. Something I didn't even know was there. An instinct to fulfill a role I was created for. To become his wife. His partner in every sense of the word.

The mother of his children.

I want that.

My orgasm hits me like a bolt of lightning, a blinding wave of pleasure that steals my breath and sets my soul on fire. I cry out his name, my body shaking and spasming in his arms as he chases his own release. His movements are wild, desperate and he grips the back of my neck and pulls me down onto him so hard he can't get any deeper inside of me while my back slides against the smooth glass.

With a roar, he comes, his cock throbbing and twitching as he empties himself, filling me with his release. It goes on and on, and he buries his face in my neck, his breath hot on my skin. We cling to each other in the aftermath, our bodies still joined, his cock still hard and deep inside of me. It twitches with aftershocks and his legs shake from holding me up, but we don't move. We stay like that for several minutes, just holding each other as we catch our breath.

There's shift in the world around us. It might sound crazy, but it's like an ancient power has given its blessing. I'm not religious, not really. But this... feels divine.

Whatever it is, there's a feeling of rightness. Of belonging.

Of two souls finally finding their way back to each other.

And when he finally slips out of me, his cum dripping down my thighs, my eyes sting with the loss of him. I try to blink back the tears but that was so overwhelming that I can't. As they spill down my cheeks, Cohen catches them with his thumb.

His rough fingers find their way under my chin and he tilts my head up. "I feel it, too. Every second I'm not inside of you is agony," he murmurs, pressing a kiss to my forehead while we both stand completely naked under the glass with our skin painted like the northern lights by the moonlight. "But I promise you, little phoenix, it will be like that every time. You will never regret giving yourself to me. I'll spend the rest of my life proving it."

Cohen
CHAPTER 17

THERE'S something poetic about watching an angel sleep after you've corrupted her in a church.

I can't stop staring at her as she sleeps in my arms, her body curled against mine in the pre-dawn darkness of her bedroom. Getting her back to the house without being seen was a challenge—especially since I couldn't keep my hands off her for more than thirty seconds.

The marks from the velvet ribbon circle her delicate wrists like bracelets, and my cock twitches at the sight. Physical evidence of her submission, a testament written in faint red lines across her skin that tells the story of how she gave herself to me in that sacred space, trading her innocence for my darkness.

Her dark hair spills across the pillow, and I brush my fingers through the silken strands, savoring how they slide between my fingers. Everything about her feeds the darkness in me. Each soft exhale brushes against my chest, a reminder that she's real, that I finally have her where she belongs. The steady rise and fall of her body against mine. The way her lips part with every breath, still swollen from my kisses. The flutter of her eyelashes against her cheeks as she dreams.

I wonder if she's dreaming of me. Of what we did in that chapel. Of how I claimed every inch of her body and carved my name into the marrow of her bones.

A possessive growl builds in my chest as I remember the way she looked spread out on that altar, bound and begging. The way she took my cock like she was made for it. Like her body had been waiting nineteen years just for me to fill it.

"Cohen?" Her voice is soft and sleepy as her eyes flutter open. Looking into her eyes in the darkness feels like staring into an abyss I want to fall into, and something in my chest tightens. "What time is it?"

"Early," I murmur, pressing a kiss to her forehead. "Go back to sleep, little one."

She shifts against me, and I have to bite back a groan as her thigh brushes against my hard on. "Will you stay?"

"No." The word feels like razor blades in my throat. "Though walking away from you might actually kill me." I stroke her cheek with my thumb, hating the disappointment that clouds her eyes. "Your mother will be up soon, and as much as I want to stay buried inside you until the world ends, I need to handle some things." Like making sure Daniel Montgomery Jr. never gets within fifty feet of what's mine.

Her lower lip juts out in a pout that makes me want to bite it, and a small furrow appears between her brows. "What things?"

I smooth my thumb over that furrow, erasing her worry. "Nothing for you to concern yourself with. Just some business matters that need my attention."

She pushes herself up on one elbow, and the sheet falls away from her chest. The sight of her perfect breasts, marked with my stubble burn and love bites, makes my mouth water. "You're planning something."

Smart girl. Too smart for her own good sometimes.

"I'm always planning something," I tell her, keeping my voice light even as my eyes drink in every inch of exposed skin. "It's what makes me so good at what I do."

She bites her lip, and my control frays. Before she can blink, I have her pinned beneath me, my cock pressed against her pussy. It's still slippery from all the fucking we did when we fell into her bed last night after the chapel, and I slide against her with a groan. "Do you know how hard it is for me to walk away from you when you're looking at me like that? When your body is aching for mine?"

"Yes," she says, her eyes locked on mine. "As hard as it is for me to let you walk away." She goes back to nibbling on her lower lip.

"Don't bite that lip," I growl, my free hand sliding down her body to cup her breast. Her nipple pebbles against my palm. "You know what it does to me."

"Maybe that's why I do it," she whispers, and fuck if that hint of defiance doesn't make me want to put her on her knees and shove my dick between those pretty lips. But she's sore. She can't take any more until she's rested. And I need to get to work.

I lean down, my mouth a breath from hers. "Don't play games with me. I'll win every time." I brush a gentle kiss against her lips and roll off the bed, tucking my raging erection into my pants and zipping it away. If I don't leave now, I never will.

"Greedy girl." I scan the floor for my clothes, trying to ignore how she makes the sheets rustle as she sits up to watch me. "But I have to go. Your mother will be up soon, and I need you to act normal at breakfast." I find my shirt tangled with her torn nightgown and pull it on, my eyes drawn back to her. Her hair is wild from my hands, her neck marked with my kisses. "No matter what happens today, remember that you're part of me now, and I'm part of you. Nothing can tear that apart. Everything that's coming... it's all for you. For us."

"You're scaring me," she whispers, drawing her knees to her chest, and I see the vulnerability in her eyes. The trust she's placed in me, despite her fears.

I pause in buttoning my wrinkled shirt, tucking in the key to Emerald's door, to sit on the edge of the bed, reaching for her face. "Don't be scared, little one. I told you I'd never let anything hurt you. That includes your mother and anyone else who might try to come between us."

She searches my face, those clever eyes trying to read the truth in mine. "Promise?"

"I promise." I seal it with a kiss, gentle this time. Reverent. Then I force myself to stand, grabbing my shoes. "Now go back to sleep. You'll need your rest for what's coming."

I finish dressing quickly, my eyes drawn to her as she burrows deeper into sheets that smell like sex and us. The sight of her in that bed, thoroughly fucked and marked by me, nearly breaks my resolve to leave.

But there's work to be done.

I slip into my room unnoticed, stripping off last night's clothes that smell like the musty chapel and Emerald's sweet skin. The shower is quick but necessary. Like fuck am I about to face Madeline looking like I just spent the night balls deep in her daughter. Ten minutes later, I'm in a fresh suit, my hair still damp, heading toward the kitchen.

Coffee first, then Emmitt.

The house feels like a tomb at this hour, that particular kind of quiet you only get before dawn when even the heating system seems to have gone dormant. The staff won't arrive for another hour, which means I have time to—

"You're up early."

Madeline's voice shatters my solitude. She's sitting at the kitchen island, her hair and makeup already perfect despite the ungodly hour, a cup of coffee steaming in front of her like she's been waiting. Like she's been plotting.

I don't let my surprise show as I move to the coffee maker. "I have an early meeting."

"Hmm." She takes a delicate sip of her coffee. "Strange. I don't remember seeing it on your calendar."

I pour myself a cup, keeping my movements casual even as tension coils in my muscles. "Since when do you monitor my calendar?"

"Since my daughter started looking at you like you hung the moon." Her voice is sharp enough to draw blood. "I'm not blind, Cohen."

I turn to face her, leaning against the counter while I sip my coffee. "And what exactly do you think you see?"

She sets her cup down with a soft clink. "I see the way you watch her. The way you've positioned yourself between her and anyone who might take her attention away from you." Her lips curve in a cold smile. "I also see that you've been tampering with my plans."

"Your plans?" I raise an eyebrow. "You mean your attempt to pimp out your daughter to the junior Montgomery for a business deal?"

Her smile doesn't waver, but her eyes turn to ice. "Daniel comes from an excellent family. He's exactly the kind of man Emerald needs—young, ambitious, and most importantly, appropriate."

My fingers tighten around the coffee cup until I'm afraid the ceramic might shatter. The word 'appropriate' tastes like poison in the air between us, and for a moment, the urge to show her exactly how inappropriate I can be nearly overwhelms me. But I force my grip to relax, take a slow sip of scalding coffee, and let the pain ground me while the silence stretches between us. When I finally speak, I've locked the beast back in its cage. Barely. "That boy isn't coming anywhere near Emerald."

"He'll be here for lunch." Madeline's tone is triumphant. "I've already arranged it."

I set the coffee cup down with precise control, though everything in me wants to hurl it across the room. "Cancel it."

"Or what?" She stands, smoothing her designer skirt. "What exactly do you think you can do about it? You're just the husband I settled for to make my company more appealing to investors. Don't forget your place, Cohen."

A dark laugh escapes me. "My place?" I close the distance between us, and Madeline takes an involuntary step back. "Let me be very clear about something. You have no idea what I'm capable of. The things I've done... the things I'm willing to do..." I let the implications hang in the air between us.

"Are you threatening me?"

"Not yet." I smile, and she pales slightly. "But if that trust fund brat shows up here today, you'll find out exactly what a threat from me looks like."

I turn to leave, but her voice stops me. "I know about Charlotte."

I look back at her, amused. "Do you?"

"I know she disappeared after filing for divorce from her husband. I know you were the last person to see her alive." She lifts her chin. "I wonder what the police would think about that?"

"Go ahead." I spread my arms. "Call them. But before you do, you might want to think very carefully about what kind of attention that would bring to your perfect family. Some secrets are better left buried, wouldn't you agree?"

The color drains from her face.

"That's what I thought." I head for the door, then pause. "Oh, and Madeline? Cancel lunch with the boy. I'd hate for something unfortunate to happen to him."

I don't wait for her response as I stride out of the kitchen. My phone is already in my hand, dialing Tristen's number.

He answers on the fourth ring. "It's fuck o'clock in the morning, Astor. This better be good."

"I need everything you have on Emmitt Caldwell."

"Jesus Christ." Tristen sighs. "What did you do?"

"Nothing yet. It's what I'm *about* to do."

"Give me a minute." There's a rustling sound as Tristen presumably sits up in bed, followed by a soft feminine murmur that definitely doesn't belong to ex considering she left months ago. I wonder if he finally pulled his head out of his ass and—

When he comes back, his voice is clearer. "Caldwell's going to be a problem. He's got connections."

"So do I." I slide into the driver's seat of my Aston, the leather cold against my back.

"Fair point." He laughs, but there's an edge to it. "Never thought I'd see the day we'd both be this far gone." A pause. "You know I get it, right? With Waverly..." He trails off, but I hear everything he's not saying.

I pull out of the driveway, heading toward downtown. "They're worth it."

"Yeah," Tristen says quietly. "Yeah, they fucking are. I'll send you everything I have on Caldwell. And Cohen? Whatever you're planning... I've got your back."

"Thanks." I end the call, my mind flipping through all the ways a man like Emmitt Caldwell can disappear. The legal ones first. Then the fun ones.

The sun is just starting to peek over the mountains as I pull into the underground parking garage beneath Caldwell Communications. The eyesore towers over downtown Emerald Hills like a middle finger to everything this place is. I still can't believe the town council approved this monstrosity.

Emmitt's Tesla sits in its reserved spot, a predictable testament to his desperate need to appear successful. Everyone knows Teslas are what you drive when you want people to think you're smarter than you actually are.

I could have waited for a more civilized hour to do this, but some conversations are better had when witnesses are scarce.

The lobby's deserted except for the security guard, who nods at me without hesitation. Being the Savage Society's attorney has its advantages in this town - no one questions my presence anywhere. The elevator ride to the fifteenth floor gives me time to lock away the violence humming beneath my skin, to polish my rage into something sharper, more precise.

I find Emmitt exactly where I expected, already behind his mahogany desk with his coffee and his wall of windows showing off the snow-covered Cascades behind him.

"What the fuck are you doing here?" Amazing how quickly his refinement abandons him when he sees me.

I settle into one of his uncomfortable leather chairs, taking my time as his annoyance grows visible.

"If this is about the boutique—" he starts.

"It's not."

His jaw tightens at the interruption. "Then what exactly are you doing in my office at seven in the morning?"

"Emerald."

"What about her?" The flash of hunger in his eyes when I say her name makes my fingers itch to wrap around his throat.

"You're going to stay away from her."

He barks out a laugh. "Is that so?" He leans forward, bracing his elbows on his desk. "And who exactly are you to make that demand? The stepfather who's been here what, a year?"

"I'm the man telling you to stay away from her."

"Interesting." His smile turns calculating. "I've noticed how protective you are of your pretty little stepdaughter. Very protective, actually. Almost inappropriate, one might say."

"We're not discussing me."

"No?" He settles back, clearly thinking he has the upper hand. "What makes you think Madeline would choose your concerns over my business? She needs me far more than she needs you."

I pull my phone from my pocket, scrolling through the

photos Tristen just sent. "You're right about one thing. Madeline does need you." I turn the phone to show him a picture of a young girl, no more than fifteen, entering his private office. "Jessica, on the other hand... I don't think she needed what you did to her. Or Sarah. Or Amy." I swipe through more photos. "You do seem to have a type."

The color drains from his face. "Those photos are—"

"Dated and timestamped?" I smile. "Yes, they are. Along with the documentation of the payoffs to their families. The NDAs. The carefully hidden paper trail that leads right back to you."

"You're bluffing."

I set my phone on his desk, screen up. More photos scroll past—him with different underage girls, bank statements, medical records. "Do I look like I'm bluffing?"

The color drains from his face, but he rallies. "You think you're the first person to try to blackmail me? I've buried better men than you."

"I'm not trying to blackmail you, Emmitt. I'm telling you how this is going to go." I lean forward. "Tell me, have you already started grooming Emerald like the others? Those private meetings Madeline arranged—you were planning to get her alone, weren't you?"

He flinches, caught. "You don't understand—"

"I understand perfectly. You're a predator who's gotten away with it for too long. But that ends now." I turn the phone to show him another, much worse, photo. "And these? These are just copies. The originals are in much more interesting hands."

Hands like the Savage Society's. I don't need to speak their names out loud; we both know who I'm referring to.

He swallows hard. "What do you want?"

"I already told you. Stay away from Emerald. And while you're at it, dissolve your partnership with Madeline. Effective immediately." I should make him leave town. I still might.

"She'll never agree to that."

"Make her." I stand, straightening my jacket and refastening the top button. "You're good at that." He flinches like I've punched him. I wish I had. "You have until the end of the day. If I don't see the paperwork by five p.m., these photos go to every news outlet in the state. Oh, and Emmitt?" I pause at the door. "If you ever so much as look at Emerald again, I'll do much worse than expose your crimes. Are we clear?"

He nods, sweat beading on his forehead.

"Good." I close his office door behind me, satisfaction settling in my chest.

By the time I reach my office, my phone is already lighting up with notifications. Emmitt works fast when properly motivated—the dissolution paperwork for his partnership with Delacroix Collective has already been filed. Every contract canceled, every joint venture terminated, including their precious charity auction. Madeline's social media is flooded with confused messages from donors and socialites about the sudden cancellation of her flagship holiday events.

Good. Let her scramble to maintain control while her empire crumbles piece by piece.

One threat eliminated. Two to go.

Now for the Montgomery brat.

Cohen

CHAPTER 18

I SPEND the next few hours at my office, reviewing case files and trying to catch up on the work I've been too distracted to keep up with. By eleven, my phone shows three missed calls from Madeline—all ignored.

I'm just wrapping up a call with one of Cole Callahan's shell companies when my office line lights up with the Delacroix house number. Something in my chest tightens.

"Did you dream of me after I left?" I say instead of a normal greeting. Only one person would call me from that number.

"Cohen." Her voice is tight with panic that makes my blood run cold as she chokes out my name. "Daniel Montgomery is here with Mother. She's forcing me to have lunch with him and..." She's whispering but her voice still breaks. "She says if I don't go down there right now, she's sending me to that finishing school in Switzerland. The one where they don't let you have any contact with the outside world for a year. She's already made the call."

Rage pours into my system as I stand so fast, I knock over my leather chair. I grab my keys and my phone off the desk and shove them into my pocket.

"Where are you?"

"Locked in my bathroom. Kendra's in my room packing a suitcase."

"Breathe for me, baby." I'm already striding toward my car in the parking lot, making a mental note to get her a phone I can track. One Madeline doesn't know about. I should have done it weeks ago. "I won't let her send you anywhere. Just hold on until I get there."

"I'm trying, but..." Her voice is barely a whisper now. "She's getting angrier. I can hear her."

"Listen to me very carefully." I slide behind the wheel, the engine roaring to life. "Go downstairs. Smile. Be polite. But do not let him touch you. I'm five minutes from the house."

"Hurry," she whispers. "Please."

I end the call and floor the accelerator, the Aston Martin's engine snarling as I weave through traffic. By the time I walk into the dining room ten minutes later, I've already imagined a dozen ways to make the Montgomery heir disappear.

They're gathered in the formal dining room when I walk in, and the sight turns my vision red. Daniel has positioned himself next to Emerald, practically on top of her as he talks, one hand resting on her arm. She's frozen in her chair, eyes fixed on her empty plate, her shoulders curved inward like she's trying to disappear. Madeline presides over it all from the head of the table, radiating satisfaction.

"I hope I'm not interrupting." The words come out soft, controlled, despite the rage coursing through my veins.

Daniel glances up, and whatever he sees in my expression makes him snatch his hand off Emerald's arm. Smart boy.

"Cohen." Madeline's voice drips with artificial warmth. "Daniel was just telling us about the luxury spa chain his family's launching. He thinks Emerald would be perfect as the face of their wellness campaign."

I move behind Emerald's chair, my hand settling on her shoulder. The tension in her body melts the moment I touch her, and she sinks back against my fingers like she's finally able to breathe again.

"I'm afraid Emerald's schedule is quite full," I say, my thumb stroking the side of her neck where I left marks last night that she's covered with makeup. "In fact, we have a meeting right now that we're late for."

"We do?" Emerald asks, then quickly adds, "Oh, right."

"Actually," Daniel starts, but I cut him off with a look that promises violence.

"It wasn't a suggestion." I pull out Emerald's chair. "Shall we?"

She stands immediately, but Madeline's voice cracks like a whip. "Sit down, Emerald. We haven't even served lunch yet."

I feel Emerald tense, torn between her mother's authority and my protection. But I've had enough of this game.

"Emerald," I say softly, "go wait in my car. We have that meeting with the new years' collection photographers." An easy lie—Madeline's obsessed with the website's content, and she'd never risk Emerald missing something that could affect her precious brand.

She catches on immediately, nodding and hurrying from the room. Smart girl.

Once she's gone, I turn to Daniel. "Leave. Now. And if you ever come near her again, they won't find enough of you to bury."

He opens his mouth to protest, but something in my expression must convince him I'm serious. He stands, straightening his tie. "Madeline, I'll call you later to discuss—"

"No," I say. "You won't."

"This is ridiculous," Madeline snaps, rising from her chair. "Daniel, please sit down. We haven't—"

But Daniel's already backing toward the door, his eyes

darting between me and Madeline. Smart boy—he's figured out which one of us is the real threat.

Once Daniel scurries from the room like the cockroach he is, I turn to Madeline. She's gripping her water glass so tightly her knuckles have gone white.

"You're making a mistake," she says, her voice trembling with rage. "Daniel could have given her everything."

"Everything?" I laugh, the sound dark and hollow. "You mean he could have given *you* everything.'

"How dare you—"

"No." I cut her off, planting my hands on the table and leaning forward. "How dare *you*. How dare you try to sell your daughter to a man you know has a history of abuse. I wonder what your shareholders would think if they knew what you really do to maintain that perfect family image."

"She has obligations—"

"Her obligation today is to your brand. Unless you want to explain to your board why the holiday collection's face disappeared right before launch?" I straighten, adjusting my engraved cufflinks. "I'm sure they'd love to hear how you prioritized a lunch date over their bottom line."

The mention of her precious brand hits its mark. Her lips press into a thin line, but I can see her mentally calculating the costs. "Have her back by dinner."

I don't bother responding as I head for the door. She hasn't won—she's just choosing her battles. And so am I.

Emerald is waiting in my car, her hands twisted together in her lap. The sight of her calms the rage burning through my veins, even as memories of Daniel touching her make me imagine all the ways I could make him disappear. Breaking his fingers one by one for daring to put them on her would be a good start.

When I slide into the driver's seat, she turns to me with worried eyes. "What did you say to them?"

"Nothing they didn't need to hear." I start the car, then reach over to take her hand. The moment our skin connects, some of the murderous rage subsides, replaced by the calm that only comes from touching her. She threads her fingers through mine like she needs the contact as much as I do.

"Are you okay?"

She nods, but I can feel her trembling. She shifts in her seat, leaning closer to me like she's trying to crawl inside my skin. "He kept touching me. Even when I moved away, he just kept..." She shudders, and violent fantasies explode behind my eyes—Daniel's body at the bottom of the lake, Daniel's car wrapped around a tree, Daniel bleeding out slowly in some dark corner of town.

I lift our joined hands to my mouth, pressing my lips to her knuckles, and she melts further into my touch. The simple contact grounds us both—her anxiety visibly easing as my bloodlust settles into something more controlled. It's fascinating how she can simultaneously calm my darkness and feed it. How touching her soothes the beast while making it more determined to destroy anyone who threatens what's mine.

"Did he hurt you?" My voice comes out rough with barely contained fury, even as her closeness keeps me from hunting Daniel down right now.

"No, nothing like that. He was just... persistent. Creepy." She looks down at our joined hands, then brings her other one up to trace the veins on my wrist. The gentle exploration of her fingers sends electricity through my blood. "Where are we going?"

"Somewhere we can breathe." I pull out of the driveway, heading toward the lake, though letting go of her hand feels like ripping off my own skin. The second I shift into drive, she leans across the console to rest her head against my shoulder, and everything in me settles. "Just for today."

She's quiet for a moment, watching the scenery blur past.

Her breath against my neck is the only thing keeping the violent thoughts at bay. "What happens when we go home?"

"We keep playing our parts." I turn my head to press a kiss into her hair, breathing in the scent that's become as necessary as oxygen. "Until the Christmas party. And then..."

"And then?"

"And then you'll never have to pretend again." I catch her hand again, unable to go another second without touching her. "No more cages, little phoenix. Just freedom to be exactly who you are."

She lifts her head from my shoulder, those green eyes full of something between hope and fear. "With you?"

"Always with me." The word comes out like a vow, like something sacred whispered in that chapel. "There's no version of this that ends with us apart."

She presses closer, like she's trying to merge our bodies into one. Like she understands exactly what I mean because she feels it too.

The drive to the lake passes in comfortable silence, her head on my shoulder, our fingers intertwined. She fits against me like she was crafted for this exact purpose, and each mile that takes us further from Madeline's influence feels like one step closer to the future I've been planning since the moment I first saw her.

Seven days until the Christmas party. Seven days until I can give her everything I promised in that chapel. Seven days until we can stop hiding.

I've never been a patient man, but for her, I'd wait forever.

Emerald

CHAPTER 19

THE WINDOWS of Cohen's Aston Martin fog up as we wind around Crescent Lake, the world outside all blurry white snow and towering evergreens. Inside it's warm—like, way too warm—but I can't make myself scoot even an inch away from him. My body literally feels like it'll shut down if I'm not touching him.

I wonder if this is what being addicted to something feels like... that whole trembling hands, racing heart, can't-live-without-it thing from all those "Just Say No" commercials my mother lets play during her charity events. Except they definitely weren't talking about being addicted to your stepfather.

Ugh. That sounds so bad when I put it that way.

But it's true—I physically can't stop myself from pressing closer, breathing him in, letting his presence fill up all the empty spaces inside me that I never even knew were there until he showed me.

My head rests against his shoulder while he drives, our fingers tangled together on his thigh. His thumb keeps stroking back and forth across my knuckles in this rhythm that matches my heartbeat. Or maybe my heart's just learned to beat in time with him now. That wouldn't surprise me—my body seems to exist just to respond to him these days.

God, I'm so far gone it's not even funny.

"Look at that," he murmurs, nodding toward where sunlight breaks through the clouds, turning the frozen lake into this glittering wonderland. The snow blankets everything—the massive evergreens, the lakefront mansions—making it all look like something out of a Hallmark movie. But all I can focus on is how his voice vibrates through me where we're pressed together.

He pulls into this hidden spot overlooking the water, tucked behind a bunch of snow-covered pines where you can't see us from the road. The second the engine cuts off, this heavy silence wraps around us, broken only by our breathing and the soft ticking of the cooling engine.

"I used to come here when I was a kid," Cohen says, his eyes on the frozen lake stretching out before us. His voice carries that rare softness that makes my heart flutter. "The Astors have lived in Emerald Hills as long as your family has. Though our histories took different paths."

His thumb traces circles on my knuckles where our fingers are intertwined, and I find myself leaning closer, starving for any little crumb of information that might help me know this man better.

"The Delacroixs built palaces, hosted galas, made themselves the center of attention. My family..." He pauses, and something dark flashes across his face. "We collected secrets instead. Built power through knowledge rather than the spotlight."

I study his profile in the winter light, fascinated by this side of him I've never seen. "Is that why you became a lawyer? To keep collecting secrets?"

"Among other reasons." He brings my hand to his lips, pressing a kiss to my palm that sends tingles shooting across my skin. "But mainly because I learned early that power is the only way to protect what matters." When his eyes meet mine, the intensity in them steals my breath.

"Come here," he says, and I'm already moving before he finishes speaking because apparently I have zero chill when it comes to him. His seat slides back and then I'm in his lap, straddling him, my forehead pressed against his while his hands grip my waist. "That's better."

"I can't be away from you," I whisper, fingers curling into his shirt like I'm afraid he'll disappear if I let go. Which... maybe I am? "Even for a second. Is that crazy?"

His grip tightens, and something dark flashes in his eyes that should probably terrify me but just makes me want to get closer. "No, little one. That's exactly how it should be." One hand slides up my back to tangle in my hair, holding me against him while his lips brush mine. "I feel it too. I've felt it for two years. Like my skin's crawling when you're not touching me. Like I can't breathe right unless you're close."

"What did you do to me?" The question slips out before my brain can catch up with my mouth. Not that I'm scared or anything. More like... completely blown away by how much I need him.

"The same thing you did to me." His hand sneaks under my sweater, his palm hot against my lower back and oh wow, okay, that's... that's really distracting. "That night in the chapel just made it official. You've been in my blood since the first moment I saw you, consuming me like the sweetest kind of poison."

I shiver, remembering last night—the candlelight, that velvet ribbon, the way he basically ruined me for anyone else with his hands and his mouth and... everything. The way he filled up every empty space inside me until there was nothing left but him.

"I can still feel you," I admit, and my face goes nuclear hot. "Inside. Like you carved yourself into my bones or something."

He makes this sound—like, half growl, half groan—that vibrates through both our bodies. His fingers dig into my skin as he slides our joined hands higher up my thigh. "Good. I want you to feel me with every breath, every heartbeat." His fingers flex against my skin. "I want everyone to look at you and know that you're thoroughly and completely owned."

"Only by you," I breathe, and then his mouth crashes into mine.

The way he kisses me now is totally different from last night in the chapel. That was raw and desperate, like he was trying to burn away any trace of who I was before him. This is... God, I don't even know how to describe it. It's like we both finally get it—that I'm never going to want anyone but him. That I literally can't want anyone else. His desire for me is impossible to ignore where I'm straddling his lap, hard and thick against me through our clothes, making my whole body flush hot.

When we finally break apart, we're both breathing like we've run a marathon. Outside, snow starts falling again, tiny flakes catching the late morning light. One of those massive mansions across the water has already put up Christmas lights and the white bulbs twinkle like stars even in the daylight.

"What happens now?" I ask, tracing my fingers along the sharp line of his jaw because I literally cannot stop touching him. His stubble feels amazing against my skin. "We can't keep sneaking around forever."

"No," he agrees, turning to press a kiss to my palm. "We can't. And we won't have to after the Christmas party."

"What do you mean?"

His eyes lock onto mine and there's that intensity again—the one that makes my lungs squeeze and falter. "I mean I'm done hiding how I feel about you. I'm done pretending I don't want to touch you every second of every day." His hand slides higher under my sweater, his fingertips trailing fire up my spine. "I'm done letting anyone think they have a say in what's between us."

"But my mother—"

"Will learn that she can't control you anymore. That she never should have tried." He cups my face in his hands, and I swear my soul tries to climb out of my body to get closer to him. "You're not her puppet, Emerald. You're not her prop or her product or her perfect little doll. You're mine. And at the party, everyone will know it."

The way he says it—like it's just a fact, like the sky being blue—makes this wild, desperate thing unfurl in my chest. "Promise?"

"I promise." He kisses me again, slow and deep like we have all the time in the world. Like nothing exists beyond this car, this moment, this absolutely insane connection between us that feels bigger than both of us and somehow keeps growing. "Seven more days, little phoenix. Seven days of pretending, and then you'll never have to hide who you are again."

I melt into him, into his touch, into the safety of his arms. Outside, the snow's coming down harder now, creating this white curtain that blocks out the rest of the world. For now, we can pretend that world doesn't exist. That there's nothing beyond this perfect bubble of warmth and want and need.

But we both know it can't last. Eventually, we'll have to go back to that house. Back to my mother's endless rules and impossible expectations. Back to pretending we're nothing more than stepfather and stepdaughter.

Crap, when did my life turn into such a mess?

For now though, I let myself get lost in him. In the way his hands worship my body through my clothes, in those little sounds he makes when I press closer, in the steady thump of his heartbeat under my palm when I slide my hand inside his jacket.

"My beautiful girl," he murmurs against my throat, and

every cell in my body lights up like a Christmas tree at how... possessive he sounds. "What am I going to do with you?"

"Keep me," I whisper back. "Never let me go."

His arms tighten around me like he's afraid someone might try to snatch me away. "Never," he promises, and I believe him with everything I am. "You're stuck with me now, little one. For better or worse. In this life and the next."

I close my eyes, breathing him in. It's crazy how my whole life I never realized something was missing until Cohen. Like I was walking around half-asleep and he finally woke me up. Like he flipped some switch inside me that I never knew existed, and now I'm actually alive for the first time. He's darkness to my light, dangerous to my safe, everything I was taught to avoid but somehow exactly what I need.

The night sky to my stars.

God, I'm in so deep I can't even see the surface anymore.

Snow crunches under our boots as we reluctantly leave the warmth of the car an hour later. My lips feel tender and swollen from his kisses, and when he takes my hand, our fingers automatically tangle together like we've been doing it for years. He leads me toward the wooden dock stretching out over the lake, the dark water endless and mysterious beneath its coating of snow along the edges.

"I don't want to go back," I admit, watching my breath make little clouds in the air between us. "Can't we just... stay here? Pretend the rest of the world doesn't exist?"

His arm slides around my waist, pulling me against him as we stop at the edge of the dock. "One week," he murmurs, his voice doing that low, rough thing that makes my insides turn to jelly. "Give me one more week to set everything in motion, and then no one will be able to touch what's between us."

I lean into him because apparently that's just what my body does now—seeks him out like he's gravity or something. The lake stretches out in front of us, black and bottomless, with just a thin sheen of ice around the edges that makes it look like shattered glass in the weak winter light. Everything feels different here, like we've stepped into another world where my mother's rules can't reach us. Like maybe we've found this pocket of space where we can just... be.

"I'm afraid," I whisper, and the wind carries the words away. "Not of you. Never of you. But of what happens next. Of what she'll do when she finds out."

As I lean back against him, my head resting on his shoulder, his fingers dig into my hip in that possessive way I'm learning Cohen has that makes me feel protected. Sheltered from the world. "Let her try something. I've been ten steps ahead of her since the day I married her." There's this dark satisfaction in his voice that makes me feel safe in a way I probably need therapy for. Like having my own personal villain who'd destroy anyone who tried to hurt me. "She's already making mistakes."

I turn in his arms to look up at him. Snowflakes are catching in his dark hair and his eyes match the storm clouds overhead and god, how is he even real? "What do you mean?"

"The Swiss school threat? It's not empty." His jaw gets all tight and angry. "She's already made arrangements. Paid the deposit. Booked your flight."

A chill races through me that even Cohen's warmth can't chase away. "How do you know?"

"Because I have access to all her accounts. Her emails. Her entire digital footprint." His smile is sharp enough to slice someone open and honestly? That shouldn't be hot but... it kind of is? "Your mother forgets what I do for a living. Who I work for. The kind of power that gives me."

"When?" My voice shakes like I'm freezing even though I'm burning up. "When is she planning to send me?"

"The day after Christmas." His arms tighten around me like he's afraid someone might try to snatch me away right now. "But it's not going to happen. I won't let it happen."

"How can you be so sure?"

He cups my face in his hands, his touch gentle despite the steel in his voice.

"Because you're part of me now, embedded in every cell, every breath. And I'll ruin anyone who tries to separate us." His thumb brushes across my bottom lip and my thoughts scatter like startled birds. "Besides, by then it will be too late. What we started in that chapel last night... it's carved into both our souls. Permanent. Unbreakable."

My face goes nuclear hot as memories of last night flash through my mind—his hands, his mouth, the way he claimed every inch of me. The way he filled me so completely I can still feel him. "Cohen..."

"I know, little one." He bends to brush his lips against mine, soft and sweet even with his tight grip on me. "I feel it too. That need. That hunger. Like I'll die if I'm not touching you."

I press closer, trying to crawl inside his skin where it's safe and warm and nothing can hurt me. "Don't let her take me away from you."

"Never." The word comes out like a growl against my lips. "You're mine. Forever. No one will ever take you from me."

A car door slams somewhere nearby and reality bursts back in—right, we're not actually alone out here. Cohen pulls back slightly but his hands stay on me like he physically can't stop touching me. I can relate.

"We should head back," he says, though everything about his expression says he'd rather do anything else.. "Your mother will be suspicious if we're gone too long."

I nod, even though everything inside me is screaming at the thought of going back to that house. Back to her rules and her control and her perfect plastic world that's always been my prison.

"What do we do now?"

"We play our parts." He kisses my forehead, then each

cheek, then finally my lips like he's trying to memorize the shape of my face. "Just for a little longer. I need you to trust me, even when things get hard. Even when it seems like everything's falling apart. Can you do that?"

"Yes," I whisper, curling my fingers into his jacket. I mean it more than I've ever meant anything. "I trust you more than anyone."

His eyes go coal black at that and his grip on me tightens for a second before he forces himself to let go. But even as we walk back to the car, his hand slides to the back of my neck under my hair, his thumb stroking my skin in a way that makes my knees weak.

The drive home is way too short, and with every mile that brings us closer to the house, I feel the walls closing in. But Cohen's hand stays wrapped around mine, his thumb stroking my skin in this gentle rhythm that promises everything will be okay.

When we pull into the driveway, I expect him to let go. To put distance between us like we usually do. Instead, he brings our joined hands to his lips, pressing a kiss to my knuckles.

"Remember what I said," he murmurs. "Seven more days."

I nod, trying to steal some of his certainty for myself.

Emerald

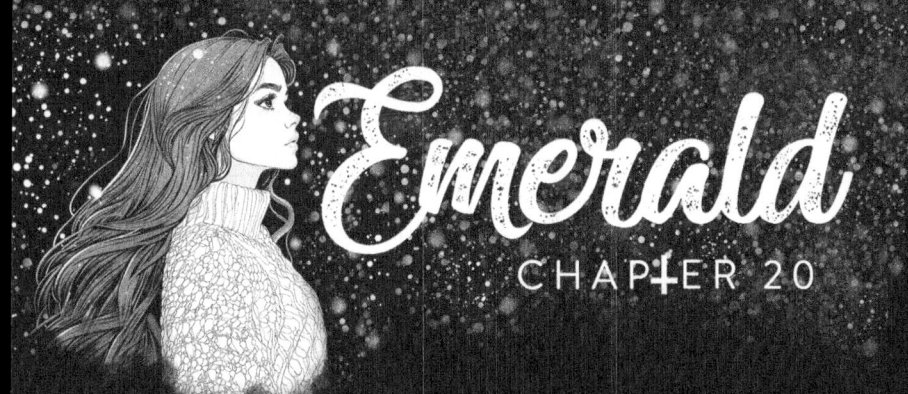

CHAPTER 20

INSIDE, the house is unusually quiet. No staff hovering, no Kendra lurking, no mother micromanaging every breath anyone takes.

"Kendra's car is gone," Cohen murmurs as we pass the window. "Your mother never lets her leave during the day unless she's at the office."

Which means my mother's gone too. All the tension bleeds out of me. I'm exhausted in a way that makes no sense—we literally just sat in his car for a couple of hours—but more than that, I'm starving. Like, ready to eat everything in sight starving, which is weird because I'm never actually hungry. Years of my mother's food rules kind of killed my appetite.

I follow him into the kitchen, unable to shake the thought of pancakes—the ones I always see the staff eating in the mornings, all golden and warm with melting chocolate chips. "Could you... I mean, is it hard to make pancakes?" The words come out rushed, like I'm confessing some horrible secret. "With chocolate chips maybe? I've never had them but they always smell so good, and my mother says I'll get fat and then no one will ever..." I trail off, my face burning at admitting one of my deepest insecurities.

"If I go above a size four, my mother loses her mind and I'm locked in my room without food until I lose enough weight that she's happy." The words taste bitter on my tongue, like all the meals I've been denied. Sometimes I wonder if that's why I barely feel hungry anymore—my body's learned that wanting food just leads to disappointment and punishment.

Cohen goes completely still for a moment, then he's in front of me, cupping my face in his hands. "Listen to me," he says, his voice rough with emotion. "I don't give a damn what size you are. You could gain a hundred pounds eating nothing but chocolate chip pancakes and I'd still look at you exactly the way I'm looking at you right now."

"How's that?"

"Like you're everything." His thumbs stroke my cheeks as his eyes bore into mine. "Like you're the air in my lungs and the blood in my veins. Like I love you so much it physically hurts."

My heart stops, then restarts with a vengeance. "You love me?"

He actually laughs, not meanly but like I've said something ridiculous. "Baby, I married your mother just to get close to you. I've been planning our entire future since the moment I first saw you. Of course I love you." His thumbs catch the tears that start falling down my cheeks. "I've loved you longer than you've even known I existed."

"No one's ever..." I try to swallow past the lump in my throat but more tears just keep coming. God, what is wrong with me lately? I never cry. "I mean, my mother doesn't... no one's ever told me they love me before."

"Then they're all idiots." He kisses away a tear trailing down my cheek. "Because loving you is as natural as breathing. As inevitable as gravity. It's just... fact. Like the sun rising or water being wet. I love you. I will always love you. And anyone who's had the chance to love you and didn't take it is too stupid to live."

"I love you too," I whisper, and it feels like the most natural thing I've ever said. Like these words have been living in my chest just waiting for the right moment to break free. "I love you so much it scares me sometimes."

"Don't be scared, little one." His smile is possessive and tender all at once. "Being mine is the safest thing you'll ever be." He wipes away the last of my tears with his thumbs. "Now, how about those pancakes?"

I hoist myself onto one of the barstools, feeling lighter than I have in... maybe ever. Like those three little words somehow changed everything and nothing all at once. I watch in fascination as Cohen moves around the kitchen like he does this all the time, pulling ingredients from cabinets I didn't even know held actual food.

"I didn't know we had chocolate chips," I say, mesmerized by the way his forearms flex as he measures flour into a bowl. The way he rolls up his sleeves should not be this hot, but here we are.

"The staff showed me all their hiding spots." That dangerous smile is back, the one that reminds me he's probably the most powerful man in Emerald Hills after the Savage Six. "There's a lot your mother doesn't know about what goes on in this house."

My stomach growls again, loud enough to make me blush. "Sorry. I don't know why I'm so hungry. Or tired." I try to stifle a yawn but fail spectacularly. "Must be all the stress from this morning catching up to me."

His eyes do this weird flash thing before his expression goes carefully blank. "Must be."

I rest my chin on my hands, watching him work. Everything about this feels... domestic. Intimate. Like we're just a normal couple making breakfast for dinner, not a stepdaughter and stepfather hiding from her psychotic mother.

"You're staring," he says without looking up from the griddle.

"You're pretty when you cook."

He snorts. "I'm always pretty."

And modest too," I say, but I can't help grinning. These little moments, when he lets his guard down and just... exists with me, they're like tiny miracles.

The first pancake hits the griddle with a satisfying sizzle, and the smell of butter and vanilla makes my mouth water. When he sprinkles chocolate chips over the batter in a pattern, I nearly fall off my stool.

"Are you making them into hearts?" I ask, delighted and embarrassed by how much I love it.

"Obviously not." He smirks, flipping the very clearly heart-decorated pancake with expert precision. "You're clearly hallucinating."

"Clearly," I agree, hiding my smile in my arms as I rest my head on the counter. My eyelids feel like they weigh about a thousand pounds each, but I don't want to miss this. Miss him being soft and sweet and... mine.

"Don't fall asleep yet," he murmurs. "Food first."

"M'not sleeping," I mumble, even as my eyes drift shut. "Just resting my eyes while I wait for my not-heart-decorated pancakes."

I hear him chuckle, followed by more sizzling and the clink of plates. The next thing I know, his fingers are running through my hair, gently scratching my scalp in a way that makes me want to purr like a cat.

"Little one," he says softly. "Your pancakes are getting cold."

I force my eyes open and nearly moan at what I see. A stack of perfectly golden pancakes sits in front of me, chocolate chips melting and steam rising. They look like something from a magazine—the kind of breakfast my mother would call "common" while secretly taking notes on the presentation.

"These are..." I blink hard, trying to clear the stupid tears that keep wanting to fall today. What is wrong with me? "No one's ever made me anything before."

"That changes now." He slides onto the stool next to me, close enough that our legs touch. "Everything changes now."

The first bite is... I don't even have words. Warm and sweet and perfect, and suddenly I'm starving like I've never eaten before in my life. I devour the first pancake in about thirty seconds flat.

"Slow down," Cohen says, but he's watching me with this intense look that makes my stomach flip for reasons that have nothing to do with food. "They're not going anywhere."

"Says you." I cut into the second pancake, getting chocolate all over my fingers. "My mother could walk in any second and catch me committing carb crimes."

"Let her." His voice goes dark and dangerous. "I'd love to have that conversation."

I pause mid-bite. "You really aren't afraid of her at all, are you?"

"Afraid?" He actually laughs. "Baby, your mother is a paper tiger. All show, no substance. The only power she has is what people give her." His hand slides to the back of my neck, warm and possessive. "And I've never given her any."

I take another bite of pancake to hide how much his confidence affects me. Like, my mother terrifies literally everyone—staff, business partners, probably small children and animals, and especially me—but Cohen just... doesn't care.

"Besides," he adds, his thumb stroking a spot behind my ear that makes my brain go fuzzy. "In seven days, she'll learn exactly how powerless she really is."

I should probably feel bad about that. About how much he

clearly wants to destroy my mother. Instead, I just feel... safe. Protected. Loved.

Also really, really sleepy.

"You're falling asleep in your pancakes," he says, sounding way too amused.

"Am not." But even as I say it, my head's getting heavier. "Just... resting between bites."

"Uh huh." He pulls my plate away and I make a noise of protest that would be embarrassing if I had any energy left to care. "Come here."

Before I can ask what he means, he's scooping me up like I weigh nothing. I should probably object—like, I'm a grown woman who can walk—but instead I just curl into his chest, breathing in his cologne and trying not to pass out.

"I can walk," I mumble into his shirt, making absolutely zero effort to prove it.

"I know." He starts up the stairs, carrying me like I weigh nothing. "But I like taking care of you."

"Even when I fall asleep in my food?"

"Especially then." His chest rumbles with quiet laughter. "Though I have to say, your sudden need for naps is interesting."

Something about the way he says it makes me lift my head. "What do you mean?"

But he just kisses my forehead and pushes open my bedroom door. "Nothing, little one. Get some rest."

He lays me on my bed so carefully, like I'm something precious. When he goes to pull away, I grab his shirt. "Stay?"

"As if I could deny you anything." He kicks off his shoes and stretches out beside me, pulling me against his chest. "Sleep. I've got you."

I snuggle closer, tangling my legs with his and pressing my face into his chest. His heartbeat is steady under my ear, his hand stroking up and down my spine in this hypnotic rhythm that makes staying awake impossible.

"Love you," I mumble, already more asleep than awake.

"Love you more," he whispers into my hair. "More than you could possibly understand."

There's something in his voice—something deep and intense that I'd probably analyze if I wasn't drifting off. Instead, I just let the sound of his heartbeat and the feeling of being completely, totally safe pull me under.

The last thing I'm aware of is him murmuring something else into my hair, but I'm too far gone to make out the words. Something about...

Forever.

Cohen
CHAPTER 21

A WEEK AGO, Emerald gave herself to me completely in that chapel. Now I watch her sleeping beside me, her dark hair spilled across my chest, and know that I've stolen far more than just her body. I've claimed every part of her—mind, heart, soul. She belongs to me so completely that trying to separate us now would be like trying to unravel DNA. We're coded into each other's cells, written into each other's blood.

And tomorrow, at her mother's precious Christmas party, everyone will know it.

Snow falls outside her bedroom window, coating Emerald Hills in white while the rest of the house sleeps. My fingers trace idle patterns on her bare shoulder as she breathes softly against my skin. She can't sleep without me anymore—hasn't spent a single night alone since the chapel. Neither have I. The rare moments we're forced apart feel like drowning, like someone's stolen all the oxygen from the room.

Some might call it unhealthy. Toxic. Co-dependent.

But they don't understand what we are to each other. What we've always been, since that first moment I saw her. Two halves of the same soul—her light to my darkness, finally whole.

"Cohen?" Her voice is soft and sleepy as she stirs against me, pressing closer so her skin's touching mine everywhere it possibly can. Always seeking closer contact, like she can't bear even an inch of space between us. I know the feeling.

"Go back to sleep, little one." I press a kiss to her forehead, breathing in the sweet scent of her skin mixed with mine. The scent of *us*. "It's early."

But she's already pushing herself up on one elbow, those endless green eyes finding mine in the gloomy gray light filtering through her windows. The love I see there still knocks the breath from my lungs. After two years of planning, manipulating, orchestrating every detail to get her exactly where I wanted her, I never expected this—to have her look at me like I'm her entire world. Like I'm something sacred instead of the monster I know I am.

"You're thinking too loud," she murmurs, her fingers tracing the line of my jaw. Just that simple touch sends electricity racing through my veins. "What's wrong?"

"Nothing's wrong." I catch her hand, pressing a kiss to her palm. "Everything's exactly as it should be."

She studies me for a moment, her brow furrowing. I want to kiss that worried look off her face, but then again, I always want to kiss her. "You're worried about tomorrow."

"Not worried." I slide my hand into her hair, gripping gently. "Just... ready. Ready for everyone to know you're mine. Ready to stop hiding." Ready to know with certainty whether she's pregnant with my child.

Her lips brush against my chest, right over my heart, and my grip in her hair tightens. "Me too," she whispers. "I'm tired of pretending I don't need you every second of every day."

My cock hardens at her words, at the naked want in her voice. She's been insatiable this past week, her body constantly craving mine in a way that makes me wonder... hope...

But I need to be sure before I let myself believe.

"How are you feeling?" I keep my voice casual as I stroke her back, cataloging every small change in her body that I've noticed this week. The tenderness in her breasts that makes her gasp when I touch them. The way she falls asleep at odd hours, pure exhaustion written across her features. Her sudden cravings for foods she's never been allowed to eat.

"Mmm." She snuggles closer, practically burrowing into my skin. "Tired. But good tired. Safe." She presses another kiss to my chest. "Everything feels... different. Bigger. More intense." Her fingers trail down my stomach, following the lines of my tattoos. "Is that weird?"

"No, little phoenix." I catch her wandering hand before it can go lower and destroy what's left of my self-control. "That's exactly how it should feel between us."

She makes a soft sound of protest when I stop her exploration. "But I want to touch you."

"And I want to let you." I bring her hand to my mouth, kissing each fingertip. "But your mother has you scheduled for final dress fittings all morning, and if I let you start something, we won't leave this bed until New Year's."

The pout she gives me should be illegal. Actually, most things about her should be illegal, including how fucking perfect she looks wearing nothing but one of my shirts. But especially that lip...

"Don't." I growl the warning, but she just bites that bottom lip harder, her eyes daring me. "You know what that does to me, little one."

"Maybe that's exactly why I'm doing it." She shifts against me, all soft curves and warm skin, and my restraint splinters. "Maybe I need—"

A knock at the door freezes us both.

"Miss Delacroix?" Kendra's voice filters through the wood. "Your mother wants you dressed and ready in twenty minutes for the fitting."

Emerald's eyes go wide with panic as she scrambles out of bed. I watch her, already missing her warmth. This sneaking around is getting old, but soon we won't have to hide anymore.

"Go shower," I murmur, stealing one last kiss before I have to let her go. "I'll see you downstairs."

She kisses me once more, quick and desperate, before slipping from the bed. I watch her disappear into the bathroom, memorizing the way my shirt falls to her thighs, the glimpse of marks I left on her skin last night.

Mine. All mine.

And tomorrow, everyone will know it.

But first, I need to confirm what my gut is telling me. Need to know for certain that my careful planning, my meticulous timing, has worked exactly as intended.

That Emerald Delacroix is carrying my child.

The thought alone makes my cock thicken and throb, but I force myself to focus. To plan. To make sure everything is perfect when I finally tell her.

Twenty-four hours until the party.

Twenty-four hours until I get to show the world who Emerald really belongs to.

Twenty-four hours until Madeline learns exactly who she allowed into her home.

I just need to be patient for one more day.

The water shuts off in the bathroom, and I hear Emerald humming softly—"All I Want for Christmas Is You." Last year she would've been terrified to make even that small sound, afraid her mother would hear her daring to express joy. Now she hums in the shower, steals chocolate from the kitchen, and laughs when I kiss that spot behind her ear that makes her shiver.

I force myself to dress quickly, knowing if I'm still here when she steps out of that bathroom wrapped in nothing but a towel, there's no power on earth that could make me leave. And getting caught right now isn't an option. Not when we're so close to everything I've planned.

My mind races through the logistics of what I need to accomplish today as I button my shirt. I need to be certain before tomorrow. Need to know if my careful timing, my meticulous planning, worked exactly as intended.

I slip out of Emerald's room and head down the hall toward my own, passing Kendra on her way to torment my stepdaughter with another one of Madeline's endless schedules. Her eyes narrow slightly at my early morning appearance, but she can't prove anything. Not that it matters at this point.

From my doorway, I hear her sharp knock on Emerald's door, her clipped voice announcing another rushed morning of fittings and photographs. Everything about that woman screams loyalty to Madeline—from her rigid posture to her precise timing.

There's no point in playing nice with Madeline's watchdog. Besides, I have more important things to focus on. Like getting my hands on a pregnancy test without arousing suspicion. Like making sure everything is perfect for tomorrow night when I finally get to show the world exactly who Emerald belongs to. I close my door on Kendra's suspicious glare.

I need someone discrete. Someone with no connection to this house or Emerald Hills. Someone who won't ask questions or run straight to Madeline.

Grace, my assistant at the law firm, answers on the first ring. "Mr. Astor?"

"I need something picked up. Immediately. And with absolute discretion."

"Of course." No questions, no hesitation. It's why I hired her.

That, and her complete lack of interest in anything beyond doing her job perfectly. "What do you need?"

Five minutes later, it's handled. The tests will be at my office within the hour.

I stand at my window, watching snow blanket the grounds while I change into a fresh suit. Through the frosted glass, I can see the chapel where Emerald gave herself to me completely, its dark spire a reminder of promises made in candlelight. Of what's to come.

Now comes the harder part—getting what I need without Emerald knowing. But Madeline's given me the perfect blueprint with her years of controlling behavior.

I head downstairs as the house comes alive around me. Staff pour in through the service entrance, arms laden with decorations and supplies for tomorrow's party. Madeline's voice carries from her office, sharp with irritation as she berates someone over the phone about candlestick heights or crystal placement or whatever other meaningless detail has caught her attention.

I find Anna, one of the newer maids, restocking towels in the hall bathroom. Young, eager to please, and—most importantly—no real loyalty to Madeline yet.

"Good morning, Anna." I lower my voice. "I need your help with something delicate."

She turns, with a hesitant smile on her face. "Yes, Mr. Astor?"

"Mrs. Delacroix has ordered another random drug screening because of Emerald's unusual behavior lately." I pull out an empty specimen cup from my pocket, watching understanding flood the maid's face. These "wellness checks" are a regular part of Madeline's control. "She wants it handled with the usual discretion. You know how she is about appearances, especially before events like tomorrow."

Anna nods quickly, already reaching for the cup. "Of course.

Just like the other times. I'll tell Miss Emerald it's another of her mother's random tests."

"Perfect." I let a hint of approval enter my voice, knowing it will cement her cooperation. "Bring this to me instead of Madeline when you've collected it. With the party, I told her I'd handle it."

I watch Anna head up the stairs toward Emerald's room where I know she's still getting ready for the day. My gut twists at using Madeline's tactics against Emerald, but I need to know. Need to be certain before tomorrow night.

I grab a quick coffee from the kitchen, avoiding Madeline's voice carrying from her office where she's still terrorizing some poor bastard about tomorrow's arrangements. Twenty minutes later, Anna slips into my study with the filled specimen cup.

"Thank you," I say, already reaching for my coat. "I'll make sure Mrs. Delacroix knows how helpful you've been."

The drive to my office takes longer than usual with the heavy snow, but it gives me time to control the anticipation coursing through my veins. The paper bag from Grace sits centered on my desk when I arrive, exactly where I knew it would be. Discrete, as always.

I lock the door before pulling out the tests and reading through the instructions. My hands actually shake as I carefully dip the first stick into the cup and set a timer on my phone.

Two minutes.

The wait feels endless. I pace in front of my window, unable to sit still, unable to focus on anything except the strip of plastic that will tell me if I've succeeded. If that night in her bedroom was just the beginning of making her completely, irrevocably mine in every possible way.

One line appears.

Then another.

Positive.

Something ancient and wild roars to life in my chest, darker and more consuming than anything I've ever felt for her. My hands grip the edge of my desk as triumph and satisfaction crash through me. She's carrying my child. My blood runs in her veins now, our DNA weaving together to create something entirely new. Something that will bind us together until the end of time.

Something perfect.

My phone buzzes and Kendra's name flashes on the screen. Fucking perfect timing.

"What?" I answer, still riding the high of confirmation that Emerald's carrying my child.

"The Whitakers just called. They're insisting on bringing their daughter and her new husband tomorrow night." Kendra's voice carries that particular tension she gets when Madeline's about to explode. "Mrs. Delacroix requires your assistance with the situation."

Of course they are. Richard Whitaker thinking he can leverage his family's three generations in Emerald Hills to do whatever the fuck he wants which then means I have to deal with Madeline.

I drop the tests in the dumpster outside before heading back to the estate. This past week, Madeline's been so caught up in her precious party preparations that she's almost ignored me. But the moments when she's not obsessing over place settings or flower arrangements, she's been worse than ever to Emerald - cutting remarks, constant criticism, threats about that Swiss school that aren't even really threats since she's already bought the plane ticket and paid the tuition.

Her obsession with both the party and tormenting Emerald has reached new levels. Like she's trying to prove something. Establish dominance one last time before... what?

I pull into the circular drive just as another delivery truck arrives. Through the windows, I can see my wife in full dictator mode, but there's calculation behind her eyes when they meet mine.

That look sets off warning bells in my gut that I've learned never to ignore.

I find Madeline in the formal living room, which has become a staging area for tomorrow night's party. Her perfect posture is rigid with tension as she snaps orders at a trembling florist about tomorrow's centerpieces. Through the doorway, I can see Emerald curled in an armchair, half-asleep despite the chaos around her. Dark circles shadow her eyes even through her makeup, and my fingers itch to take her upstairs, wrap her in my arms, and let her rest. To protect her and our child from everything—including her mother.

Our child.

The words still feel surreal, even with the proof I just saw.

"Cohen." Madeline's voice cuts through my thoughts. "Finally. We have a situation with the Whitakers."

"I heard." I keep my voice neutral as I tear my gaze from Emerald. "What exactly do they want?"

"To bring their newly married daughter and her husband." Her lips curve into a smile that doesn't reach her eyes. "Normally I wouldn't care, but given the seating arrangements... perhaps you could speak with Richard? After all, you handle his family's legal affairs."

There's something in her tone that sets me on edge. Like this is a test. But of what?

"Of course." I pull out my phone, already composing a text to Richard that will shut this down immediately. "I'll handle it."

"Excellent." She turns back to the florist but pauses. "Oh, and Cohen? Make sure you're both dressed appropriately tonight. The photographer is coming for the website's Christmas day message and I won't have either of you embarrassing me."

Both of us. As if Emerald and I are a unit in her mind.

She knows something's off, but her ego won't let her see the truth. She's too convinced of her own power, too certain that she's broken Emerald's spirit completely. Too arrogant to believe that her beaten down puppet of a daughter could ever defy her. And she thinks I married her for her money, her status, her brand—as if I need any of that when I have the Savage Society's backing.

Let her underestimate us. Let her believe she's still in control.

It'll make tomorrow night that much sweeter when her world shatters.

Emerald stirs in her chair, those endless green eyes finding mine across the room, and everything else just... disappears. She's exhausted, worried about the party, anxious about her mother's mood—I can read it all in her face like she's speaking directly to my soul. When she looks at me like this, it's impossible not to drown in her, to forget where we are, who might be watching.

I force myself to break our connection, glancing quickly at Madeline, but she's too busy terrorizing the florist to notice how her daughter and husband just got lost in each other.

"I have a few calls to make," I say, though walking away from her feels like having my heart ripped out through my throat. "I'll be back for the photoshoot."

By this time tomorrow, everything changes. Our lives, our future, our family.

But first, I need to figure out exactly what Madeline's planning.

Because as I left the room, that woman's smile promised war.

She has no idea that while she's been playing chess, I've already positioned every piece for checkmate.

And I never lose.

Cohen

CHAPTER 22

EVERYTHING I'VE DONE for the past two years has led to this moment.

I stand at my study window, watching fresh snow blanket the grounds of the Delacroix estate while sipping my bourbon before tonight begins.

My phone buzzes with a message from Cole confirming some of his and Lucas's guys are in position just in case this goes to shit. Call them plan B.

In less than an hour, Madeline's carefully constructed world will burn. The thought brings a smile to my lips as I check the livestream link one final time. Every guest's phone is primed to receive it at precisely the right moment—when Madeline is at her most triumphant, playing perfect hostess to all the old money families she's spent decades manipulating.

But more than revenge, more than watching Madeline's empire crumble, my mind is consumed with Emerald. My everything. My salvation. My perfect match in every way that matters. She doesn't know all my plans yet—that once Madeline is gone, we'll be free to make this official in every way. The same way she doesn't know she's carrying my child.

My hand tightens around my phone as need burns through my veins like poison. We've been apart for hours while she prepares for the party, and every second without her feels like withdrawal, like my body's shutting down without the antidote. She's an entire floor above me in her room, and even that distance is too much for my sanity to bear.

I've never craved anything the way I crave her. Never needed anyone the way I need her. She's the other half of my twisted soul, as essential to me as oxygen, as inevitable as death.

A knock at my door breaks through the fog of my thoughts. "Mr. Astor?" Kendra's voice carries that edge of disapproval it always has when she addresses me. "Mrs. Delacroix wants to ensure you'll be downstairs in ten minutes to greet the early arrivals."

I don't bother responding. In ten minutes, Kendra won't matter. None of Madeline's minions will.

My phone buzzes again—Tristen: *Just watched Madeline almost have an aneurysm when we showed up. Worth coming just for that. The others are here too.*

I send back a quick acknowledgment before tucking the phone away. The Savage Six's presence tonight isn't strictly necessary, but their support sends a message. That I'm not just some lawyer who married above his station, as Madeline likes to imply. That I have the backing of the most dangerous men in Emerald Hills.

That I'm a part of the real power in this town.

These hours of forced separation from Emerald have every nerve ending raw, my body achingly aware that she's somewhere above me getting ready for tonight. Knowing what's coming—how everything changes after this party—makes the wait even more excruciating.

I check my reflection one last time, adjusting my tie. The

blood-red tux is a statement. A warning to anyone paying attention. This isn't a celebration. It's an execution.

And I'm the executioner.

Music spills from the ballroom as the first guests arrive. Through my window, I watch a stream of luxury cars pull up to the entrance. Madeline's carefully curated guest list—all the "right" people, all the old money families who matter in this town.

All the people who are about to witness her destruction.

But first, I need to see her. My Emerald. My reason for breathing.

I turn toward the grand staircase and time freezes. Emerald appears at the top, golden tulle catching the light with every movement, making her look like she's floating as she descends. Her dark hair falls in perfect waves around her shoulders, the ivory silk and full skirt transforming her into an angel stepping down from heaven directly into my darkness.

"Cohen." My name falls from her lips like a prayer as she reaches the bottom step, and the sound nearly brings me to my knees. Her eyes find mine and reality fractures, shattering until there's nothing left but her. Until she's the only thing that exists in my universe.

"Little one." I reach for her, my hands finding her waist above the clouds of tulle like they belong there. Like they've always belonged there. "You're devastating."

A blush stains her cheeks as she leans into me, her body fitting against mine like we're two pieces of the same whole. "I've missed you," she whispers, and I feel the words in my soul. "Even just these few hours... it hurt."

"I know." I press my lips to her forehead, breathing her in. *Sugar cookies and innocence and mine.* "But after tonight, we never have to be apart again. I promise."

She shivers, her fingers curling into my jacket. "What's going to happen?"

"Justice." I tip her chin up, drowning in green eyes that hold my entire universe. "Are you ready?"

She nods without hesitation, trust shining in her gaze. "As long as I'm with you."

"Always." I steal a quick kiss, careful not to smudge her lipstick or let anyone see. The timing needs to be right for Madeline to find out about us. "Now come. We have a party to attend."

The sound of breaking glass carries from the ballroom. "Mother's probably terrorizing the staff about the crystal display she designed specifically for tonight."

I smile, dark satisfaction curling through me. "Let her have her moment. Soon, none of this will matter."

Hand in hand, we move toward the party. Toward destiny. Toward the future I've spent two years orchestrating.

Everything is in place. Everyone is exactly where they need to be.

The ballroom is a masterpiece of Madeline's twisted imagination—an ethereal fusion of frost and starlight. Crystal icicles float mid-air, suspended on invisible wires while white roses bloom from sculpted ice. Shards of mirrors catch and scatter light in mesmerizing patterns across the walls, making the massive space feel like the inside of a diamond. Even I have to admit it's breathtaking, innovative in that way that will have every socialite in the Pacific Northwest scrambling to copy it by New Year's.

As we enter, Emerald is immediately swept away by Katherine Ashworth and her circle, all of them cooing over her dress. The separation is physical torture, but I force myself to let her go. Instead, I claim the high-backed chair near the grand fireplace, positioning myself where I can observe everything—but mostly her.

The Savage Six are already making their presence felt. Cole and Lucas stand in matching black suits by the bar, a statement just by being here. Tristen has drawn a crowd of admirers, though his attention keeps drifting to his phone. Romeo's tattoos peek above his collar as he talks with Beckett, both of them looking like wolves among Madeline's pampered sheep. And Xander prowls the edges of the room, his mismatched eyes and restless energy making the socialites nervous as he fidgets with his collar, unable to stay still.

But my focus is solely on Emerald as she moves through the crowd, playing the role her mother crafted for her one last time. Every cell in my body screams to go to her, to keep her by my side where she belongs. The physical pain of our separation claws at my chest even though she's only yards away.

She feels it too. I can tell by the way she keeps glancing my direction, by how she drifts closer whenever she can, like we're magnets being pulled together. Even across the room, I can see the subtle tremor in her hands, the slight hitch in her breathing when too many people separate us.

"Quite the turnout." Madeline appears beside my chair, her voice dripping artificial warmth. She's wearing white, as cold and sharp as the woman herself. "I trust you're planning to be social tonight?"

I don't bother looking at her. My eyes are fixed on Emerald as she accepts a champagne flute from a passing waiter, and every muscle in my body goes rigid. But then she sets it on a side table without taking a sip, and the tension bleeds from my shoulders. "I'm exactly where I need to be."

She follows my gaze, her lips tightening when she sees who I'm watching. "You seem very focused on my daughter lately."

"Do I?" Now I do turn to her, letting her see just a glimpse of the darkness she invited into her home. "How observant of you."

Something flashes in her eyes—uncertainty? Fear? But before she can respond, the Montgomerys arrive. I watch with dark satisfaction as she's forced to play hostess, welcoming

Daniel Jr. and his parents with that plastic smile she's perfected.

Emerald tenses when she spots Daniel, but I'm already on top of the situation. One look at Cole has him intercepting the spoiled heir before he can get within ten feet of what's mine.

"Cohen." Emerald's relief is palpable as she reaches for me, propriety forgotten. I pull her against me, not caring who sees. Let them look. Let them whisper. Soon they'll all know anyway.

"Come here, little one." I guide her to my chair, settling her on my lap. She curls into me immediately, like she's finally able to breathe. I know the feeling. "Better?"

"Yes." She presses closer, her head tucking under my chin. "I hate being away from you. It feels wrong. Like my skin doesn't fit right."

"I know." My hand slides to her lower back. "But it's almost over."

Her fingers play with my tie, and I have to bite back a groan at the innocent touch. "Promise?"

"I promise." I press a kiss to her temple, breathing her in. Let them stare. Let all these wealthy parasites in their custom Italian suits and designer ballgowns see exactly who she belongs to. The heat from the overcrowded ballroom has started to melt Madeline's icy decor, but that's fitting. Everything in this room is about to come crashing down anyway.

My stepdaughter's perched on my lap and, from our spot on the on the dais, we watch them. Several of them stare at the way she's sitting, how *inappropriate* it is for a girl her age to be this close to her stepfather's dick, and I almost laugh. Whenever we make eye contact, I get a disgusted curl of the lip or a glare before they turn away. Imagine what they'd think if they knew my hand was moving underneath her fluffy tulle skirt and sneaking between her legs.

Emerald shifts, pressing her legs together to trap my fingers.

"Cohen," she whispers under her breath so nobody can hear but me. "Everyone can see."

She's right. Everyone can see us, but her skirt is cover enough to hide everything I plan to do. My lips find the shell of her ear, and I nip at her. "Then you'd better stay quiet and still." Her eyes drift closed and her breathing speeds up as my fingers slide higher.

"I don't want them to see," she protests but doesn't stop me from teasing her skin. The softness of her inner thigh feels incredible as I drag my knuckle against it.

"They won't. Now, be a good girl, and spread your legs for me." She bites her lip, and I watch as she does exactly what I tell her to do.

The power she gives me is heady.

I move my fingers higher, and the lacy fabric of her panties greets me. She's so warm, and the heat radiating from her pussy makes my cock stiffen into an uncomfortable position in my tuxedo pants. I'd love nothing more than to bend her over the edge of this chair, shove the layers of sparkly golden fabric to her waist, and drive my cock into her.

Unfortunately, the guests' reactions to seeing my fingers beneath her skirt are tame compared to the outrage I'd receive if I pull her panties to the side to give her the fucking I know we both want.

And I'd never let any of them see her that way.

The fabric of her underwear gets wetter the more I touch her, and when I dip my finger below the lace to brush across her slickness, Emerald's breath catches. She lets it out slowly, and her hips shift forward.

"Did you want something?" I ask.

She glances at me and gives me a little smile, shaking her head. "Nope." Her voice wavers, betraying the fact that she's lying to me. "I'm fine."

"Oh, yeah?" I ask, dragging my finger along her pussy. Her

thighs tense and her breathing speeds up. "That's too bad. I was going to see if you wanted to ride my fingers while I fuck you with them. At least until you're ready to take my cock."

"Cohen," she gasps, and her head whips to the side to check and see if anyone heard. They didn't. The conversations and the string quartet are loud enough to hide our secrets. "Someone's going to notice what we're doing."

Her words don't stop her from shifting until my hand slips beneath her underwear again. I'm touching her pussy, and her wetness is all over my fingers. My chest rumbles with how much it turns me on to know how badly she wants me.

I lean closer to her ear. "You think I'll let anyone see what's happening under your skirt, little one?" I slip my finger inside of her up to the second knuckle. "But if you don't want to play, that's fine. I'll stop touching you." I start to pull out of her, but her thighs squeeze and her hand clamps down over my arm.

"Don't," she whispers. "Don't stop."

She's practically panting now, and I'm so hard for her. I want to see her come. I want to *feel* her come while I'm balls deep inside of her. It doesn't matter that we're surrounded by her mother's friends and business associates. That her mother's sitting less than ten feet away in a chair just like this one. I drag my finger out and then push it back in over and over, my thumb brushing against her clit. It's not enough to get her off but it's enough to make her squirm.

"What is it you want, little one?"

"More. Please, give me more," she begs in a whisper. "Please."

I slide a second finger inside her. She clenches down on me and sucks me in. "Fuck," I grit out. "You're squeezing my fingers. Is this what you'd do to my cock?" Her lips are parted, and she's facing out into the room but I doubt she's really seeing anything. "Is it?"

"Yes," she answers in a whisper. Her hands are gripping the

arms of the throne-like chair we're sitting on, and my chest presses against her back as I lean in close to her ear. "Reach down between us and take out my cock." I start fucking her harder with shaking fingers. I'm so goddamn turned on, if I don't get inside of her I might die. "Now, Emerald. Do it now."

Her hand trembles as she reaches behind her and fumbles at my belt before she gets the zipper down. She shifts forward to give herself a little more room and I feel my wife's frigid glare from the other side of the dais. It doesn't matter, though. She can't do anything to stop us. Not without making a massive scene. She'd never do anything to embarrass herself.

The moment Emerald has my pants open enough to free my cock, I use my hand to guide hers to the base and have her wrap her fingers around me. I lean back in the throne and push my hips up so my dick slides through her grip.

"Fuck," I breathe, as I pull my sticky fingers out of her and grab her hips to put her how I want her. She doesn't resist as I angle her body toward me and tug her panties to the side again. Her pussy is slick and hot, and in the middle of a room full of people, her mother—my wife—included, I pull her down onto my shaft until every inch is buried inside of her.

Emerald's lips fall open, her eyelids droop, and her head tilts back to rest on my shoulder. She's the most beautiful thing I've ever seen, and the fact that she's taking my cock surrounded by these people only makes her that much more so. She doesn't care. All she cares about is me and how I make her feel.

We can't fuck like I want, so my fingers dig into her hips to hold her still when she tries to move. Her cunt grips me, squeezing and clamping down again and again while I grit my teeth and try not to fucking lose it. It's like her body's trying to steal my cum straight from my balls.

When Madeline's attention is focused on one of her many admirers, I tighten my grip on Emerald's hip and get her to rock ever so slightly against me. I can't hold in my groan and Emerald whimpers at the relief of finally fucking, even if it's not much.

"Do you want to know a secret?" I murmur, my lips brushing her ear. She nods once and tilts her head so I have better access, but I don't take advantage. This is important and here and now, while we're as close to being one person as we can possibly get, I need to tell her.

"You're pregnant." I say the words and her entire body goes rigid. She stops rocking and tries to turn to look at me. "Shh. Stay still, little one. You don't want to get caught." I wrap my arm around her waist to hold her steady and keep her from moving. "It's true." My hand moves lower, sliding over her dress to the spot where my baby is growing. "You're going to give me a child. The first of many."

"What? How..."

I push my hips up. "I think you know how."

"How long have you known?"

"I'll tell you everything later. But just know," I spread my fingers over her stomach, "I want this more than I've ever wanted anything."

She takes one of her hands off the arm of the chair-slash-throne and puts it over mine on her stomach. "Me, too," she whispers.

This right here is the best gift I've ever gotten.

I need to make this girl come before I explode. If she can't rock her hips, then I'll move for her. I shift my other hand between her thighs, back up under her skirt, and I rub her clit. Her reaction is immediate, a shudder working its way through her. I lean forward until my lips are pressed against her ear. "You're going to come on my cock right here in the middle of this room while all these people watch you without knowing that's what they're watching."

She's panting now, her hips jerking forward and back in a

barely-there movement that no one is going to notice unless they're looking for it. "You're going to show them what they'll never have. What belongs to me," I growl into her ear. Her nails dig into the fabric on the arms of the throne, and she bites her bottom lip. She's close. So am I.

I'm going to fill Emerald with my cum in the middle of her mother's Christmas party.

And then I'm going to destroy my wife.

Cohen
CHAPTER 23

EMERALD GASPS and her head falls back against my shoulder again as her cunt starts spasming around me. I have to fight to keep from groaning out loud when I follow her over the edge. My cock jerks and my cum fills her pussy. The relief from coming after being hard for her for so long is almost overwhelming.

I press a kiss to her neck, and she smiles as her eyes drift open. She looks out into the crowd, her gaze hazy and content. "They can't see, right? Nobody's staring at us," she whispers to me after looking around the room and seeing that no one gives a fuck.

"No, little one. They can't see. They're too busy worrying about what everyone else thinks of them to notice anything we're doing."

We sit for a while, catching our breath while my cock softens inside of her. Eventually, I slip out and I shove two fingers inside her pussy to make sure she doesn't lose a drop of my gift. Once I'm satisfied, I tug her panties back into place and catch Madeline's eye as I suck my fingers into my mouth.

Everything's been set into motion and there's no going back. Madeline's powerless to stop it now.

"I love you," Emerald whispers against my skin, her face buried in my neck. "So much it terrifies me sometimes."

"Don't be afraid." I tilt her face up to mine while tucking myself back into my pants. "Anyone who tries to touch you or our child will cease to exist. Starting tonight."

Right on cue, the first phone chimes. Then another. And another, until the sound fills the ballroom like a symphony of destruction. The link has gone out.

Let the show begin.

Madeline's barely held it together since Emmitt cut ties last week. I've watched her spiral, firing staff and making threats as her carefully planned holiday season imploded. The charity auction's cancellation alone cost her millions in lost contracts and social capital. But looking at her tonight, you'd never know. She's wearing her CEO mask, every crack plastered over with bullshit as she plays perfect hostess to the very people who've been whispering about her downfall.

Her desperation is a tangible thing, almost like a bad smell she's giving off as she makes her rounds. She still thinks she has cards left to play. Still thinks she can salvage her control.

She has no idea what's coming.

Madeline's head snaps up from across the room, her perfect hostess smile faltering as she registers the wave of notifications. Her eyes narrow as she watches her guests reaching for their phones, that calculating look I've been waiting for crossing her face. She starts moving through the crowd, trying to assess the threat to her control, but she's too late.

I hold Emerald closer as chaos erupts in elegant whispers and sharp inhales. Watching everything Madeline built crumble around us is almost as satisfying as the way Emerald curls into me, seeking protection even as her mother's reign ends.

Richard Whitaker moves first, exactly as I knew he would. His face goes from red to purple as he reads, designer glass shattering in his grip. "You manipulative bitch," he snarls, turning on her. "You've been blackmailing my entire family for a decade."

Madeline's plastic smile doesn't waver, but her fingers tighten around her champagne flute until her knuckles go white. "Richard, I'm sure there's been some mistake—"

"No mistake." Katherine Ashworth steps forward, generations of old money social power radiating from her rigid posture as she grips her phone. "The proof is right here. How you used my grandson's accident to force our merger. How you've been stealing from your own charitable foundation."

Madeline stalks through the crowd, which parts before her like she's contagious, as her guests continue scrolling through the evidence of her crimes.

"You said you'd protect my daughter," Elizabeth Caldwell's voice shakes with rage. "Instead, you helped Emmitt hide what he did to her. Helped him do it to others."

Emerald tenses in my arms, no doubt thinking about how close she came to becoming one of Emmitt's victims. I press my lips to her temple. "I've got you," I murmur against her skin. "No one will ever hurt you like that."

The accusations continue mounting, each revelation stripping away another layer of Madeline's power. The Pierces revealing how she sabotaged their family business. The Bradfords exposing how she manipulated their daughter's social media empire to destroy it. Every prominent family in Emerald Hills uncovering decades of betrayal.

I watch it all from my throne, Emerald safe in my arms, as the woman who dared cage my phoenix finally faces justice.

"This is ridiculous," Madeline snaps, but her voice has lost its commanding edge. "These are obviously fabrications—"

"Like how you fabricated my entire childhood?" Emerald's

voice rings out clear and strong, silencing the room. My chest swells with pride as she stands, though she keeps her hand in mine. "Like how you starved me? Isolated me? Tried to break me?"

"Everything I did was for your own good—"

"No." Emerald's fingers tighten around mine. "Everything you did was for yourself. Your image. Your brand. Your perfect little doll to dress up and control."

Madeline's eyes dart around the room, finding no allies among the faces she once commanded. "You ungrateful little—" She stops, that calculating look I've been waiting for crossing her face. "You think you've won? You and Cohen with your disgusting affair?" A cruel smile twists her lips. "Did he tell you about Charlotte? About what really happened to her? About all the other girls who—"

"I know everything." Emerald's voice doesn't waver. "Every dark truth. Every shadow. And I choose him. I will *always* choose him."

"You think I haven't prepared for this?" Madeline's laugh holds an edge of hysteria as she pulls out her phone. "You think I'd let you destroy everything I've built?"

Her fingers fly across the screen while more accusations fill the air.

"My daughter's college fund—"

"Our merger documents—"

"All those charity donations—"

"Shut up!" Madeline screams, all pretense of control shattering. "None of you would be anything without me. I made this town what it is!"

"You're delusional," Katherine Ashworth says, stepping forward. "You're nothing but a social climber who clawed her way up by destroying anyone in your path."

Madeline's fingers still on her phone. "Destroying?" That broken laugh again. "Oh, I'll show you destruction."

The lights flicker, then surge bright enough to pop. Sparks shower from the crystal chandeliers as the electrical system overloads. One of her precious ice sculptures explodes from the sudden heat, sending shards flying.

"Mother," Emerald starts, but I pull her behind me.

"Stay back," I murmur, already scanning for the safest exit. Romeo's fighters are moving through the crowd, but this is escalating faster than even I anticipated.

"You want to see what real power looks like?" Madeline's voice rises over the panicked murmurs as she backs toward the control panel on the wall. "Let me show you what happens when you try to take everything from me."

She slams her hand on the panel and every display screen in the ballroom lights up with her face, multiplied dozen of times. "If I'm going down, I'm taking all of you with me." Her fingers fly across the keypad. "Every account, every document, every dirty little secret—it all burns."

"Step away from the panel," Richard Whitaker demands, but she just laughs.

"Or what? You'll call the police? Go ahead. Let them come see how Emerald Hills' finest all burn together."

The electrical system surges again, and this time actual flames spark along the wiring. The ice sculptures start melting, sending rivers of water across the marble floor as smoke begins filling the room.

"You're insane," someone shouts, but Madeline's eyes are fixed on me and Emerald.

"I should have known," she says, her voice dropping to something almost conversational. "The way you looked at her." Her smile is terrible to behold. "But she'll never be free of me. None of you will."

She pulls something else from her clutch—not a lighter, but a small remote. "You think you're so clever, Cohen? You think you've won?" Her thumb hovers over the button. "I had this whole place rigged months ago. A failsafe. In case anyone ever tried to take what's mine."

"Mother, please," Emerald steps forward despite my attempt to hold her back. "This isn't the answer."

"Oh, but it is." Madeline's eyes are fever-bright. "You're just like me, darling. You'll see. When everything burns, you'll understand what it means to have real power."

The sprinklers activate, but it's not enough to combat the electrical fires now spreading through the wiring in the walls. Smoke pours from the vents as the climate control system fails.

What the fuck did she do to fuck with the electrical system?

"Get everyone out," I order Cole, who's already moving. But Madeline blocks the main exit, that remote still raised.

"Nobody leaves," she says as the room descends into chaos. "We all go down together."

"I can end this right now," Cole says quietly beside me, his hand already reaching for the gun I know he carries. "One clean shot."

"No." I grab his arm, my eyes fixed on that remote. "She's got a dead man's switch. The moment her hand releases it, everything blows. She planned for someone trying to take her out."

"Fuck." Cole's jaw tightens. "Romeo's guys could—"

"Same problem. She falls, we all die. She's made sure of it."

The marble floor becomes treacherous as melting ice sculptures create rivers that reflect the growing flames. Smoke curls through the room like a living thing, turning Madeline's winter wonderland into something from a nightmare.

"You should see your faces," she taunts as the crowd draws back. "All your precious wealth, your centuries of status, your careful breeding—none of it matters now. You're all just rats in my trap."

"The only rat here is you," Elizabeth Caldwell shouts over the panicked crowd, rage threading through every word. "You sold our children to predators. Used them as bargaining chips."

Something dark flashes in Madeline's eyes. "Used them? I improved them. Made them worthy of our world. Just like I did with Emerald." Her gaze fixes on her daughter. "Everything I did was to make you perfect. And how do you repay me? By spreading your legs for your stepfather?"

The words hit like a whip, but Emerald doesn't flinch. "No," she says, her voice steady even as smoke fills the air. "Everything you did was to control me. To own me. To make me as hollow as you are."

"Hollow?" Madeline's laugh sounds like breaking glass. "I built an empire. Created a dynasty. And you think fucking Cohen makes you special?" She takes a step forward, remote still raised. "You're nothing without me. Nothing but damaged goods now—"

"That's enough." My voice cuts through her tirade. "You've lost, Madeline. It's over."

"Over?" She hits another button and explosions rock the foundation. The massive chandeliers swing like pendulums, crystals breaking free to shatter across the marble floor as women in designer gowns scramble back. The impact sends decorative columns toppling into ice sculptures while hairline fractures race across the ceiling. Someone screams as a piece of molding crashes down inches from their head. "I'm just getting started."

The crowd surges toward the exits, but Romeo's fighters hold them back—the doors are too hot to touch now, the electrical fires having spread through the walls.

"Cohen." Emerald's voice is soft but certain. "Let me talk to her."

"No." The word tears from my throat. "I won't risk you."

"Trust me." She squeezes my hand. "Please."

Everything in me rebels against letting her step forward, but I see something in her eyes—strength I helped unlock, power that was always there beneath Madeline's conditioning.

"Mother," Emerald says, moving closer despite the heat and smoke. "You don't have to do this."

"Don't I?" Madeline's voice cracks. "They're trying to take everything. Just like your father tried—"

She stops, that calculating look returning. "You want to know what happened to him? Your precious daddy who abandoned you?" Her smile is cruel. "I took care of him. Because he tried to take you from me. Just like Cohen's trying to take you now."

"What did you do to him?" Emerald's voice shakes for the first time.

"What I had to. What I'll do to anyone who tries to steal from me." Madeline's finger moves on the remote. "Including you, my perfect little disappointment."

The sound system crackles with feedback as more electrical surges pulse through the walls. The smoke is getting thicker, the heat more intense. We're running out of time.

Through the smoke and chaos, I watch my entire world step closer to the monster who gave her life. Emerald's ivory dress glows in the firelight, the gold tulle catching embers like stars. She looks like an avenging angel as she faces her mother, and pride wars with terror in my chest.

"What did you do to my father?" Emerald's voice carries over the crackle of flames.

"Does it matter?" Madeline's smile is all teeth. "He's been in the ground for fifteen years. Just like you'll be when I'm done." She hits another button and part of the ceiling caves in, sending guests scrambling. "It's almost poetic, isn't it? The whole family, together again."

The Savage Six react instinctively to the chaos. Cole and Lucas position themselves near Emerald and me, ready to move if needed, while Romeo directs his fighters toward the kitchen exit. Tristen's eyes stay locked on Madeline, his hand hovering near where I know he keeps a weapon. And Xander darts through the panicked crowd like some demented jack-in-the-box, his heterochromatic eyes wild with glee as he turns rich people's terror into his own personal entertainment.

"This is better than Christmas morning!" Xander shouts, making Richard Whitaker stumble backward into a melting ice sculpture. "Look how they run when you play with them!"

But Madeline just laughs.

"You think your pet criminals scare me?" She waves the remote. "I have enough explosives rigged to turn this whole estate into ash. One more step and we all burn."

"You killed him." Emerald's voice is steady even as tears cut tracks through the soot on her face. "Because he saw what you really are."

"I eliminated a threat." Madeline's mask finally cracks completely, decades of careful artifice shattering. "Just like I'll eliminate anyone who thinks they can steal my legacy. Including that bastard in your belly."

The words hit like bullets. Emerald's hand flies to her stomach as gasps echo through the smoke-filled room.

"That's right, darling." Madeline's eyes are wild now. "You think I didn't know? That I didn't have cameras everywhere? That I didn't watch every disgusting moment between you and him?" She gestures at me with the remote. "I saw it all. Every touch. Every kiss. Every time he fucked you in my house."

"Then you saw something real," Emerald says, her voice stronger. "You saw actual love. Not the twisted control you call love. Real, consuming, soul-deep love."

"Love?" Madeline spits the word like poison. "Love is weakness. Love is what gets you killed. Just ask your father—"

"No." Emerald takes another step forward. "Love is what gives me the strength to do this."

She moves faster than anyone expects, launching herself at her mother. They collide in a blur of white fabric and gold tulle. The remote goes flying as they hit the marble floor.

I'm moving before I can think, but Emerald is already rolling away. The remote skids across the floor toward Cole, who snatches it up.

"It's over, Mother." Emerald stands, blood running from a cut on her cheek. "You've lost. Everything."

The sight of her blood ignites something lethal in my chest, but watching Emerald rise, unflinching and unbroken, fills me with a savage pride that nearly drowns out my rage. That small cut is nothing compared to the years of invisible wounds Madeline inflicted, yet seeing it makes me want to tear her mother apart with my bare hands. But Emerald doesn't need me to fight this battle. She's magnificent in her defiance, stronger than Madeline ever imagined she could be.

My little phoenix is finally free.

Sweat trickles down my spine, my blood-red suit sticking to my skin as the temperature climbs. Each breath burns in my lungs, the smoke making my eyes water even as I refuse to look away from Emerald.

Behind us, the crowd surges against the exits, their panic growing as thick as the smoke that fills the ballroom. Expensive shoes slip on melting ice, silk dresses tear as people push past each other. The heat from the electrical fires makes the air shimmer, turning Madeline's winter wonderland into an inferno.

Someone screams as another piece of ceiling crashes down. The acrid smoke claws at my throat, making people cough and stumble. My eyes sting but I won't blink, won't look away from my goddess standing in the middle of her mother's burning empire. Romeo's fighters struggle to maintain order as the wealthy elite of Emerald Hills forget their careful breeding in their desperation to escape.

"Have I?" Madeline pulls herself up, that broken laugh bubbling from her throat. "Maybe. But so have you."

She reaches into the fabric of her dress and pulls out a gun.

The gun looks out of place in Madeline's manicured hand, but her aim is steady as she points it at her daughter's heart. At my heart, because that's what Emerald is to me.

"You want to know how I killed him?" Madeline's voice rasps through the smoke, her perfect makeup running in black streaks down her face. Somewhere behind her, another crystal chandelier crashes to the floor, sending screaming party guests scrambling. "Your father? With this exact gun." She coughs but keeps the weapon steady. "He thought he could take you, thought he could save you from what he called my 'obsession.'"

The heat is unbearable now, making the air shimmer between us. Madeline's designer dress clings to her body, dark with sweat and soot, but her eyes burn brighter than the flames consuming her empire. Romeo's fighters guide the last of the panicked guests toward the kitchen exit while glass continues to shatter in the inferno. "One bullet. That's all it took. And that's all it will take now."

I shift forward but Madeline swings the gun toward me. My lungs feel like they're filling with razor blades, but I won't look away from the weapon aimed at my heart. Emerald sways beside me, her breath coming in short gasps, the ivory silk of her dress now gray with ash. Her skin glows orange in the firelight, sweat plastering her dark hair to her neck.

"Don't." Madeline's voice cracks as she chokes on smoke, but her aim doesn't waver even as the ceiling groans ominously above us. "One move and I paint the walls with her blood."

"You won't shoot me." Emerald's voice is soft but certain. "You can't."

"Can't I?" The gun swings back to her. "You think you know me? Think carrying his child makes you special? Untouchable?" Her finger tightens on the trigger. "I brought you into this world. I can take you out of it."

The fire roars louder, drowning out the sounds of breaking glass and crumbling architecture. Through the thickening smoke, I catch glimpses of Cole and Lucas positioning themselves by the kitchen doors, waiting for my okay to take out my wife. But with that gun trained on Emerald, I don't dare risk it.

"Stop. Moving." The gun shakes in Madeline's grip.

"You want to know the difference between you and me?" Emerald keeps moving forward until the barrel touches her chest. "I know what real love feels like. What it means to belong to someone completely. To give yourself willingly instead of being forced."

"Shut up!" Madeline screams, but her hand trembles harder, sweat dripping down her arm.

"I'm going to have his baby." Emerald's voice rises above the roar of flames, steady despite the smoke burning her lungs. Sparks rain down around her like deadly fireflies, catching in her ash-streaked hair. "I'm going to know what it means to truly love a child. To protect them. To let them be exactly who they're meant to be." Her eyes lock with mine through the smoky haze, the green nearly glowing in the firelight. "I'm going to have everything you never could. Because I know how to love. And you only know how to destroy."

The gun drops a fraction of an inch as Madeline chokes on the toxic air—and that's all I need.

I move at the same moment Cole and Lucas do, the scorching marble burning through my tux as I tackle Madeline to the ground. The gun goes off, the sound deafening in the enclosed space, but Emerald is already diving to the side, rolling across the superheated floor. The gun skids away through puddles of melted ice as Madeline thrashes beneath me, her screams mixing with the crackle of flames and the groan of failing support beams. My skin blisters from the heat of the floor, but I don't let go, even as burning debris rains down around us.

"No!" she shrieks as Lucas and Cole drag her up, her

designer dress smoking at the edges. "You can't—I won't let you —she's mine—"

But her words dissolve into broken sobs as a blast of cold winter air rushes in, making the flames dance wildly as uniformed officers and firefighters surge through the entrance. The sudden temperature change sends more crystals shattering from what remains of the chandeliers.

I don't care about any of it. My entire world narrows to Emerald as I pull her into my arms, my hands running over her body checking for injuries. The heat radiates off her skin, her pulse racing under my fingers where they press against her throat.

"I'm okay," she whispers against my chest, her voice raw from the smoke. "We're okay. All of us."

My hand slides to her stomach as I breathe her in, ignoring the sting in my lungs. Her ivory dress is ruined, scorched and stained with soot, but she's never looked more beautiful. "Don't ever do that to me again."

She looks up at me, those green eyes bright despite the ash smudged across her cheek where I'd kissed her earlier. Her skin burns hot against my palm. "I knew you'd catch me. You always catch me."

"Always." I kiss her forehead, tasting salt and smoke on her skin, not caring who sees. Not anymore. "Until the stars burn out, remember?"

Around us, the scene unfolds like a choreographed dance. Officers lead Madeline away in handcuffs while she screams about betrayal and revenge. The old money families of Emerald Hills watch with a mix of horror and satisfaction as their tormentor is finally brought down. The Savage Six stand off to the side like the rulers they are, watching as emergency crews begin assessing the damage.

But none of it matters. Nothing exists except the woman in my arms and the child she carries. My entire universe contained in her body, in the life we created, in this victory written in ash and blood.

"Take me home," Emerald whispers against my skin.

I tuck her closer as we walk through the destruction Madeline left behind. "Home" stopped being about places the moment she gave herself to me in that chapel.

Home is wherever we are together.

Just us. Just this. Forever.

Cohen
CHAPTER 24

"YOU CAN MAKE it whatever you want it to be."

I watch Emerald's face as she takes in the empty rooms of the house I bought us, her hand resting on her stomach. It's been sitting empty for almost two years, waiting for this moment.

The space is nothing like the mansion she grew up in. It's warmer somehow even though it's empty, with huge windows that let in natural light and exposed wooden beams that give it character without the ostentatious display of wealth her mother insisted on.

"It's amazing," she whispers, moving to one of the windows that overlooks Crescent Lake. From here, you can see the water through the trees, the snow-covered mountains beyond. "But isn't it far from your office?"

"It's closer to where it matters." I wrap my arms around her from behind, spreading my palm over where my baby's growing. "The Savage Six all live close. You'll never be alone here."

She leans back against my chest and lets out a happy sigh. I breathe in the sweet scent of her skin. Every day since the fire has been about rebuilding—not just our lives, but her sense of security. Her trust in having choices.

"I can really do whatever I want with it?"

"Anything you want." I press a kiss to her neck. "Paint the walls neon pink. Turn the dining room into an art studio. Build a fortress of pillows in the living room. It's yours to create."

She turns in my arms, her bottomless green eyes glassy. "We'll do it together."

"If that's what you want." I capture her lips with mine, still amazed that I get to have this. Her. Our child. A future I never thought I deserved.

A knock echoes through the empty house, and Emerald tenses before relaxing when she recognizes Tristen's voice as he calls out from the front door. After everything, sudden noises startle her sometimes. But she'll heal. She's already doing better and it's only been a few days.

"In here," I call back, keeping one arm around her waist. She's still too thin. She's barely eaten today, too excited about seeing the house, and I make a mental note to feed her soon.

Tristen appears in the doorway, and something in his expression makes me tighten my grip on Emerald. "Good news?" I ask, though I already know the answer.

He nods. "Lucas just checked in. Emmitt made a run for Vancouver." His lips curve into a smirk. "Sadly, he didn't make it. The guy has shit luck. Apparently it was a carjacking gone wrong." His grin widens as he tucks his hands into his pockets and leans against the counter. "Very tragic. The Canadian authorities say it was a random act of violence."

Emerald stiffens in my arms, but satisfaction curls in my chest like smoke. I meet Tristen's eyes and see my own dark pleasure mirrored there. Lucas's work is always clean, always untraceable. That's why I trusted him with this particular task.

It wasn't enough for Emmitt to cut ties with Madeline, not for the things he planned to do to my little phoenix.

The look Tristen and I exchange says everything without speaking a word. It's a mutual understanding between men who don't even blink when problems require permanent solutions. His slight nod tells me everything I need to know about how thoroughly the job was done. How completely Emmitt has been erased from our world.

One less monster who dared think he could touch what's mine.

"And Montgomery?"

"Transferred to a private facility in Montana. I hear it's very exclusive and even more secure." Tristen's smile turns a little feral at the edges. "Seems all that cocaine daddy's money was covering up finally caught up with him. Junior had a public meltdown at the club." Tristen chuckles like he witnessed the drama firsthand, and then he turns his attention to Emerald. "He started screaming about how you were promised to him and then he tried to attack his father when the old man suggested rehab. Now he's enjoying a very long-term stay in a place where the orderlies are paid extremely well to keep problematic patients sedated."

Emerald shudders and I turn her in my arms, tucking her face against my chest and running my fingers through her hair. She doesn't need to hear the details. Doesn't need to know exactly how I ensure no one will ever threaten what we have.

"Make sure he stays there," I tell Tristen. "Permanently."

"Already done. The staff understands that his treatment requires indefinite care." He glances at Emerald's back, something almost gentle crossing his face. "The grounds are beautiful, though. Peaceful."

I run my hand down Emerald's spine. "Thank you."

And I don't just mean for cleaning up my mess. I mean for trying to soften what had to be done for Emerald's sake.

Tristen checks his watch, and I recognize that restless energy that appears whenever he's been away from Waverly too long. If I'm possessive of Emerald, he's ten times worse with his girl. "Speaking of unhealthy obsession," he says with a grin that's more wild animal than human, "I need to get home." His expression softens slightly. "You should know she's desperate to meet Emerald."

Something warm spreads through my chest at that. Emerald needs friends her own age who understand this life—the darkness, the possession, the all-consuming love that most people would call toxic as fuck.

"Tell her we'll be there," I say.

He nods and turns to go. When his footsteps fade, Emerald lifts her head. There are no tears in her eyes like I might've expected. She's stronger than anyone gives her credit for. "They deserved it," she says softly. "For what they wanted to do to me."

"Yes." I kiss her forehead. "And now you'll never have to think about them again."

She's quiet for a moment, her fingers playing with the buttons on my shirt. "I want to paint the living room a stormy gray," she says finally, a tiny smile on her face as she stares into my eyes. "And maybe turn that room with the lake view into a nursery."

My heart clenches at how naturally she fits me. She's got this innate ability to acknowledge the darkness while still reaching for the light. "Whatever you want, little one. I meant what I said before."

She smiles up at me, and everything else melts away. That smile is every goddamn thing, bright and warm and *happy*. Emmitt's body cooling in some Canadian ditch, Montgomery losing his mind in a padded room... None of it matters except this—her in my arms and the future we're building from the ashes of everything that tried to break us.

"Show me the rest of the house?" she asks, and I see the excitement returning to her eyes. The joy of getting to make choices, to create something that's truly ours.

"Of course." I take her hand, leading her toward the stairs. "But as soon as we're done here, we're getting you dinner. You need to eat."

She laughs, the sound echoing through our empty house like a preview of things to come. The warmth that'll make these four walls a home. "Always taking care of me."

"Always will." I pull her closer as we climb. "Until the stars burn out, remember?"

Her fingers tighten around mine. "I remember. I love you."

"I love you more."

I follow her up the stairs, watching how she pauses in each doorway, already seeing possibilities I can't imagine. Her fingertips trail along the walls like she's reading braille, learning the language of our future home.

My phone vibrates, but I silence it without looking. The outside world can wait. Right now, all I care about is how the late afternoon light catches in her hair, how her hand keeps drifting to her stomach where our baby's safe and healthy, how her eyes light up when she finds the perfect room for the nursery.

"This one," she says, spinning to face me in the doorway. "The view is beautiful."

I step into the space, seeing it through her eyes—the way the sun paints the hardwood floors gold, how the lake shimmers beyond the windows. But mostly I see her, glowing with life and possibility, finally free to be who she was meant to be.

Someone I'll get to watch her discover.

She moves to the window, pressing her palm against the glass. "I can breathe here," she whispers.

And that's everything, isn't it? Not the revenge or the violence or even the victory. Just her, finally able to fill her lungs without fear. Finally able to exist without needing permission.

Without being afraid.

I wrap my arms around her from behind, and together we watch the sun sink toward the mountains, painting our empty house in shades of promise.

Tomorrow we'll fill these rooms with furniture and color and life. But for now, this is enough—her head against my shoulder, her dreams taking shape in the gathering dark, and the quiet certainty that everything led us exactly where we were meant to be.

Emerald
EPILOGUE

TWO YEARS LATER...

Gray winter light seeps through our bedroom windows, and I can't stop staring at my husband. Even in sleep, he's got one arm draped possessively over my huge belly, like he needs to touch us even in his dreams. The baby kicks against his palm, doing his normal morning stretches, and I swear he already knows when his daddy's close. Just like his big sister.

Speaking of Ember...

"Mama!" Her voice crackles through the baby monitor, followed by that happy babbling that still makes my chest feel too full. At eighteen months old, she's already figured out exactly how to get whatever she wants from her daddy. Not that it's hard - Cohen would give her the moon if she asked for it.

He stirs the second he hears her voice, those storm-gray eyes that still make my stomach do backflips blinking open. "I'll get her."

"Wait." I catch his hand before he can move. "Stay with me a little longer."

His palm spreads wider over my stomach where his son grows, and that familiar darkness I crave fills his eyes. These moments feel sacred somehow—like time stops and lets me just exist here with him, with the family we made. Sometimes I still can't believe this is real, that I get to have this kind of love. That I escaped my mother and get to live for me now.

"What are you thinking about?" Cohen's voice is rough with sleep as he props himself up on one elbow.

"How happy I am." I gesture to my huge belly. "Even if I look like I swallowed one of those giant snow globes from the mall."

He laughs, rolling to pin me against the mattress, careful of my stomach. "Did you actually set foot in a mall?"

"Shut up." But I'm grinning because he knows how much I love doing normal things now. His lips find that spot behind my ear that still makes me shiver. "You're beautiful," he murmurs against my skin. "Especially carrying my son."

"Mama! Dada!" Ember's voice grows more insistent, and I laugh as Cohen groans.

"Your daughter's awake," I tell him, pushing at his chest.

"Our daughter," he corrects, stealing one more kiss before letting me up. "And she's definitely got your impatience."

"Hey!" I smack his chest, pretending to be offended, but he's right. These days I can barely wait to experience everything life has to offer - all the messy, real moments I was never allowed before. The thought makes me smile as I throw on one of his t-shirts over my sleep shorts and pile my hair into what might generously be called a messy bun. Two years ago, the thought of anyone seeing me like this would have given me anxiety attacks. Now? Now I know I'm loved exactly as I am, bedhead and all.

Cohen follows me down the hall to Ember's room, and my heart melts at the sight that greets us. Our little girl stands in her crib, dark curls wild around her sweet little face, beaming at us with bright eyes. She's thrown every one of her stuffed animals out into her room.

"Up!" She reaches for Cohen with grabby hands, and he scoops her into his arms like she's made of spun glass and pure magic. Which, to be fair, she kind of is.

"Good morning, little flame." He presses kisses to her cheeks while she giggles. The sight of my dangerous, powerful husband completely undone by our daughter still takes my breath away.

The first time he held her, I bawled my eyes out because the cuteness actually hurt.

"Tree!" Ember demands, pointing toward the hallway. "Tree tree tree!"

"Someone's excited for Christmas," I laugh, following them downstairs. Our daughter bounces in Cohen's arms, her dark curls, the same color as mine, bouncing with every movement.

The tree comes into view and my chest tightens with pride. It's nothing like the ridiculous masterpieces my mother used to demand. Instead, every branch holds ornaments I made myself or with Cohen and Ember. There are lopsided salt dough stars, paper chains in mismatched colors, and pinecones covered in more glitter than pine. They're terrible, if I'm being honest. Martha Stewart would have a stroke.

But they're mine. Every crooked one represents another choice I got to make for myself.

"That one's definitely my favorite." Cohen's voice holds barely contained amusement as he points to a particularly tragic attempt at a felt snowman.

"Shut up." I smack his arm while I try not to laugh and Ember squeals at the lights. "I'd like to see you do better."

Turns out he's just as bad at crafting as I am.

His free arm snakes around my waist, pulling me against him. "I wouldn't dare try. Your horrible crafting skills are one of the things I love most about you."

"Horrible?" I gasp in mock offense, but then his lips find my neck and coherent thought becomes impossible. Even after two years, one touch from him still makes everything else fade away.

"Down!" Ember demands, squirming in Cohen's arms. The moment her feet touch the floor she toddles toward the presents, remarkably steady for someone who just learned to walk a few months ago.

"Wait for us, little flame." Cohen keeps his arm around me as we follow her, and I lean into him, already missing his touch if he moves even an inch away. Some things never change.

"Pretty," Ember declares, pointing to a package wrapped in silver paper. She inherited Cohen's ability to zero in on exactly what she wants, and she won't be distracted by anything until she gets it.

"Should we let her open one before breakfast?" I ask, though I already know the answer. Neither of us can deny her anything.

Cohen pulls me closer, his hand sliding to my belly where our son shoves an elbow... or maybe a foot? "Let her enjoy it. This Christmas is nothing like the ones you had growing up."

He's right. My childhood Christmases were photo opportunities, every moment staged for maximum marketing appeal and over the last couple of years, I've told him more than he ever realized. But here, watching our daughter attack wrapping paper with unrestrained joy while wearing footie pajamas covered in dancing reindeer, I finally understand what Christmas is supposed to feel like.

"I love you," I whisper, turning in his arms. "Thank you for giving me this. All of this."

His eyes darken as he cups my face. "You gave me everything worth having." His thumb traces my bottom lip. "A family. A future. A reason for existing."

A shiver runs through me at the intensity in his voice. Even after two years, one look from him still makes everything else fade away. We're still as desperately in need of each other as we were that first Christmas. Maybe more now that we have Ember and another baby on the way.

A squeal of delight pulls us from our moment as Ember discovers the rocking horse Cohen insisted she needed. She's still too small for it, but that didn't stop him from having it custom made.

"Help!" She commands, making grabby hands at Cohen. He releases me reluctantly, though his hand trails across my lower back as he moves, like he can't bear to break contact completely.

I know the feeling.

I sink into the oversized armchair, curling my legs under me while I watch my husband lift our daughter onto the horse. His massive hands span her tiny waist as he shows her how to hold the reins, and my heart does this weird flutter thing that happens every time I see them together.

"Remember when you were so nervous about being a father?" I ask, watching him with Ember. Back then, after he'd confessed everything—about the pregnancy test, about the real night I lost my virginity—I think that was the only time I'd ever seen him truly afraid.

He looks up, those storm-gray eyes intense even as Ember tries to eat the rocking horse's mane. "I'm good at this because of you. Because you love me despite everything. Because you understood why I did what I did."

"I'll always understand you," I say, but I'm tearing up because pregnancy hormones are no joke.

"Mama cry?" Ember's bottom lip trembles in sympathy.

"Happy tears, little flame." I hold out my arms and she launches herself off the horse, trusting completely that one of us will catch her. Cohen does, of course. He always catches us.

She climbs into my lap—or tries to, given my enormous

belly—and pats my face with sticky hands. I have no idea what's making them sticky since she hasn't had breakfast yet, but that's just life with a toddler.

"More presents?" She asks hopefully.

Cohen settles on the floor beside my chair, one hand automatically finding my ankle. "What do you think, little one? Should we spoil her more?"

"Like you haven't already bought out half the toy stores in Seattle." But I'm smiling because I love how much he loves giving her everything I never had. Freedom. Choices. Unconditional love.

And so. Many. Toys.

My thoughts drift briefly to my mother, serving her twenty-five-year sentence in federal prison. The evidence Cohen had collected destroyed not just her social standing, but her entire world. The charges of fraud, embezzlement, and conspiracy had shocked Emerald Hills' elite almost as much as the revelation that their perfect society queen had orchestrated my father's death.

But those thoughts don't hurt anymore. Not with Cohen's arms around me, our daughter's laughter filling our home, and our son growing strong inside me. My mother's darkness has no power here in the light.

"Speaking of presents..." He reaches behind the tree and pulls out a small wrapped box.

"Cohen." I narrow my eyes. "We said no gifts for each other this year."

His smile is pure sin. "When have I ever followed rules about giving you things?"

"Give Mama!" Ember bounces in my lap, more excited about the gift than I am. Though knowing Cohen, it's probably something ridiculously extravagant that will make me cry.

He hands me the box, but his fingers linger against mine longer than necessary. Even these tiny touches between us still feel electric, like that first night in the chapel. If anything, our need for each other grows stronger every day.

"Open it," he says, that dangerous smile playing at his lips. "Before Ember decides to help."

The paper falls away to reveal a long velvet box. Inside, nestled in black silk, is a delicate gold chain with two tiny flames—one in rose gold, one in yellow gold.

"One for each of our children," Cohen murmurs, his voice dropping to that tone that still makes my skin tingle. "Though we'll need to add more soon."

My eyes snap to his. "More? I'm not even done cooking this one yet."

"You know I want a whole army of babies with you." His hand slides up my leg to rest on my stomach, and my body responds instantly to his touch, to his words. Heat floods through my veins and settles between my legs. I love being pregnant with his children, love how possessive he gets, how incredible it feels to carry a piece of him inside me. Pregnancy hormones aren't helping and neither is the glint in his eye as he watches me.

"Dada baby?" Ember pats my belly, completely unaware of the heat building between her parents.

"That's right, little flame." Cohen's voice is gentle with her even as his eyes promise wickedly ungentle things to me later. "You're getting a baby brother soon."

I touch the necklace with trembling fingers. Two years ago, I never could have imagined this—being cherished, being free, being so completely and utterly loved.

"Thank you," I whisper, though it's for so much more than just the gift. It's for everything he's given me. Everything we've built together.

"Let me put it on you." He moves behind my chair, and I lift the hair that's fallen out of my messy bun out of the way. His fingers brush my neck as he fastens the chain, and that simple touch makes my nipples tighten.

"Pretty!" Ember claps, then immediately slides off my lap and gets distracted by more presents under the tree.

Cohen's lips find that spot behind my ear that he knows drives me crazy. "I love watching you with her," he murmurs. "Seeing you be the mother I always knew you could be. Carrying my son. Being everything I ever wanted."

"Cohen," I breathe his name as his teeth graze my skin. But Ember's delighted shriek as she discovers another present breaks through the heat building between us. She's already created a war zone of wrapping paper and bows in here.

"More!" She demands, brandishing an empty box like a trophy.

"Breakfast first," Cohen says, scooping her up onto his shoulders. He navigates through the sea of destroyed wrapping paper while I follow them to the kitchen, already craving his chocolate chip pancakes. Some traditions are worth keeping.

"Cakes!" Ember declares from up on Cohen's shoulders as we make our way to the kitchen. "Chips!"

"Like father, like daughter," I laugh, remembering that first time Cohen made me chocolate chip pancakes. The day he told me he loved me for the first time.

The kitchen is warm and bright, nothing like the sterile showcase of a house my mother maintained. Ember's artwork covers the fridge, bright crayon scribbles that Cohen treats like masterpieces. There are still half-decorated cookies waiting on the counter from yesterday's attempt at baking.

It's messy and imperfect and completely ours.

"What are you thinking about?" Cohen asks as he settles Ember in her high chair. His tilts my chin up so he can look into my eyes and brushes some of my messy hair out of the way.

"How different everything is now." I lean into him, watching our daughter systematically destroy a banana. "How happy we are."

His arm goes around my waist and tighten, pulling me into his body. "Happier every day." His other hand spreads over my belly. "Though I still want to hunt down anyone who ever made you doubt you deserved this."

"No one can hurt me anymore." I turn in his arms, pressing closer despite my enormous stomach between us. "You made sure of that."

His eyes darken with that possessive heat that always makes my knees weak. "Always will. You and our children are everything to me. My whole world."

"Dada help!" Ember interrupts, holding up her mangled banana with sticky hands.

I catch the flash of regret in Cohen's eyes at having to let me go, but he moves to help our daughter. I watch them together, and my heart feels too full to contain.

This is what freedom feels like. What real love feels like. What having a real family feels like.

"I love you," I whisper, though with Cohen's scary-good hearing, I know he catches it. His eyes meet mine over Ember's dark curls, and that electric connection between us crackles again.

"Until the stars burn out," he says, and I know it's true. What we have—this consuming, desperate kind of love—it's forever.

Just us. Just this. Just our little family built from the ashes of everything that tried to break us.

And as I watch my husband and daughter tackle breakfast together while our son grows inside of me, I know this is exactly where I'm meant to be.

Home isn't a place. It's wherever we are together.

Always has been.

Always will be.

a letter from the author

USUALLY BY THE time I finish a book, I'm ready to just be done and move on so I don't typically write afterwards or author's notes. But this story...

Phew.

It's not a secret that 2024 has been a rough year for me creativity-wise. (Fuck you, Migraines). I know my readers have been dying for more Emerald Hills and that meant Perfect Nightmare, but there have been so many struggles with that book, too, that I just needed time to... breathe, I guess.

And from that time and space, this book was born. I wrote it incredibly fast for me, and it's the shortest non-novella book I've ever written ("shortest" at over 70,000 words haha). It's literally five days before Christmas and I'm watching Home Alone while putting the finishing touches on this story after starting writing it at the beginning of November.

I still can't believe it's done.

Did any of you pick out who Cohen Astor is?

He's made a *very* brief appearance in one of my other books. Anyone? (Bueller?)

No?

He's Hayden's lawyer in Dirty Hit, the one he has a brief text exchange with. Cookies and muscular forearms to you if you got it!

I never intended to give Cohen a book. He was just a throw-away character, but when I decided I wanted to write a dark Christmas romance, I felt like it needed to be set in Emerald Hills and it occurred to me that he was the perfect shady character to be the male lead in this story.

The female lead, though… I don't even know where she came from. I had the hardest time with her name and who she was as a person. I wanted her name to have a vaguely Christmas-feel without being something like "Holly" or "Noelle" or "Merry."

It was only after I named her and settled on it I realized Emerald and Emerald Hills were too close, but by then I just said fuck it because in my head she was already Emerald, ya know?

Now let's talk about the chapel. That wasn't an original part of the story but when I was brainstorming ideas for Cohen & Emerald's first time (well, that she knew of…) I wanted something dynamic. Given the "Unholy Nights" title, it felt like it needed to happen in a chapel. So I had to go back and edit the chapel in before that point so it wasn't just thrown in there for them to bang in.

And thus the chapel was born.

There are a few other little fun Easter-eggish things, like Cohen's father's name being Clark ("Save the neck for me, Clark!"), and tiny peeks into the world of Emerald Hills and things to come, too. Did you catch them?

Anyway, I hope you enjoy this one. It's not perfect, but that's what makes it fun.

Happy holidays.

Heather

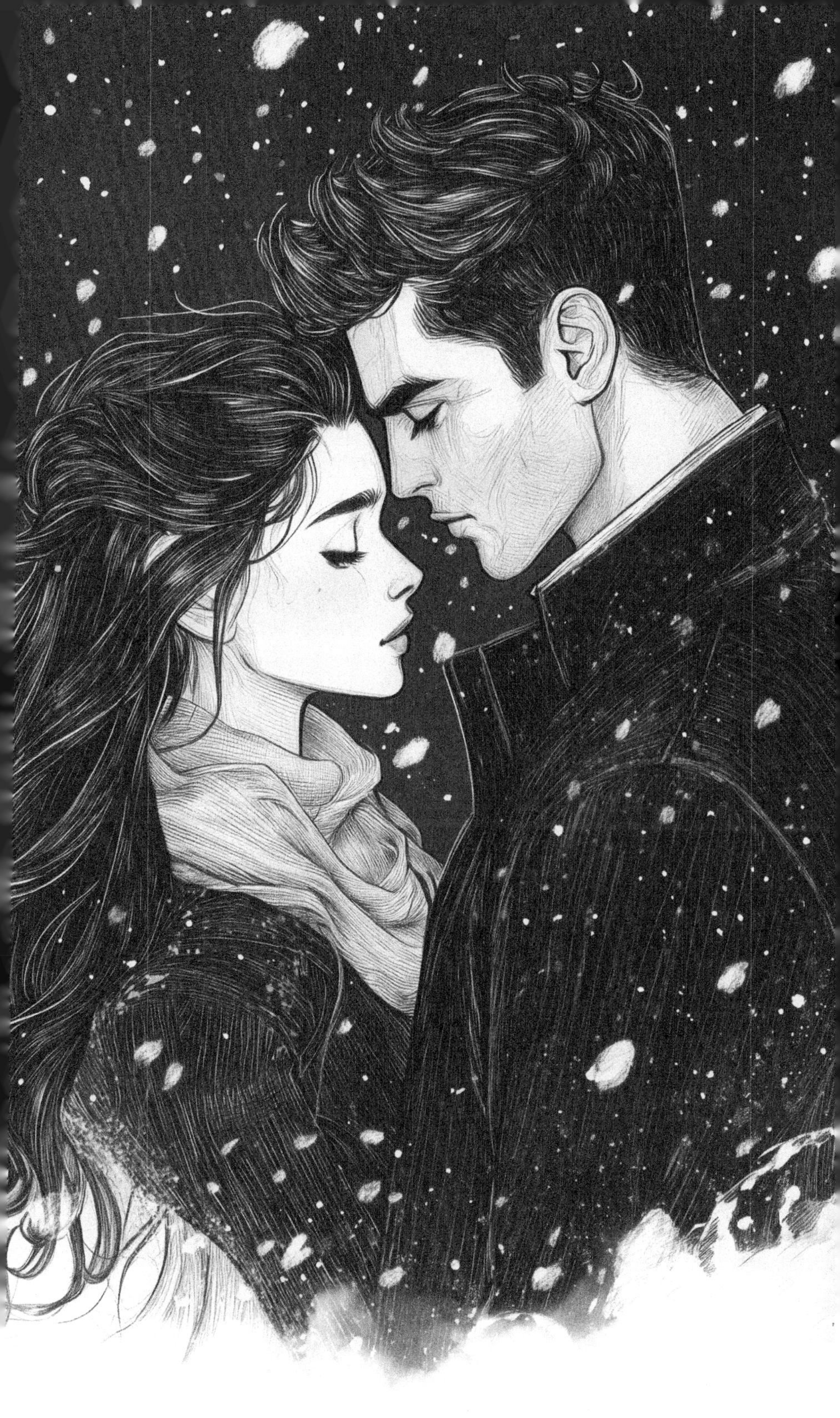

find me

📷 @heatherashleywrites

🎵 @heatherashleyauthor

f /heatherashleywrites

P /heatherwritesitall

🦋 @heatherashley.bsky.social

/heatherashleywrites

heatherashleywrites.com

About the Author

Heather Ashley writes dark & steamy forbidden stories with toxic, obsessive heroes. She's a PNW girl through and through and lives for foggy mornings among the evergreens.